where t

Rive
Flowed

OTHER BOOKS AND AUDIO BOOKS
BY JENNIE HANSEN

Abandoned

All I Hold Dear

Beyond Summer Dreams

The Bracelet

The Emerald

The Topaz

The Ruby

Breaking Point

Chance Encounter

Code Red

The Heirs of Southbridge

High Country

High Stakes

Macady

Run Away Home

Journey Home

Coming Home

Shudder

Some Sweet Day

When Tomorrow Comes

Wild Card

a novel

JENNIE HANSEN

Covenant Communications, Inc.

Cover image: *Cowboy* © The Palmer

Cover design copyright © 2013 by Covenant Communications, Inc.

Published by Covenant Communications, Inc.
American Fork, Utah

Printed in the United States of America
First Printing: February 2013

19 18 17 16 15 14 13   10 9 8 7 6 5 4 3 2 1

ISBN: 978-1-62108-226-2

This book is dedicated to my family, the people who have been there for me through all of life's ups and downs, who have stayed in touch no matter the distance, and who share the memories that make up my life. It's a salute, too, to the exceptional editors I've had at Covenant: Darla Isaakson, Giles Florence, JoAnn Jolley, Shauna Humphreys, Valerie Holladay, Christian Sorensen, Kathryn Gordon, Kirk Shaw, and Stacey Owen. Thanks, too, to my first readers: Eva Jensen, Mindi Battraw, Janice Sperry, and Lezlie Anderson.

Chapter One

1889

ILIANA TERESA ANJELICA MEDINA SEBASTIAN stood before the gilt-edged mirror eyeing herself critically. Today she was fifteen, a woman, but the eyes staring back at her in the ornate glass lacked the calm acceptance she was accustomed to seeing in the eyes of her maid or the other adult women about the hacienda or in the village church. She knew, in truth, that she was not a woman, but a frightened girl, a mere child. It was Grandfather who insisted she don a ball gown, wear her hair up, and fasten her mother's diamond-encrusted crucifix about her neck.

With one hand she brushed a stray tendril of dark hair back into the elaborate upsweep Amaya had fashioned from her waist-length locks. The small action sent one of the long dangling earrings, which matched the cross nestled at her throat, shimmering and twisting in the light reflected in the mirror from two thick candles on the heavy table before her.

She knew of Grandfather's concern. There was no son to inherit the vast land grant to which Grandfather had devoted his life. The Sebastian heir, her papa, was no more. He had died with Mama at the hands of marauding Apaches over a decade ago. Grandfather's only hope of continuing the Sebastian dynasty was through Iliana. He was old now and believed his time was short, lending an urgency to the necessity that she acquire a husband and produce the needed heir.

Tears shimmered in her eyes as she thought of her beautiful mother, who should have been at her side for this party that marked her emergence into womanhood. She wondered if she would ever stop missing her mother; something in her heart said she would not.

She had coaxed to be allowed to wait a year, but Grandfather had explained that he was old and there were *Americanos* anxious to drive him from his land. Only marriage to a man strong enough to hold the land could guarantee a home for her and an inheritance for the sons she would one day bear.

"You must hurry." Amaya returned to Iliana's bedroom from checking on preparations taking place in the kitchen. "The guests are beginning to arrive and you must be at your *abuelo's* side to welcome them."

Bowing her head in submission, the young girl gathered up a scrap of lace that served as a handkerchief and made her way through the hallways and arches to the patio where Grandfather stood, proud and unbent. She frowned to see that the men from the Purdy Ranch were the first arrivals. Their ranch had once been the Medina Rancho and had belonged to her maternal grandfather until Jacob Purdy had wrested it away from him through questionable means. She reflected with sadness that the law, the little that existed in New Mexico, seldom favored the original settlers of that vast land.

She schooled her features to remain neutral as a handsome young Americano approached. Ben, Jacob's son, was only a few years older than she, but he always laughed and smirked at her as though he knew something she didn't. He no longer threw rocks at her or attempted to frighten her horse as he had done when they were children, but the leering smiles somehow seemed worse. She turned her head and lifted her chin, pretending she didn't notice his blatant attempts to catch her eye.

* * *

On a high point leading to a small village in New Mexico, Ross Adams raised up in his saddle for a better look. In the distance a steady trail of rolling dust appeared to move toward the mountains. Curious, he moved closer and followed a stream of riders and wagons. Mexico had lost the war, the land now belonged to the United States, and he'd heard land was available in New Mexico to those strong enough to take it from the Spanish land grant claimants. Spanish land grants formed the basis of many of the large ranchos across New Mexico and California, and while they were supposed to be honored, few actually were.

He'd heard about the vast Sebastian Rancho, the apparent destination of the villagers. The almost fifteen years spent in Texas after the war had taught him enough Spanish to understand that the travelers were headed toward a fiesta of great significance. He considered attending the party without an invitation; such parties didn't require specific invites. It might be the opportunity he'd been looking for to examine the ranch belonging to the Spanish aristocrat. He'd heard rumors in the last town that the old man to whom the land grant belonged couldn't hold onto the land much longer. He was old and frail and had no sons. Expectations were that the rancho would soon be absorbed by its neighbor to the north. If the rancho proved to be all it was rumored to be, Ross Adams meant to be first in line to place his claim, one way or another.

Ross rode onto the vast estate with a crowd of noisy caballeros and mingled with the crowd. By keeping his ears open and paying attention to whispered words around him, he'd learned how one rancho after another in the fertile mountain valleys had slipped from Spanish hands to those of Americanos and that a neighboring rancher, who was rumored to be a Confederate-soldier-turned-outlaw, was set on acquiring el Rancho de Sebastian for his son. No doubt others were equally ready to stake a claim to the vast acres. Rumors of competition for the land didn't worry him. If the ranch proved to live up to its reputation, he didn't doubt he could outmaneuver other claimants.

The Spanish rancher, Don Rodrigo Ignacio Renteria Sebastian, had a formidable reputation and had managed to stave off eviction longer than most of his countrymen. He was rumored to have lost his only son during a skirmish with the Apaches years ago, and his daughter-in-law had died with her husband, leaving behind a small daughter. It was considered only a matter of time until the ranch fell into the hands of an American. Looking at the rolling, grass-covered hills and the fat cattle, Ross spied a corral of the most magnificent horses he'd ever seen and made up his mind. The Sebastian Rancho would be his.

* * *

Ross stood in the shadows cast by the large trees surrounding the house that, though two stories high, appeared low and close to the ground. His previous experience with such houses, made of adobe, assured him it would be cool inside even on the hottest days. While most of the guests at the party spoke Spanish, his ears caught a smattering of English, revealing that he wasn't the only gringo in attendance, though he might be the only one attending without an invitation. The food he sampled was hot and spicy, far better than the beans and biscuits he usually prepared for his evening meal.

He lifted his eyes to the grassy hills stretching out beyond the hacienda and observed the cattle grazing in the distance. He'd dreamed of raising cattle such as these since the day he'd surrendered his weapons with General Lee at Appomattox. A feeling of coming home at long last wrapped him in pleasant dreams. This ranch was his destiny, something he felt deep in his bones. From somewhere close, the sound of music brought his thoughts back to the present. He needed a plan.

He stood watching for several minutes then joined a circle of men dancing with slow, deliberate steps around a circle of women moving in the opposite direction. As the steps grew faster, whistling and clapping kept pace with the music. Swirls of color flashed from the women's swirling skirts.

A young woman stepped from the shadows and moved with hesitant steps toward the lanterns circling the dance floor. Ross was stunned. He hadn't spent much time with young women since the war, but even his inexperienced eye told him this one was a rare beauty. She was also much too young for him. Something about her slender waist and wide skirt; the long, dark curls that brushed her waist; and her warm, doe-like eyes sent an unfamiliar shiver rushing down his spine and caused his heart to pound. She was the most beautiful creature he'd ever seen. If he were seventeen instead of a few years past thirty, he'd ask her to dance.

Ross watched as a young man not much older than the young woman bowed before her and lifted her hand to lead her onto the dance floor. The unexpected jolt of jealousy left him scowling at the pair and annoyed with himself for his interest in the young woman. She was beautiful, but he'd never before experienced the sharp sting of resentment over a woman. It took considerable effort to turn his thoughts from the girl to the intricate steps of the dance.

When the dance ended, he headed for the refreshment table; it was the only excuse he could think of for moving closer to where he could continue to watch the young Spanish woman with the long ebony curls and doe-like eyes. His maneuver was useless as she was immediately claimed by another partner. He shook his head to clear thoughts of her from his mind. He wasn't looking for a woman; he needed to concentrate on finding a way to obtain the land.

* * *

The evening confirmed Ross's first impression that the Sebastian Rancho was everything he'd dreamed of owning. Something deep inside him told him the grass-covered hills and sparkling streams could be his if he played his cards right.

He'd been disappointed at first to learn the fiesta was a *quinceanera*, a party to celebrate the *grandee's* fifteen-year-old granddaughter's entrance into society. When the beautiful, dark-eyed senorita he'd admired earlier danced by in the arms of her silver-haired grandfather, he felt the jolt of an idea begin to form.

He stood in the shadows watching as the young woman danced with one guest after another. She seldom smiled and seemed almost fearful of the guests who swarmed around her. Something about her touched his heart, a place that had not experienced much tenderness for many years, and he wondered if the young woman could be more than a means to an end. Was it possible he might find with her the happiness that had somehow eluded him since the war? He scoffed at his own fantasy; no woman, not even the tantalizingly beautiful senorita, could bring him the satisfaction that thousands of acres of rich grassland and open sky could.

A young man, scarcely old enough to be called a man, held her too close, and his proprietary air grated on Ross's nerves, especially when Ross observed her futile struggle to widen the space between her and her possessive dance partner. He contemplated cutting in on the couple when he noticed her embarrassment and felt a surge of anger as the young man forced her into the dark shadows beyond the lanterns. Some impulse, or perhaps the need to safeguard his plans, sent him into the darkness after them.

At first he couldn't determine where the young couple had gone until the muffled sounds of a scuffle drew his attention to a hidden alcove in a walled garden. He crept closer, taking care to make no sound. The young man held the senorita crushed to him, his mouth pressed to hers while one hand tore at her blouse. Unable to scream, she kicked him and struck at him with two small fists.

Stopping short of the struggling pair, Ross felt a consuming rage, much like he'd felt that day long ago when his company had been overrun by Yankees and he'd watched one friend after another fall to the ground in pools of their own blood. His hand went to the revolver at his hip. Faster than a blink of an eye it was in his hand.

"Let her go." His voice was low, but there was no mistaking the threat behind his words.

"Mind your own business!" the young man snarled without releasing his captive.

"I said, let her go!" Ross stepped closer. The man had no idea how much Ross considered the woman his business.

She gulped for air, but the tight hold the man retained on her choked off her voice. The only sound she made came out more sob than scream.

Ross swung his heavy revolver in a swift upper cut that slammed into the predator's jaw; the sudden action caught the senorita's captor off guard, causing him to stumble backward. He came back swinging but halted when he saw the gun leveled at his chest.

"I suggest you leave quietly." Ross spoke in a low, menacing voice. "If you touch the lady again, you will live only long enough to regret your stupidity."

The senorita made a strangled sound before fleeing toward the two figures Ross was aware had moved into his peripheral vision. The young man seemed about to deliver some scathing remark; instead, he turned and scurried toward the music and lights.

Once Ross felt certain the stymied Romeo wasn't about to return, he turned to assure himself that the young lady was no longer in danger. She stood weeping in the arms of a woman he suspected was her *duenna*. A tall, stately man Ross recognized as the grandee of the rancho stepped forward. Ross didn't miss the gleam of silver as the gray-haired man placed something Ross suspected was a small pistol inside his jacket.

Perhaps this was his chance. The proud Spaniard knew as well as anyone that his fight to retain his land for himself and his granddaughter was futile, but something in his bearing told Ross that the Spaniard would fight to the end to secure his granddaughter's inheritance and to ensure a succession of his descendants retained their right to the land. Ross's conviction grew that the granddaughter was the key to securing both the old man's and his own dream.

He felt a grudging respect for the elderly man and began executing his plan by extending a hand toward the aging Spaniard. A few whispered words proved Ross's premise and gained him the old man's ear.

Late that night in the lavish library of Don Sebastian, a bargain was struck. Ross would have the land and stock he craved; the Spanish aristocrat was guaranteed the land would remain in the hands of his granddaughter's sons.

* * *

Ross sometimes compared himself to the ancient prophet Jacob, who had labored seven years to claim his chosen bride, but in fact, the agreement he'd struck with Don Rodrigo Ignacio Renteria Sebastian required but one year and most of the funds he'd accumulated in the years since the war ended—he thought the prize worth the price. Arrangements were made for him to live in a small adobe house a short distance from the main house, and Ross took over the day-to-day management of the rancho while he waited to claim his betrothed and the thousands of acres that comprised the Sebastian Rancho.

The elderly caballero who served as foreman was nearly as old as Don Sebastian and seemed content to play a smaller role in the management of the huge tract of land and the cattle that grazed on it. He continued to live in an adobe house similar to the one Ross claimed and served as Ross's right-hand man. Ross went out of his way to treat the elderly cowboy with dignity and respect. The ranch hands accepted Ross as foreman, knowing the assumption of authority by a gringo had become inevitable. In time, when their fears that he would replace them with drifting gringo cowboys weren't realized and he exhibited unwavering fairness toward them, they accepted him and became fiercely loyal. Ross took care, too, to keep Don Sebastian apprised of every action he took. Little by little as the months passed, genuine respect and friendship grew between Ross and the elderly patron. In each other they found a shared devotion to the land.

His relationship with Iliana wasn't going as well. Though he and Iliana were formally engaged, Ross felt uncertain about how to court the young woman. He ate dinner each evening at the hacienda and often invited Iliana to walk with him following dinner. Always they were accompanied by Amaya, Iliana's formidable housekeeper and personal maid, who he learned had served as a surrogate mother to his fiancée since the girl was orphaned at a young age.

Getting to know the shy young woman was proving harder than Ross had expected, but as he learned the workings of the rancho, he knew the vast holding was all he had yearned for since he'd struck out on his own after the war. He'd be the first to admit he didn't know nearly as much about women as he did about ranching. He couldn't even remember his ma; she'd died birthing him. He'd been just sixteen when he rode out with Pa and his brothers to enlist in the Confederate Army, and when the war ended and he learned none of his family had survived, he'd ridden far and hard, giving little thought to women or his future for a long time. The few women he'd known since then weren't the sort he wanted to spend the rest of his life with. It was land and the ever-expanding cattle industry that had won his heart and pulled him away from the hard life of a wandering cowboy. With the fulfillment of his ambition within reach, he threw himself heart and soul into the management of the Sebastian Rancho. He wanted Iliana, but it was the land that held his heart. There were a few skirmishes with the rough gringos that rode for the Purdy spread, but he soon proved he could hold his own with any of them.

One evening the following spring as he sat in Don Sebastian's library, the older man spoke of his concerns. "My grandfather claimed this land in the name of the king of Spain. We have worked it and fought for it. First the Indians and now the Americanos, who bring documents with false claims, have tried to take it from us. You must keep abreast of what is happening in this new country and you must keep careful records."

"I can read and write. Pa made sure my brothers and I could read the Good Book; then when I served in the army, an officer took a liking to me and made me his scribe. He'd been a schoolmaster before the war and felt it his duty to educate me."

"*Bueno*. That is good. There are plans for a telegraph office in Two Creek Junction next summer and I think it will be just the beginning of new opportunities. Someday the railroad will reach this far. You must see that your sons are educated and prepared to take their place as leaders in both the matters of my people and yours. As of today you will begin to manage the rancho's books and one day pass them on to my grandson."

Ross felt uncomfortable discussing his sons' future when he'd never so much as touched the hand of the woman who would be their mother. Between Iliana's shyness and her duenna's constant presence, he knew Iliana little better than he had almost a year ago.

"The time draws close that you will wed my granddaughter," Don Sebastian went on. "You have proved yourself capable of managing the rancho, and I trust your judgment in preparing my grandsons to take over their responsibilities and to honor the Sebastian name when the time comes, but I fear you do not fully understand the threat posed by Jacob Purdy and his son. They will stop at nothing to take over this land. You must be ready."

"We've had a few words. I think Jacob knows I won't put up with any incursion onto the rancho."

"The real danger lies with the water," the old man warned. "El Senor Purdy is too smart to wage war with guns. When I was a young man, there was plenty of water pouring down from the mountains. My friend once held the grant for the ranch now claimed by Jacob. He shared the water without complaint, but our fathers spoke of a time when two rivers came from the mountain. The larger one ran unfettered to Sebastian lands. Always I planned to make the long journey to the mountain to learn why the river ceased to flow. First it was unsafe to journey to the mountains because the Apache guarded the trails, then I became too old for such journeying. One day you must go to the mountains to make certain there will always be water for the rancho. If you do not, one day Jacob Purdy will cut off the water supply and all I, and my father before me, sacrificed to build will return to worthless dust."

Chapter Two

1891–Utah Territory

If there was one thing Travis Telford hated more than anything else, it was the cold—and it would be fine with him if he never saw another snowstorm in his life. He removed one glove and blew on his fingers, warming them enough so he could loosen the cinch on his saddle. His movements were clumsy, but at last he succeeded in removing the saddle from the horse that appeared as worn out as he felt.

The logs formed a haphazard shed piled against one side of the derelict cabin and would provide some shelter for the exhausted animal. The horse would be all right, but he wasn't so sure about himself. It took the last of his waning strength to lug his heavy Mexican saddle through the sagging door of the cabin before collapsing on the hard, cold, dirt floor. He lay still for several minutes thinking how easy it would be to give up, to just go to sleep.

"Quittin' ain't a choice. Cowboys been buckin' hard times all our lives, so jist git yourself up an' git a fire goin'."

He might have known his former partner wouldn't let him even die in peace. He was just rational enough to know old Treadwell wasn't really there in the cabin, but he wouldn't be too surprised if the irascible old man's ghost hadn't managed somehow to find a way to push and prod him into taking the next step, just the way the old man himself had on the long trek across the plains into Montana from Texas, trailing two thousand head of the orneriest cattle God ever saw fit to bestow upon the earth.

He'd been lucky to find the thatch-roofed jumble of logs. The storm had struck with such sudden ferocity that it had left him despairing of seeing another day. The squat structure had appeared out of the swirling snow like the answer to one of Treadwell's prayers. Travis sensed he was a long way off the road that wound around the side of the mountain and eventually led to Salt Lake City, but if he and his horse could survive until the storm blew itself out, they had a chance. He'd given his word that he'd go to Salt Lake and personally deliver Treadwell's few worldly goods to his sister just before Treadwell died from the wounds he'd received from a rampaging bull along the Bitterroot Range in Montana.

Forcing himself first to his knees, then to his feet, he took a few stumbling steps until he reached a wall. Inching his way along the wall, he explored the darkness until he stumbled into a hard object a brief exploration proved was a small stove. If he hadn't been so tired and cold, he would have shouted for joy. Deciding it was his lucky day after all, Travis continued to examine the room, finding in the area around the stove a nearly full wood box.

There was a chance the chimney had been knocked off by the storm or was full of debris or a bird's nest and his efforts to light a fire would burn the ramshackle cabin down around his ears, but he felt an urgency to try. If the cabin burned, he'd be warm for a few minutes. Digging through the box of wood produced a few bits of kindling. He stuffed them in the firebox then peeled off his coat to search an inside pocket for the sulfur matchsticks he kept in an oiled cloth inside the coat for emergencies. This was definitely an emergency!

He breathed easier once the fire was burning. The chimney seemed to be drawing just fine, and leaving the lid off the firebox so the flames could leap and dance, lighting the room, he got his first look at the interior of the cabin. The walls were dirt for the first few feet over what was probably a natural depression in the ground that had been dug out further and squared before logs had been used to extend the walls another four feet. There were no windows, and packed dirt sufficed for a floor. Rusty traps hung on one wall, and a crooked shelf held a fry pan, a kettle, a bucket, and a tin plate. A few ragged garments hung from nails beside the door. A wobbly table sat near the stove with one lonely chair, and in a corner of the room was a wooden bed frame covered with a thin mattress. Closer inspection revealed the mattress stuffing was grass, not straw.

He eyed the mattress with longing and trepidation. He longed to sleep, but the mattress was probably the habitation of a colony of rodents. So long as the grass stuffing wasn't moldy, it would probably be better fodder for his horse than comfort for his tired body. The cabin was warming up fairly well, so he decided to risk going back out in the storm to carry an armload of the mattress stuffing to his horse along with a bucket of melted snow.

Finding a pile of old sacks in a corner, he used one to wipe down the young stallion, one of his mama's stallion's many offspring. When he left Mr. Sorenson's ranch in Texas to accompany old Treadwell on a trail drive to Montana, he'd entered into an arrangement with the former trail boss. In exchange for Sorenson's feeding and sheltering Travis's other horses, the rancher would keep all but every fourth colt or filly sired by his mother's old stallion.

He regretted that his plans to start a ranch in Montana where he could keep his horses hadn't worked out. He patted the horse he called General Jack and wondered if the stallion might be the last horse from old Zeus he'd ever own. When he was satisfied the animal was as comfortable as he could make him, Travis returned to the cabin.

Going straight to the stove, he huddled before the fire until he nearly fell over from fatigue. He added two thick chunks of wood to the fire and withdrew his bedroll from the back of his saddle. With his ground cloth spread across the much-depleted mattress, he wrapped himself in his blanket and was asleep before he had time to wonder if he was sharing his bed with a nest of rats.

Travis awoke with the barrel of a shotgun jabbing him in his abdomen. He opened his eyes to see a small, elderly man wearing buckskins and sporting a full, bushy, salt-and-pepper beard peering down at him.

"Best you crawl outta my bed and hightail it down the trail." The bewhiskered old man poked him hard with the gun barrel.

"All right. Take it easy." Travis edged toward the side of the cot.

"Keep your hands where I can see 'em, too."

Sliding his legs out from under the blanket he'd pulled over himself, he felt with his toes on the dirt floor for his boots. He wasn't about to argue with the shotgun, but inside he fumed as he slid around trying to right himself while keeping his hands above the blanket. He gave a despairing glance toward the pants he'd hung over the back of the chair near the stove before calling it a night, not wanting to crawl into bed in cold, clammy, wet pants.

"I thought the cabin had been abandoned and I was just trying to get out of the storm," Travis attempted to appeal to the old man's better side—if he had one.

"This cabin ain't nowhere near the trail."

"I don't know if it is or it isn't. I got turned around in the storm and don't rightly know where I am."

"You're where you don't belong. This is my cabin and I been livin' here 'most twenty years."

Travis stood, his legs shaking, feeling the cold cut through his long johns. "Mind if I put on my pants and boots before I leave?" A kerosene lantern cast a dim glow, making the contents of the room just visible.

The old man looked from him to the pants folded over the back of the solitary chair. He twisted his pursed lips from one side to the other as though deep in thought.

Probably trying to figure out if he could make use of the pants himself. Travis hoped the old goat could see he was a foot shorter and considerably thicker through the middle than Travis. The man nodded toward the pants and Travis made his way toward them, taking slow steps.

"I already confee-skated yer guns. You'll not be findin' 'em. You one of them gunfighters?"

Travis kept his face straight as he shook his head. He had no intention of revealing that he'd spent almost every coin he had acquiring one of the new repeating rifles from the army or that the set of silver pistols in his saddlebags were left to him by old Treadwell. The guns and five gold pieces, his wages for trailing the Texas herd to Montana, were all he had to get himself back to Texas and the rest of his horses.

"You running from the law?" The question caught Travis by surprise.

"No, I'm just trying to get to my former partner's sister's house."

"She live around here?"

"No. She and her husband live farther north and on the other side of this range of mountains. I missed the pass and traveled too far south." He concealed his annoyance with the old man's questions.

"Durn near didn't make it through the pass myself. Iffen it warn't fer ole Cindy Lou, tha's my mule, I'd still be lookin' fer the trail. Reminds me of my first winter here. Owe my life to an ornery Indian and his squaw. They took me in—"

"I'll get my horse and be on my way." Travis cut the man's story off, fearing that if the old coot didn't shoot him, he'd talk him to death. He stepped toward his saddle, which still rested on the floor. He had no intention of leaving without his guns, but he hoped to lull the old mountain man into thinking he would.

"Now, let's not be hasty. I'm not for sending a man out into the snow without somethin' warm in his belly. You got any coffee?" The old man was practically drooling as he eyed the fat saddlebags Travis had tossed on the floor beside his saddle.

"No coffee, but I've got a slab of bacon and the makin's for biscuits."

By the time the two men were half way through eating breakfast, the shotgun was lying across its owner's lap and Travis was wondering if it might have been a better fate if the old man had just shot him. He'd listened to bear stories, "Injun" stories, gold strike stories, blizzard stories, Mormon stories, and trapping stories until he felt his eyes glaze over.

"I suppose I ought to be on my way." Travis rose to his feet, attempting to end the loquacious man's tales.

"Now don't git yourself in a dither," the man Travis secretly called Whiskers protested. "I ain't plannin' to shoot ya. I was jist leadin' up to askin' if you'd like to buy this cabin an' the blamed mountainside it's sittin' on."

"Buy it? I just stopped here to get out of the storm and keep from freezing to death."

"It's a good cabin. It'd do fine for a young fella like you. You got a wife an' youngins?"

"No, no family other than a brother." The old trapper didn't protest when Travis retrieved his pants. He reached for his boots and felt a measure of relief to find the bulge that was old Treadwell's leather pouch in the boot pocket designed to hold a spare gun.

"I was jist like you when I wuz a young buck. Always wantin' to see the other side of the mountain. I saw plenty, but I put off findin' a good woman. Shoulda had a passel of youngins to look after me in my old age. Too late now, but I got plans to settle in Californy, where the sun don't never quit shinin'."

"Good luck with that!" Travis edged closer to his saddle.

"Blame it! Hold still whilst I'm talkin' to ya."

Travis froze, eyeing the shotgun on the old man's lap.

"Now don't go gettin' all edgy on me. I ain't never shot a man I broke bread with. I can see you ain't quite to the settlin' down place yet, so I'm gonna make ya a deal. I'll give you back your guns and a paper what says this place is your'n in a couple a years. You jist give me two o' them gold pieces you got in that bag, an' when you come to claim this ol' homestead, you can give me a couple more. Til then, I'll take good care o' this cabin."

Travis stared at the old man in disbelief. He knew about the gold pieces and was trying to weasel a few out of him, when he could have easily just taken them. It seemed the man had a code of honor that forbid outright stealing but didn't prohibit him from scamming any fool that passed his way.

A half hour later, Travis rode out of the secluded mountain valley with the silver pistols in their holsters and his rifle in its scabbard. In his pocket was the deed to sixty acres of timber and brush. His purse now held only three of the gold coins he'd placed there upon leaving Montana. He wrapped his scarf around the lower portion of his face and pressed his heels into his horse's side. The snow had stopped, but if he didn't reach Salt Lake by nightfall, chances were he'd freeze to death.

Chapter Three

HOLDING HIS MOUNT TO A steady walk, Ross soon reached the stream that gave life to the dusty, baked soil in the valley. He stepped down from his mount to study the trickle of water at his feet. It was July, far too soon for the creek to be running so low. He recalled the old don's words concerning the water. He knew at once who was responsible for the diminished water flow. The Purdys had somehow blocked the channel to divert the water for their own use, ignoring the fact that the stream that flowed from the nearby mountains had provided adequate flow for both ranches before disappearing into the hot sands for many years and that there was a written agreement that spelled out the Sebastian Rancho's right to half of the water that came from the distant mountains. One day Ross would follow the stream to its source in a high mountain canyon, but right now he couldn't spare the time such an expedition would require.

He'd soon have to do something about the flow of water that had been diminished from the preceding year. He suspected Jacob Purdy was testing to see whether Sebastian's agreement with Ross would hold. Iliana had turned sixteen three months ago, and still a date had not been set for their wedding. He hadn't pushed the issue, knowing his fiancée was young and had been sheltered from life's realities, but he was getting anxious to move on to the next stage of the bargain he'd struck with the don and to serve warning to men like Purdy that he was in charge of the vast rancho.

Remounting, he started back toward the ranch buildings. As he neared the stable, he saw two mounted figures start at a fast trot toward the trail that led to a high mesa. Even at a distance he recognized the gelding favored by the former ranch foreman, Javier, and Iliana's spirited roan mare. On an impulse, Ross decided to join them. Javier would serve as chaperone, and it might give Ross an opportunity to speak with Iliana without Amaya's disapproving presence. Only for a fast ride with Javier a couple of times each week did Amaya allow Iliana to leave the house without her.

Ross leaned low across his mount's neck as he raced to catch up to the pair who were almost out of sight.

* * *

Iliana stopped as soon as she noticed that Javier had reined in his horse. She trotted her mare back to him when she saw him swing stiffly to the ground.

"Is something wrong?" she asked as her horse danced, anxious for the swift run she'd come to expect from their forays to the mesa. Iliana, too, was anxious for an invigorating run.

"No, just a pebble." Javier pulled a small knife from his pocket. "I'll be ready in just a moment."

Iliana debated whether to continue on without him or wait the few minutes it would take for him to be ready to continue the ride.

Hearing the sound of another horse scrambling up the rocky trail, they both paused to watch Ross's horse climb toward them. He waved and Javier returned the wave before bending to lift his horse's hoof. Iliana suddenly felt shy. Ross Adams was a fine-looking man and he always treated her with respect and courtesy. They'd dined at the same table and taken innumerable walks during the past fifteen months, but she still knew him no better than when he'd arrived on the ranch. Though she understood her grandfather's agreement with him, he was still a stranger, and she felt awkward in his presence. They were betrothed, so shouldn't she be more comfortable around him by now? She had so little experience being around men other than her grandfather and the men who worked for him.

Ross continued toward them and Iliana made up her mind. "Since that should only take a few minutes, I will ride ahead," she announced to Javier, and without waiting for a response she tapped her heels against the mare's sides and the fleet-footed animal was off like a streak.

* * *

Ross watched Iliana disappear into the brush as he paused beside Javier. "Need any help?" he asked.

"I've got it." Javier folded up his knife and tucked it back into his pocket. Then taking the reins, he began to move toward the trail. "I think I should walk him for a few minutes to be certain there's no soreness."

Ross didn't dismount but paced his horse to match Javier's steps. He glanced once toward the trail, remembering how insistent Iliana's grandfather had been that she never be left alone for a moment when she rode. The old man's caution was derived partly from the attack on his son and daughter-in-law and partly from an incident that occurred when Iliana was about ten and had been pelted by rocks thrown by Ben Purdy that left her frightened, bruised, and bleeding. The Purdy ranch was only a short distance beyond the upper mesa, but it wouldn't take long for Javier to be back in his saddle, and Ross knew Amaya would disapprove if he rode ahead and was alone with Iliana for even the few minutes it would take for Javier to catch up to them. He'd like a few minutes alone with his future bride, but he didn't wish to run afoul of Amaya.

A scream rent the air, followed by a second scream that was cut off before it reached full crescendo.

Without a word Ross dug in his heels and his horse shot forward. He had no doubt Javier had mounted and was pounding after him. When he reached the top of the trail, he did a hasty scan and saw no sign of Iliana.

"Go left!" he shouted to Javier and sawed at the reins, urging his own horse to a sharp right. Before the animal had once more reached its stride, it reared, pawing at the air as a dark shape raced from a copse of stunted junipers. Even as he fought for control, Ross recognized Iliana's mare. By the time he had his horse settled down, Ross's mind had assimilated the few facts and he plunged into the trees, expecting to find a crumpled body on the rocky ground. He traveled only a short distance before spotting two figures struggling beneath a twisted juniper tree.

Fury coursed through Ross's veins. Leaping from the saddle, he charged at the larger figure. Swinging his fist, he connected a solid blow to the man's jaw, sending him sprawling backward. As the man fell, he released Iliana's hands, which he'd held gripped in one of his much larger hands, causing his frightened captive to also fall to the ground. From Ross's side view, he was aware of Iliana jerking a wadded kerchief from her mouth as she sat up. She released an ear-splitting scream just as he delivered another blow, this time to her attacker's belly. He ducked a fist aimed at his own face and swung again. Iliana's assailant staggered backward, but Ross continued to rain blows toward the other man's face and midsection. When the man fell to the ground and lay still, Ross turned to see about Iliana. Before any words could leave his mouth, a command came from behind him.

"Drop the gun!"

Startled, Ross turned back to see Ben Purdy with a wavering gun in one hand. He was looking beyond Ross to where Javier sat astride his gelding, pointing his Browning toward their neighbor. Ben seemed uncertain whether he should be aiming at Ross or Javier. Slowly he released his grip on the pistol and let it slide to the ground at his feet.

"Get on your horse and get out of here before I decide to shoot you." Ross scarcely recognized easygoing Javier in the steel-laced order. There was no doubt Ben understood the threat as he walked warily toward his mount, which was tethered to a nearby cedar tree. Neither Ross nor Javier took their eyes from the man who was their closest neighbor's only son. Though neighbors, Ross felt no fondness for the arrogant young man, whom he'd long suspected had his own plans for Iliana, but he'd never had a direct confrontation with Ben since the night of her quinceanera.

"You'll regret this," Ben muttered as he neared Javier. "No greaser is going to get away with telling me what to do."

Javier's only response was a well-aimed boot to Ben's face, which sent him rolling on the ground with blood spurting from his mouth and nose.

Ross reached for his own rifle and trained it on Ben as he crawled toward his horse and grasped a stirrup to pull himself up. Ross had never before felt so strong an urge to shoot a man, and it took all of the self-control he could muster to refrain from squeezing the trigger that itched beneath his finger.

When Ben was mounted, Javier looked after Iliana, while Ross remounted to follow at a careful distance until he was certain her attacker had crossed onto Purdy land. He then closed in on Iliana's mare as it grazed near the stream that cut across the plateau. A well-placed rope brought the mare to his side.

When Ross returned to the grove of trees where he'd left Iliana and Javier, he saw she was wearing Javier's shirt, and a strip of rawhide held her sagging riding skirt about her waist. Deep gouges marred her hands and one eye was swollen almost shut. He found himself regretting he hadn't shot the sorry excuse of a man who had done this to her, or at least pounded him more thoroughly. He looked at Javier, who gave an almost imperceptible shake of his head, and Ross felt some of his tension ease.

Ross helped Iliana mount and the three turned back toward the hacienda. He took the lead and Javier reined in behind Iliana. They rode at a steady pace without speaking for some time. Once or twice Ross thought he heard a soft sob, and his mouth formed a grim line and his bruised knuckles turned white where his hand gripped the leather reins. He suspected Iliana ached physically as well as emotionally from the ordeal she had endured and that the ride was a painful nightmare for her. He knew, too, that she wouldn't ask him to slow his pace nor would she complain about her injuries.

It was dusk when they reached the barn. Ross was aware of the pain Iliana attempted to hide as he helped her dismount, but taking his cue from her, he said nothing, though his lips formed a stern grimace to keep from saying the words he longed to say to comfort her.

"Go to the house," he told her. "I'll take care of your horse and tack." She hesitated only a moment then, with careful steps, moved toward the light streaming from the sprawling hacienda. He watched her go and regretted that there was nothing he could do to ease her pain.

When she was out of sight, Javier paused with a heavy saddle in his arms to ask, "What are you going to tell Don Sebastian?"

"Nothing. I think it's up to Iliana to tell him as much as she chooses and I suspect that won't be much. She'll blame herself, and there's not much we can say that will convince her she did nothing wrong in wanting a brisk run across the mesa. Besides, she knows as well as we do that if her grandfather finds out what happened, he'll confront Jacob, and Jacob will then dam up the creek that runs across his land, and this ranch will burn up without water. The ornery old coot would likely stir up the other ranchers who share his view of the old Spanish aristocracy and Mexican laborers as well, and we'd have a war on our hands."

"He will know." Javier shook his head.

Ross knew the old caballero was right. Iliana could keep no secrets from Amaya, and Amaya would go straight to Don Sebastian.

Chapter Four

ILIANA DID NOT APPEAR AT the table for dinner that evening, and the following morning Don Sebastian summoned Ross to his library to inform him that his marriage to his granddaughter would take place in three weeks. There was no mention of the previous day's events, but Ross understood that Ben's attack had convinced the old man that marriage was the best protection against a repeated attack and would be more effective than reprisal.

Javier arrived at dawn on the day of the wedding to transfer Ross's few belongings to a suite of rooms on the second floor of the hacienda, rooms Ross understood had belonged to the don when he was a young man with a bride. He drew Ross's attention to a dark Spanish-style suit of clothes laid out in preparation for him in the new room.

Ross stood for several minutes gazing at the large bed set on a low dais, the ornately carved bureaus, and the heavy hangings at the window, a window that looked out over miles of grass and brush that extended to distant purple mountains. The land, the luxurious surroundings, and the beautiful young woman who would soon be his bride were all he had ever wished for. With eager anticipation, he threw off his clothes and donned the suit.

* * *

Iliana stood before the mirror in the room that had been hers for all of her sixteen-and-a-half years. She'd been given the room as an infant because it was near her mother. Later, when her parents were no longer there to hear if she cried in the night, Grandfather had left his luxurious rooms upstairs to claim a suite of rooms on the same floor as the nursery. After today she would no longer sleep in the familiar room. When the ceremony and celebration were over, she would return to the room that adjoined her husband's room, the grand suite that had once been her grandparents'.

Peering into the mirror while Amaya fussed with the ruffles and flounces of the gown Iliana's mother had worn to wed her father, she examined her face, wondering if the girl she saw there was ready to be a wife. She almost didn't recognize her own reflection with her hair piled high and held in place with pearl-encrusted combs. A *mantilla* of lace partially hid her face, a face that was pale in spite of the hint of blush Amaya had brushed on her cheeks and the vermillion she had daubed on her lips. About her throat was a strand of pearls fastened with a heavy diamond clasp, and from the center hung a diamond-encrusted cross. Matching earrings were hidden by the intricate lace of the mantilla. The jewels, like her gown, had adorned her mother on her wedding day.

"It is time." Amaya indicated Iliana should precede her through the door.

Iliana's heart pounded and she struggled to maintain the serene calmness Amaya had warned her grandfather would expect of her. She looked down the aisle that separated two rows of pews in the small chapel. Her grandfather's friend, Mr. Williams, along with a few neighboring ranchers and their wives and most of the ranch hands filled the pews. At the far end of the aisle stood Ross beside the black-robed priest. Dressed in clothing similar to what Abuelo wore on special occasions, Ross looked handsome and less intimidating than usual. She remembered his fierce anger when Ben had attacked her and his gentle efforts to ensure she was uninjured. Setting aside the frightened girl inside her, she stepped forward. Grandfather had explained that it was her destiny to provide an heir for the ranch. She was a Sebastian and she would do all that duty required.

* * *

Travis arrived in Salt Lake City, cold and exhausted, and made his first order of business seeking out a stable where his exhausted horse could rest and be given a generous measure of oats. Only a horse as strong and determined as General Jack could have carried his rider through the deep snow of the mountain pass. When his horse was cared for, he sought out supper and a bed for himself.

The morning was half spent when Travis at last made his way to the address his former partner had given for his sister. He rapped on the door and waited. The door was suddenly flung open and Travis was startled to see a lad of no more than ten years scowling at him.

"Ma!" The child turned to shout back into the room behind him. He didn't have to wait long. A woman appeared with one toddler riding astride her hip and another clinging to her skirt. She looked up at Travis and swiped her free hand across her face to scrape back a strand of long, blonde hair that had escaped the lopsided bun that hovered near the nape of her neck. From behind her came the shouts of several more children.

"Are you Moses Treadwell's sister?" He felt foolish asking the question. Treadwell had been pushing sixty. Surely this young woman couldn't be the sister he'd commissioned Travis to seek out.

The woman stared at him for several minutes, seeming puzzled by his question. Surely he hadn't made a mistake in following the instructions he'd received at the stable when he'd collected General Jack. A sudden smile lit her face and he felt a moment's relief.

"You must mean the widow lady who used to live in this house. She moved to California last spring to be closer to her daughter."

It was all he could do to keep from groaning. He'd given his word to a dying man to find the old man's sister and deliver to her word of his death and his small savings.

"If you want to wait for my husband, he might be able to give you her address."

"I'll be back." Travis tipped his hat and backed off of the porch.

He stood just outside the gate of the small house and debated with himself over what his next course of action should be. After a few moments, he made his way to the post office. Finding a dozen envelopes bearing his brother's return address brightened his day and he settled down to read them. After a few minutes, Travis's attention was drawn from the sheet of paper in his hand by the words of two nearby men.

"I heard some fellow near San Bernardino is hiring wranglers for an expedition into Mexico to acquire horses. Some of the California ranchers are paying good money for horses, more if they're saddle broke. Couple of us have been thinking about heading down there in the spring to see if he'll take us on."

"Not likely. I heard he don't like Mormons."

"I'd head up my own group of wranglers if I was familiar with the California/Mexican route."

Travis studied the two men and mulled over their words. If he had to travel to southern California to locate Treadwell's sister, he just might see about hiring on as a wrangler. By the time he bought supplies for the trip to California and paid for his snow-enforced stay in Utah, there wouldn't be much left of his few coins. He needed a job, and he was a long way from the Kansas bank where he'd left his share of Pa's money and most of his wages from the Sorensen Ranch in Texas, where he'd left his horses.

He'd look for lodging to tide him over until spring then make his way to California. Wrangling horses was more to his liking than herding cattle anyway.

* * *

1892

Ross touched his glass to that lifted high in a toast by his grandfather-in-law, Don Sebastian.

Less than a year had passed since his wedding. Life was good; not only were the New Mexico hills home to an enviable herd of fine cattle he could claim as his own, but now he had a son, one that shared his and the old man's blood and who would one day inherit el Rancho de Sebastian.

A faint whimper reached his ears. It wasn't the lusty cry he had hoped for, but the sound bound the two men, granting fulfillment of their bargain. Sebastian had the heir of his own blood he had yearned for, and Ross would control the vast acres that were his dream for many years to come. By the time his son was a man, he'd be ready to retire.

In the room above the men toasting the new arrival, Iliana waved the maid, Amaya, away. Though weak and exhausted, she refused to surrender her tiny new son to the maid's care. She cradled him in her arms and whispered hushing sounds in his ear until both she and little Rodrigo Gabriel Ross Sebastian Adams slept.

* * *

"Iliana." Ross knelt beside her bed, gently awakening her with whispered words. Confusion fogged her mind and she felt certain she had slept for no more than an hour. "Your grandfather sent me to bring you and our son to him."

She brushed her hair back from her face, rubbed her eyes, and struggled to sit up. Her body protested against the movement. Not a dozen hours had passed since she'd given birth. She bit her bottom lip to hold back the groan the movement evinced from her aching body.

"I wouldn't ask it of you," Ross whispered. "But the pain has come again and it is far more severe than the other times. Your grandfather insists you must go to him and allow him to hold his great-grandson and heir."

"I shall carry the little one." Amaya appeared with the infant in her arms. Since the maid's arms were full, Ross helped Iliana don her robe. She paused only long enough to slide her silver-backed brush through her hair in quick dabs before taking her husband's arm and stepping toward the door.

Iliana's steps were slow, and Ross moved his arm to her waist to support her as she made her faltering way down the stairs and toward the wing of the hacienda that housed her grandfather's rooms. She was grateful for her husband's steadying arm about her waist. At last she paused outside the elaborately carved door of Abuelo's bedchamber, and Amaya placed the baby in her arms. Looking down at the tiny scrunched face, she straightened, refusing to allow her fatigue to show. This was the heir for which her grandfather had waited so long. Ross opened the door and they made their way to Abuelo's bedside.

"Come, little one," Grandfather whispered in a feeble voice. Iliana was uncertain whether he meant her or her newborn son, who was much too small. Though she knew little of infants, her son seemed much tinier and less robust than those of the wives of the married men who worked on the rancho. Ross helped her make her way to the bed where the old man lay. They sank to their knees beside the bed, and Iliana rested the bundled infant beside her beloved abuelo. Ross carefully pulled back the satin edge of the blanket Amaya had wrapped around the infant.

The newborn stared back unblinking at the black eyes that examined him. A small smile lifted one corner of Don Sebastian's mouth and a sheen of moisture made his eyes glisten. His gaze left the infant for a brief moment and met those of his granddaughter. His voice came in short puffs of breath. "You have brought honor to the family Sebastian."

The old man's gaze returned to his heir. His stern features relaxed, becoming almost serene. Iliana couldn't say just when Abuelo ceased to breathe.

* * *

1893

Iliana knelt beside the handsome, carved stone Ross had ordered placed on Grandfather's grave. She crossed herself and bowed her head, working her way quickly along the row of prayer beads that ran through her fingers. She still missed the austere old man with an ache that would not go away. There had never been any doubt of his love for the sweeping land on which she had been born or for the granddaughter and great-grandson who were all that was left of the family he had envisioned becoming a dynasty in the new land his great-grandfather had claimed more than a century earlier. She felt a small amount of comfort in knowing she had given him his greatest desire, an heir in the form of little Gabe, before he passed from life.

As she prayed she listened for her son. He was frequently ill and often awoke from his afternoon siesta feverish and crying. Amaya said it was because he was born too soon and that if he'd waited until his proper time to arrive, he would be sturdy and strong.

Sometimes Iliana believed Amaya's excuses for Gabe's fretfulness. He had arrived early, and perhaps she did coddle him, but more often, she thought Gabe was small and fretful because she was not a good mother. She didn't remember her own mother well or know what a mother should do, so she just held her small son and begged him to grow strong. She seldom left his side except to kneel in the chapel to pray for him.

A troubling memory crossed her mind. Just yesterday Ross had plucked the tearful toddler from her arms and carried him to the stable. When she'd protested he'd said, "You should rest."

She couldn't lie on her bed not knowing what was happening to her son, so she'd paced the floor, pausing at frequent intervals to peer out a window toward the stable. When Ross returned with Gabe, asleep in the crook of his arm, no words came to her lips. He placed the little boy in his crib before striding from the room without acknowledging her or her concern. Leaning over the side of the small bed where her son slept, she caught a faint whiff of peppermint. His cheeks and hands felt sticky to her touch. She would never know what had passed between Gabe and his father, but she didn't believe she was mistaken in seeing tenderness on Ross's face for his small son, and there was a look of contentment on Gabe's small face. Calmness filled her soul. Grandfather's trust in her and in Ross had not been misplaced.

* * *

Looking over the herd of horses his men had purchased from several powerful Spanish landholders near the Mormon villages in Mexico, Travis struggled to hide his disappointment. There weren't as many horses as they'd trailed to California the previous year, and their condition was not as fine either. After one season of working for the horse trader he'd found in California, he'd struck out on his own and hired a dozen Mormons who were eager for work. After a winter spent in Salt Lake, he'd gained a large measure of respect for the family-oriented men who traveled great distances to support their families and improve their farms and communities. Together, he and his Mormon crew had built a reputation for providing the best horses to California ranchers. Travis was aware of the ugly stories that circulated about the Mormons, but his experience with old Treadwell and the rapport Travis felt with his crew told a different story.

He thought of the advice given him by Bishop Daniels in the last Mormon colony they'd visited before leaving Mexico. The frontier bishop seemed to know a great deal about horses, and when he'd remarked that it wouldn't be far out of his way to stop at the Sebastian Rancho to see if the new rancher of one of the largest ranches in New Mexico would part with some of his horses, Travis had resolved to make the ranch a stop on his return trip. If the rancher wouldn't sell any of his horses, Travis wouldn't be able to satisfy all of his contracts. The herd needed water and the ranch was the nearest place to satisfy the horses' thirst. On every count, he seemed to be pushed toward the Sebastian Rancho.

Leaving instructions for his men to hold the horses near the wagon trail that twisted toward the mountains and the oasis of trees and buildings just barely visible in the distance, Travis rode forward with two of his most trusted men. Six hours later, with the help of two Sebastian caballeros, he and his men hazed a small herd of horses toward the larger herd then drove the combined herd toward a clump of willows, where Ross Adams had said they were welcome to camp overnight and water their horses.

Travis surveyed his enlarged herd and felt a swell of satisfaction and gratitude. Surely it had been God who had prompted Bishop Daniels to suggest the Sebastian Ranch. Ross Adams was nothing like the other Americans who had been gradually taking over the old Spanish ranches. He'd asked an honest price, showed Travis a large crop of young colts, and invited the trader to stop in again on his next trip.

A few more trips, two or three more years, and Travis Telford would be ready to purchase land of his own. He might even marry and start a family. The occasional letter he received from his brother had him hungering for a place of his own and the comforts of a family. His eyes swept the mesa, filling him with something akin to homesickness for something he'd never quite known. He determined that the Sebastian Ranch would become a regular stop for his horses between Mexico and California. With horses such as the ones he'd purchased at the ranch, perhaps in time he'd be able to buy land and build his own ranch in one of the New Mexico valleys.

Chapter Five

Iliana watched from her window as a dozen riders hazed a string of horses into a corral near the barn. Some of the men looked familiar. She'd watched them before from behind her curtain. The trader stopped at the ranch a couple of times each year, sometimes to buy horses and sometimes merely to water his herd. She'd listened to the talk between her husband and old Javier enough to know a two-year-old colt would remain behind this time after the men departed to take possession of a large herd of horses farther south. She was curious about the colt. She'd heard Ross speak of it in glowing anticipation of its arrival. Ross had been expecting it to be delivered by the trader when he arrived and had commented several times that the colt was the offspring of the magnificent stallion the trader himself rode. She'd admired the beautiful stallion more than once from her hidden spot behind her deep-set bedroom window.

She wondered about the other horses the traders would be bringing out of Mexico. They'd been captured and broken by a group of people Ross called Mormons and would be driven to California, where there was a lucrative market for them. She could ask Ross about the horses, but she wanted to see them for herself. Her grandfather had insisted she stay out of sight whenever strange men visited the rancho, and Amaya demanded she still do so even though she was now a married woman, but sometimes she chafed at the restrictions that kept her far from the important happenings concerning her beloved horses.

There would be dinner guests tonight. Mr. Williams was coming from the village, and the leader of the group of horse traders had agreed to dine with them before discussing business matters with Ross. Amaya had been shocked and voiced her disapproval when Ross announced his expectation that Iliana should attend and serve as hostess for the dinner. Though meeting strangers was a somewhat terrifying prospect, Iliana was pleased to be included. From the bits of conversation she'd overheard, it seemed likely the horse trader was interested in adding some of el Rancho de Sebastian horses to the herd he aimed to sell in California, and Ross was pleased to have a steady market for the ranch's horses, whose number had grown beyond the needs of the ranch hands.

She sighed before drawing the curtains and beginning her toiletry in preparation for hostess duties that evening. She knew her role was merely ornamental and that no business would be discussed at the table. Sometimes she wished that she had been born the son and heir Grandfather had longed for.

Curbing her thoughts, she donned the gown Amaya had set out before making her way downstairs to offer the cook assistance. The dress was a shimmering blue, like the New Mexico sky, with a white lace panel extending from the high neck to the floor. The ballooned sleeves fell to just below her elbows and ended with a tiny blue bow on each. It was a beautiful dress and had been a surprise gift from her husband, carried from New Orleans when he'd traveled there on business the previous spring. Amaya brought from her mother's jewel casket long, dangling streams of diamonds to adorn Iliana's ears and set off her dark curls. The locket Ross had presented to her at Gabe's birth nestled at her throat. She sensed this dinner was important to Ross, and she wanted to look her best and ensure that all went well with the dinner being prepared for her husband's guests.

Ted Williams arrived while Ross and the horse trader were washing and changing for dinner. Mr. Williams was tall and thin, with gray hair. Though a gringo, he was always as austerely formal as Abuelo had been. Mr. Williams bent low over her hand and complimented her on her gown. She was pleased to see Grandfather's old friend, and though he had long been a frequent visitor to the hacienda, her shyness prevented her from feeling comfortable conversing alone with him. The only men she'd ever been alone with as long as she could remember were her grandfather, her husband, and old Javier. Before she had to worry much about making conversation, Ross and the trader entered the grand room, where guests were customarily greeted.

Through lowered lashes she observed the man standing beside her husband. He was younger than Ross but carried himself with the same self-confident air. He was tall, but not as tall as Mr. Williams. She'd seen few men with hair as light or eyes as blue as that of the trader. His dark suit bore the signs of having been folded into a small space for an extended period of time, yet a slight shine at the elbows and knees hinted that it was worn frequently. His damp hair testified of his attempt to wash away the trail dust from his journey before entering the hacienda.

"Dear, this is Travis Telford, who has come to acquire horses for resale in California," Ross presented their guest. Iliana dipped her head in acknowledgement and was pleased to see Mr. Telford repeat the gesture rather than attempt to take her hand, as close acquaintances were accustomed to doing.

"Pleased to meet you." He acknowledged the introduction with a wide smile that revealed white teeth and a hint of laughter. Hoping the handsome stranger didn't find her an object of amusement, she stepped closer to Ross. Ross reached for her arm and she prepared to lead the party to the dining room.

A slight commotion from the entryway heralded the arrival of two more guests. Ross stepped away from her to greet them.

Jacob Purdy, followed by his son, Ben, was ushered into the room, and it took all of the strength Iliana could muster not to turn and run for the stairs. She'd known since the day Ben had attacked her that there would be occasions when she would have to face him again, but she never felt ready. She stepped back to avoid Ben's approach, and Mr. Telford, with smooth courtesy, offered his arm to conduct her into the dining room, sparing her the ordeal of personally greeting the Purdys, before Ross could resume his place beside her. She saw the startled look on her husband's face as his guest preempted his duty to escort her to the table, but she was grateful for the quick escape the stranger offered her. Ross followed and she was pleased to find herself facing her husband down the length of the table, with Mr. Williams and Mr. Telford to her right and left. The Purdys were left to fill the seats between Ross and his other guests. Before them were place settings she suspected Amaya had rushed to add to the table upon the arrival of Jacob and Ben Purdy.

Through lowered eyelashes, Iliana saw the smug look on Ben's face as he cast frequent glances her way. Her backbone stiffened. She sent him a scornful glance much like she'd bestow on a cockroach and lifted her fork to her lips. For her family and the people who had served her family for generations, she could play the aristocrat, unbowed by any threat to her peace or personal well-being.

Ross fumed, though he hid his anger from the others seated at the table. Ben had a lot of nerve appearing for dinner at the table of the woman he had assaulted, and her husband, as though nothing had happened. He'd shown up uninvited on numerous occasions since his attack on Iliana but had never been so brash as to assume a place at the table. Jacob had approached Ross several times, hinting broadly that it would be to their mutual advantage to include the Purdys' horses in his arrangement with Travis Telford. He had spoken in glowing terms of the prices they could demand if they worked together. Unfortunately he'd arrived at the ranch earlier that day, in time to learn of Ross's dinner invitation to Telford. Ross had been naive to not anticipate that Jacob would assume the invitation included him and that he would bring his son.

Ben's smirking leer directed toward Iliana served to warn Ross that he must be more vigilant in watching over his wife. He'd noticed that she'd given up riding, which wouldn't do. He would not allow Ben to deprive Iliana of one of her few pleasures. At first he'd thought she'd given up riding because of her pregnancy, which had quickly followed their marriage, but Gabe was no longer an infant and she needed an outlet from her constant attendance upon the child. And Gabe needed to begin training for the day he would assume ownership of the rancho. Ross would have to make certain he or Javier was available to ride with her each day.

As Amaya served the dessert course, Ross became aware that Ben wasn't the only guest watching Iliana. The trader didn't seem to be able to take his eyes off her either. Ross couldn't entirely fault the man, since Iliana was indeed a beautiful woman. It would be difficult not to notice the long, shining, black curls that fell to her slender waist, her exquisite form, or the startling beauty of her patrician face and ivory skin. He'd keep an eye on the man.

"My dear," Ross addressed Iliana at the conclusion of the meal. "Don't wait up for me. The gentlemen and I have much to discuss." He turned to his guests. "You'll excuse my wife; she is anxious to return to the nursery to assure herself that our young son has truly recovered from a slight upset he suffered earlier."

Ross smiled inwardly on seeing the startled expression that hinted at disappointment on the trader's face and noted the man's red ears and instant focus on his plate. It was probably well that there had been little opportunity for the man to speak with Iliana beyond a rudimentary introduction. He had likely given the trader a false impression by not immediately introducing her as his wife. It appeared Telford had not understood that his hostess was the mistress of the household rather than a daughter. As Iliana rose to her feet with a gracious nod to her guests and left the room, Ross vowed to correct any mistaken assumptions either Ben or the trader might still harbor about Iliana. He followed her to the door and gently kissed her cheek.

When Iliana disappeared up the stairs, Ross led the party to the room that had been the old senor's library but which Ross now claimed as his own. It was time to put personal concerns aside and turn to the business of horse trading.

* * *

Travis followed his host and the other men to a generously sized room. Two walls were lined with books, most bearing Spanish titles. A massive, intricately carved desk made from some dark hardwood dominated the room. Chairs were gathered before it. He was surprised to see the young man who had made no attempt to conceal his interest in their hostess take the seat behind the desk as though he had a right to it until his father, with a nod of his head, ordered him to another chair. The young man obeyed with all the grace of a sullen, spoiled child.

Travis mentally cringed remembering his own interest in his host's young wife, though he could partially excuse himself because he hadn't known the woman was married. He should have known better than to make assumptions based on the couple's obvious difference in age. At least he'd done and said nothing to embarrass her or for which he need apologize.

Ross opened the discussion. "I don't have as many horses ready for sale as there were last summer or the summer before. I've hired more men and have need for a greater number of mounts for them."

"I'm sorry to hear that, but I'm interested in whatever number you're willing to part with. I have several customers who particularly asked for more horses from your stock."

"I have twenty horses I could be persuaded to part with to make up the difference," Ross's neighbor, Jacob Purdy, offered. He stood, leaning one hand against Ross Adams's desk, blocking Ross's view of the man he'd traded with for three seasons. "My horses are in top condition and I'll expect top dollar for them."

"How many are saddle trained?" There was something about the arrogant way Purdy had inserted himself into the discussion that raised a red flag in Travis's mind. He'd known plenty of men like Jacob Purdy before and they always meant trouble.

"They know who's boss."

"Are you saying they're rough broke?"

"Some are. Some haven't seen a rider yet, but they'll settle right down as soon as they get a strong taste of leather."

Travis kept his face from revealing his distaste for the rough kind of treatment he felt broke an animal's spirit and had little to do with actual training. "What about bloodlines?"

"I've never worried much about that nonsense." Purdy puffed out his chest. "I can tell a good horse just by looking at it. First thing I did when I took over my spread was to shoot every last one of those mincing, delicate mares the old Spaniard squatter who had previously lived there called horses."

Travis winced. He'd been around the area long enough to know that "the old Spaniard," El Senor Medina, had bred and trained exceptional dressage horses as well as started a line of race horses from a pair of fleet-footed imported horses from Arabia. The ignorantly destroyed mares had been of inestimable value.

"I don't have time to examine your horses this trip," he attempted to sidestep Purdy's offer.

"Won't take any time. I'll have my men drive them over here in the morning."

"I don't pay top dollar for horses I haven't seen nor for animals that have been abused."

"You saying my horses ain't as good as Sebastian horses?" The big man glowered at Travis, rose to his considerable height, and took an aggressive step forward.

Travis stood his ground. "Every horse I brought from Mexico and from ranches between there and here has been ridden. They're trail broken, which saves considerable time driving a herd as far as I'm going. I can't risk buying horses that may be difficult to control and near impossible to sell. I'll look at your horses the next time I come through here."

Jacob Purdy slapped his hat back on his head and stomped toward the door. His son followed. At the door, Ben stopped and with a sneer spit on Travis's boots.

Chapter Six

1894

Ross sat on the side of his bed to pull on his boots, and as they always did, his eyes went to the gently rising hills beyond the home pastures. The first streaks of light reaching over the mountains hinted at another hot day. Even without enough light to see clearly, he knew that the grass was already starting to turn brown, and he suspected that when he checked the stream, he'd find the water level a little lower than the day before. Since he'd taken over full management of the ranch almost five years earlier, each summer had seen less water reach the Sebastian Rancho. He suspected Jacob Purdy was damming the creek. Iliana's grandfather had claimed there was a place high in the mountains to the east where enough water gushed forth to keep the entire valley green. Someday, he'd explore those distant canyons to see if the old man's claim was true. His eyes lifted to the distant purple peaks. *Someday . . .*

As he passed the kitchen on the way out of the house, he heard the rattle of stove lids assuring him breakfast would be ready when he finished morning chores. He'd have just enough time for breakfast before riding to town to meet with Ted Williams to arrange for the early sale of part of the herd his men would be bringing down from the mesa today. The pastures near the barns and the low water condition wouldn't support the entire herd, making it necessary to sell what they could before the dry summer began taking its toll. The water shortage had cost too much the previous year and this year promised to exact a steeper penalty. He closed the door softly behind him and made his way to the stable, his footsteps heavy.

A young boy, instead of his usual stockman, Juan, was already measuring out oats, for the horses when Ross slid open the door and stepped inside.

"Good morning, Carlos," Ross greeted the youngster. "Where is your pa?"

"Mama has new baby. Pa say I come to help you. He come later."

The arrival of a new baby to the small houses where some of the caballeros lived with their families wasn't an uncommon occurrence, but Ross wasn't pleased with the timing. He'd been counting on Juan to have the horses ready for the caballeros who would be moving the herd of cattle from the upper mesa down to the lower creek area and taking charge of the drive. Juan's young son was a hard worker, and Ross knew he could count on the boy to finish the chores and even milk the cow his mother usually milked each morning. He'd be a great help finishing up the chores, but Juan's absence meant Ross would have to put someone else in charge of moving the herd.

Voices and the jingle of spurs alerted Ross to the ranch hands selecting their mounts from the corral. He walked to the large door at the back of the barn, where he noticed a tall, slender man he'd been told had grown up at the ranch. With the passage of years, the man had become a dependable ranch hand who worked hard and seemed to be on good terms with all of the men, though Ross had detected a toughness in him that spoke of ambition.

Ross called, "Dominic, I'm going to need your help. I'm putting you in charge of bringing the herd down from the upper mesa. Get your horse saddled while I help Carlos finish up here."

"Si, senor!" Dominic dusted his hands down the sides of his pants and hurried toward the tack room. Clearly he was pleased with the trust placed in him. He emerged a few minutes later lugging his saddle, with the bridle he'd chosen flung over one shoulder and his chaps buckled into place. He walked with rapid steps toward the corral.

Ross emerged from the stable with one hand shading his eyes against the bright glare of rays streaming from the rising sun. He gave Carlos a few last minute instructions before walking toward the horse one of the men had saddled for him. He took a few minutes to adjust the girth and test the length of the stirrups before mounting and settling into the high-backed Mexican saddle.

"Go ahead," Dominic called to him with surprising confidence. "I'll take care of everything." He touched two fingers to his hat brim and brushed his mount's sides with his heels, and as the horse began an easy trot, the other cowboys fell in behind him to begin their trek up to the mesa.

Ross watched for only a moment. *I should have given Dom more authority a long time ago. Javier is too old and too crippled with arthritis for the load I've placed on him, and though Juan is a good, dependable worker, he's not a leader.*

Ross didn't watch the other riders wend their way up the trail. Instead he spoke to Javier, advising him to watch over the hacienda and prepare for the cattle that would be streaming down to the lower pasture in a few hours. "Carlos can help you." Hoping he'd made wise choices, he headed for the village, several hours' ride away.

Ross rode into the small town shortly before noon. The single, dusty street looked sleepy and forlorn in the midday heat. Mr. Williams closed up the bank and accompanied him to the marshal's office, where they sat down for a discussion of Ross's suspicion that Jacob Purdy was damming off the creek in violation of their water agreement.

"There's not much I can do," the marshal said. "I just received word of a bank robbery and shooting in Silver City. It could be a month or more before I'm back here."

"By then it could be too late." Ross was well aware of how few marshals were sent to cover the vast New Mexico territory, and he sympathized with the communities where the local ranchers were taking the law into their own hands, but he'd rather not do so unless pushed too far. If not for the influence Jacob Purdy wielded in the valley, he'd press the neighboring ranchers to elect a sheriff, but as conditions stood, he didn't want a lawman handpicked by Purdy.

Following the brief meeting with the marshal, Ross joined Mr. Williams in his cramped office at the bank to make arrangements for the sale of the larger portion of Ross's herd. With insufficient water, it would be necessary to begin the roundup early. He had to console himself with the hope that if his stock could reach the railhead before other ranchers got there with their herds, he stood a good chance of securing a high enough price to provide for their needs through the winter. Care would need to be taken to select the best breeding stock to keep and from which to form the foundation for a new herd. He wished he hadn't been so hasty in agreeing to the old don's stipulation that the Sebastian family fortune be held in abeyance until his grandson came of age.

By the time Ross returned to the ranch and looked over the herd now milling around the scant amount of water in the lower creek, he was struck anew that the summer heat and the lack of water were beginning to take a heavy toll on the ranch's livestock. The cattle should be fat and their hides sleek, but instead they were lean and looked dusty and tired. He looked out over the yellow grass and the shallow mud holes that were all that was left of the other stream and longed for the deep grass that had first drawn him to the valley. He clenched his fists. Something had to be done. One more year without water would cost him the ranch.

It was almost dusk when he rode toward the barn. His horse showed signs of having been ridden hard. Both Javier and Dominic joined him in the barn while he was unsaddling his mount.

"Did you find the marshal?" Javier asked. Ross didn't respond at once but reached for a rag to wipe down his horse. In a motion that was almost automatic, Dominic reached for a brush and began stroking the horse's wet coat with it.

"Yes." Ross looked up from his task, a grim smile on his face. "I gave him a copy of the water agreement, and he promised to ride out to the Purdy Ranch and have a talk with Jacob as soon as he gets back from a shooting he has to deal with in Silver City; should be about a month."

"A month! Those cows need water now!" Dominic stopped brushing and stared at Ross in horror. Old Javier shook his head; his slumped shoulders indicated he hadn't expected anything better.

A week after his unsuccessful visit with the marshal, Ross waited beside two saddled horses for Dominic to join him. He removed his hat and beat it against one leg to rid it of accumulated dust, wishing his new foreman would hurry. They didn't have a lot of time. There was work to do on the ranch, and the drive to the railhead was slated to begin in two weeks, but with the shortage of water, Ross had decided it was time to follow the stream to its source and see if their suspicions concerning Jacob Purdy diverting the water were valid. His young foreman seemed a perfect choice to assist him in what he meant to do.

Checking the water was something that had to be done. The small stream that meandered through the lower end of the ranch usually went dry by mid-August, and even if it stayed steady, it wasn't enough water for the whole ranch. A dependable flow of water from the upper stream was essential to the ranch's success. Without a good watering before starting their journey to the railhead, too many cattle could be lost.

He heard the rapid jangle of spurs and saw Dom rounding a corner of the stable.

"It's about time," Ross grumbled as he fitted one boot in a stirrup and prepared to mount.

"Old Javier had much advice," was the younger man's explanation for his tardiness.

They rode for several hours, enjoying the early morning air with little conversation. When they reached the mesa, they made their way to a rugged, rocky area where water plunged downward to the lower plain when there was water in the stream. No water flowed over the series of precipices, and the rocks lay bleached and dry where there were indications that a large stream had once made its way into the valley.

Stepping down from their mounts, the two men walked through the dry, brown grass, trailing their horses behind them. The brittle grass formed small dust clouds around their feet.

"Which way?" Dom asked. "Are we going to follow the streambed across Purdy land or follow that dry wash over there?" He pointed to a depression in the land leading toward the mountains that seemed to indicate an ancient stream had once cut a diagonal pattern across the mesa, bypassing Purdy land until the two streams joined on the Sebastian side of the mesa.

Ross looked toward the distant mountains and sighed.

"There's never been water in that wash other than for a few weeks in the spring. Even Javier doesn't remember it holding water since he was a child," Dominic reminded Ross.

"We don't have time to follow it anyway. It's at least a four-day ride, maybe more, to the mountains. Let's just follow Purdy Creek until we find the problem or Purdy chases us off his range."

When they crossed onto Purdy land, they saw no sign of men or cattle. Their neighbors' high range was as dry as their own. Taking care to stay below the ridgeline, they followed the dry streambed for several miles. They weren't anxious to have any of the Purdy ranch hands spot them and become curious concerning their presence. About a mile from the ranch buildings, they dismounted. Leaving their horses ground hitched, they scooted up a brush-covered hill for a look around.

From the top of the hill, where they lay flat on their bellies, they could see an adobe hacienda only a little smaller than the Sebastian Hacienda. A single tree drooped between the house and the wall that surrounded what had once been a garden. Barns and sheds slept in the midday sun and there was a general air of neglect surrounding all of the buildings. A few horses dozed in the shade of the lone tree. The men saw no one moving about.

It wasn't on the buildings that Ross's attention lingered. He nudged Dominic and pointed. In the distance there was a shimmer of green, indicating there was water on the Purdy ranch. It appeared the Purdy's lower range was rich with grass, and a silver gleam indicated that a tributary of the main stream held abundant water, spilling over its banks to spread a carpet of grass as far as the two men could see.

Taking care not to stir up clouds of dust, the men slid backward until they reached their horses. Pouring water from his canteen into a cupped hand, Ross offered the animal a few sips of water. Dominic did the same. Then gathering up their horses' reins, they trudged on, following a path that led beside the dry stream. When they were safely beyond the ranch buildings, they remounted.

They hadn't traveled far when they found what they were looking for. Water tumbled from a fast-flowing stream toward a pool that formed behind a fork in the stream. One side of the fork led from the pool toward the green fields and pastures. Brush and rocks clogged the other arm of the stream, forming a dam that permitted almost no water to enter the fork that led to the Sebastian Ranch. Ross dismounted for a closer look.

The structure wasn't new. He guessed it had been there for several years, though there were signs it had been recently strengthened. At a glance, it was easy to see it had been designed to regulate the flow so that, in low water years, more water could be sent down the fork that fed Jacob Purdy's land than would find its way to the Sebastian ranch. With the present summer being warmer than normal and the previous winter yielding little moisture, the main stream showed signs of running lower than usual. It didn't appear to have taken much effort for someone to add more dirt and rocks to close off the Sebastian fork completely. Only a small amount of water seeped through to form a muddy puddle just beyond the dam.

Chapter Seven

"I knew it!" Ross stood beside Dominic with clenched fists. He felt like hitting someone and Jacob Purdy was the most likely target.

"What do you think we should do about it?" Dom asked.

"We're going to have to bust that dam."

"They'll just rebuild it," Dominic said with a calculating look in his eyes. "What if we were to dam off their side?"

"If you think I'm going to rebuild that dam on their side, forget it. That would probably only give us an extra day of water. As it is, we'll be lucky to get our side cleared and get out of here before they catch us."

"Yeah, you're right. Let's get it done." Dominic moved toward the makeshift dam. "But we could roll the rocks into that arroyo over there, so it will take them longer to rebuild it." He pointed to a nearby wash.

Ross picked up the first rock and dumped it over the side of the steep wash. They worked silently for several minutes. When the first trickle of water began to pour over the top of the rapidly diminishing pile of rubble he turned to Dominic with a wide grin and was met by a matching one.

It was getting dark by the time they decided they'd done all they could and a steady stream of water was moving toward the parched ground on the Sebastian ranch. The larger rocks had been rolled into the gulley, where they'd be difficult to reclaim. The men were both caked in mud; their hands were bruised, and their backs and shoulders ached, but they were pleased with what they had accomplished. They mounted and began their return journey.

"Do you hear something?" Dominic reined in beside Ross, who had stopped short of the upper mesa where the two ranches met. He sat with his head cocked to one side as though listening.

"Shh! I think someone is following us. Best we get on our own side of the mesa." Ross nudged his horse forward, and after a slight hesitation

Dominic urged his horse into a fast trot. They'd almost reached the boundary line when they heard the sharp crack of a rifle. A puff of dust erupted to one side of them. Both men leaned forward, spurring their horses to a run.

They were well onto Sebastian property and concealed by a clump of juniper trees before they brought their horses to a halt. Their mounts stood with heaving sides while the men spoke in low tones.

"There was just one shot. Do you suppose it was a warning?" Dominic asked.

"Most likely. But it's a pretty good indication someone on Purdy's spread knows what we did."

"Come on. We'd better go." Dominic gave a nervous glance over his shoulder.

"Yeah, before they block the water again." Ross's shoulders sagged. He fully expected their labor to be for naught and that they'd soon be back to struggling to keep even their breeding stock alive. They'd turn as much water as they could into the dry stock pond before the stream went dry again and hope that would get them through a few more weeks until they could get the main herd to market.

As they rode over the last ridge separating the upper mesa from the flat lower portion of the ranch where the hacienda and ranch buildings stood, Ross stood in his stirrups to better see the silver ribbon of water finding its way across the parched land to a depression that served as a storage pond. He hoped it would be nearly full before Jacob and Ben dammed the water again. Though it was now dark, he could see darker patches moving toward the water, shadows he knew were cattle.

"At least they'll drink their fill tonight," he muttered.

Ross spent most of the following morning poring over the ranch's books. From the open window beside the desk he could see young Carlos working the colts in the pole corral. Ross cast frequent glances toward the line of willows that marked Purdy Creek's distant path to where it dumped into the pond then continued on to the smaller stream. Occasionally he spotted a flash of silver and was assured the water was still flowing. He'd expected the water to be gone when he awoke that morning and was pleasantly surprised each time he caught the distant glint of flowing water.

"Senor Ross?"

He hadn't heard Javier approach the door of the library. Ross turned with a look of resignation on his face toward the small, bandy-legged caballero.

"What is it?"

"I took two men with me to the upper mesa, just as you said I should do. When we got close to the boundary line, shots were fired at us."

Ross stood and moved closer to the elderly man. "Was anyone hit?"

"No, I don't think they were trying to hit us, but they spooked the horses."

Ross left the office with Javier hurrying to keep up. In minutes they joined a group of cowboys who had gathered near the corral. As Ross approached them, he thanked Javier for losing no time in bringing back word.

He felt helpless to know how to deal with the problem. Once he would have picked up his own rifle and gone charging up to the mesa, but now he wasn't certain that would solve anything. He didn't know what to expect from their neighbors. He'd heard some wild stories about the way Jacob Purdy had taken his ranch from the Spaniard who first claimed it, and Ross vowed to be prepared for anything. He needed to come up with a plan.

"Put up your horses and take an early night, but be ready to ride if there's trouble," he told Javier and the other hands.

"The water is still flowing." Dominic said with a smug smile. He finished brushing the horse he'd ridden and gave it a scoop of oats.

"The wily old goat likely figured he'd get a call from the law and doesn't know the marshal is out of town. As soon as he learns the marshal is away, he'll divert the water again." Ross closed the stall that housed his gelding and turned to face Javier and Dominic. "When Rodrigo Sebastian was a boy, water flowed from the mountain straight onto the rancho without passing through his neighbor's land. The threat of an Apache attack kept Don Sebastian from exploring the mountain to discover why the river ceased running when he was still a young man, and since he was on good terms with his neighbor and there was plenty of water, he never made the trip. His neighbor was a generous man and the don's daughter married his son. There was no reason to worry about water until Jacob Purdy drove Senor Medina away and took over his ranch."

Javier turned his face toward the distant purple mountains.

"Someday I mean to follow that old riverbed and see if I can find out what happened to the water. Until then, we must find a way to protect our share of the water that flows across Purdy's ranch." Ross placed a hand on the old man's shoulder and followed his gaze. "Tomorrow, Javier, and in the days to come, you and young Carlos will oversee the hacienda and the barns. Dominic, Juan, and the other men will work with me to watch over the stock and our range. The men we sent to the high mesa this morning were fired on. I think it's time to send our own armed guards to the hills overlooking the mesa."

* * *

Iliana was grateful for the gleam of water she could see from her bedroom window. Her beloved horses were losing their gaunt appearance, and there was even enough water to allow a trickle of wetness to meander down the rows of corn and squash Javier had planted near his squat adobe house along the row of such houses built by Abuelo for the married ranch hands. Javier's wife had gone to her reward many years ago, but there had never been a question of returning Javier to the bunkhouse where the single caballeros and wandering cowboys tossed their bedrolls.

Amaya seemed determined to scrub every speck of dust from the hacienda and had commandeered the wives and older daughters who lived on the ranch to aid in her mission as though she expected the water to disappear at any moment. Iliana didn't know what to think of Ross's distracted air; he too eyed the distant stream as though it were an illusion that would vanish if he looked away. She knew he was troubled and planned to send cattle to market far earlier than in previous years. His concern had something to do with the men, armed with rifles, who rode toward the upper mesa at regular intervals and the exhausted men who rode into the yard on weary horses a few hours later.

A wave of sadness swept over her. Wasn't a wife supposed to share in her husband's concerns? How could she offer him comfort when he never confided in her? Her position on the ranch was exactly what it had been when she was a child.

Chapter Eight

TRAVIS WATCHED THE LAST OF his men board the train. He couldn't help envying them. They were on their way back to Utah with the meager funds they'd earned driving horses north from Mexico to California, money that would buy supplies to see their families through the winter and to put in crops next spring. It wasn't their destination he envied. The Salt Lake Valley was mighty cold in the winter and he had no love for ice and snow. It was the loving arms they'd step into when they left the train at the end of their journey he found hard to put out of his mind.

Most of his men were returning to wives and families. Lately he'd begun to despair of ever finding someone to share his life with or of having anything to offer her if he did meet a woman with whom he wanted to spend the rest of his life. He spent months with only the companionship of the men he'd hired to help with the herds of horses. He'd gotten in the habit of spending his winters in California near old Treadwell's sister, Fanny, in a small Mormon community and working at a nearby ranch. The Mormon girls he met there and in the Mexican colonies made it clear they were looking for men who shared their beliefs. He wasn't sure whether he believed the same things they did or not, but he found much to admire in their society that centered around families. His own family had always been small, and there was no one he claimed as kin anymore except his brother, and he hadn't seen Clayton for going on eight years. He didn't remember ever having an extended family except for Grandpa and memories of him weren't pleasant. Maybe next year when he finished driving horses and was ready to settle down . . .

He walked to the hitching rail where he'd tied his horse. The stallion was getting on in years and would need to be replaced in another year or two. He thought longingly of the horses he'd left at the Sorensen Ranch in Texas and his plan to start a horse-breeding ranch of his own. Next year, he planned to claim a couple of the best mares from the Sebastian herd and visit Mr. Sorensen to see if he could still claim any of the colts sired by his mama's stallion to begin his own herd. He still had money in a far-off bank in Kansas and he'd opened an account in Sacramento. Together, there should be almost enough funds to buy land and horses to establish the ranch he'd dreamed of since he was a boy in Alabama. He didn't want to wait until he was too old, like Pa had been.

Stepping astride his horse, he slapped the reins against the animal's neck and urged it toward the edge of town. He had a long ride ahead of him if he meant to reach Aunt Fanny's place before dark. The woman was a widow and had left her home in Utah to settle near her grown children in California. She wasn't blood kin, but she'd treated him like a son or favorite nephew ever since he'd carried word to her of her brother's death in far-off Montana and for that he was grateful. It was through her son Travis had met one of his best customers and landed a job that ensured he had a bed and grub through the rainy winter months. Hopefully one of the Mormons who traveled regularly from Salt Lake to California had left a packet of letters for him from Clayton with the widow. Letters weren't the same as being with his brother, but they never failed to ease his ache for family.

* * *

Ross pulled his sheepskin coat closer around him and drew the blanket he'd tied over his hat down tighter across his ears and face. Snow didn't usually arrive with such force or abundance so far south, but this was one of those once-in-a-hundred-years blizzards that pushed cattle south toward Mexico and piled them against fences or into rivers to die. Many would be lost in the mountain canyons to starve or fall prey to wild beasts or the last remnants of Indian tribes who still hid there. He glanced to his right, where he caught only brief glimpses of Dominic through the blowing snow. Dom was the best horseman on the ranch, possibly the best in the valley, but Ross couldn't help feeling concern for him. The young ranch hand had become almost a brother to him.

The storm, instead of abating, seemed to be gathering greater fury. The temperature was dropping, and with such low visibility, a rider could easily become as confused as the cattle and become lost or freeze to death.

He couldn't help wondering if he'd made the right decision to brave the storm in an attempt to rescue his cattle. Losses had been heavy due to last summer's water shortage and his finances were in no condition to sustain another deep cut in his breeding stock. Conditions had improved some since the breakup of the dam diverting water from the creek the ranch depended on, but they'd still had to trail a sizable portion of their herd to Albuquerque for early transport to eastern markets, and both weight and prices had been low.

There'd been no further disputes with the Purdys since last summer's incident. The marshal had visited the ranch, and finding no sign of the dam, he had concluded that the obstruction was a natural occurrence of piled-up debris carried by the water itself. Ross had fumed over the time he'd wasted tipping the rocks and slabs of stone into a dry gulley but had gradually withdrawn orders to post armed men above the mesa, and there had been no further incidences of Purdy gunmen firing at his men. Perhaps all he needed was to show Jacob he couldn't be pushed around.

The horse stopped and Ross realized they'd reached the fence line a sheep rancher had strung to keep his sheep from wandering onto land claimed by cattlemen. As expected, some cattle lay in heaps, already stiff, while others bawled and struggled against the wire. Dismounting, he waded through drifts of cattle and snow toward the hated barbed wire. With nearly frozen fingers he withdrew wire cutters from a pouch attached to his belt and went to work on the strands of wire. He didn't have to see them to know that Dominic, Jacob, and Ben, along with a dozen caballeros from both ranches were repeating the action as they encountered the fence. More cattle would survive if they were allowed to drift before the storm than if they huddled against an obstacle such as the fence, and the ranchers would be able to round them up in the spring.

Just as he cut the last wire, a sound reached his ears that sounded eerily like a scream. It was likely just the wind or a shout to move the cattle that were still alive, but Ross waded with care through the snow back to his patient mount, who stood with snow plastering his dark hide, nearly obscuring his presence. A sense of foreboding rode on his shoulders as he turned toward the position where Dom should be. Following the barely visible line of the fence, Ross worked his way west until a rider on horseback loomed out of the blowing snow.

Ross recognized Carlos and pulled his horse alongside the boy's, never revealing by word or action how relieved he was to see the kid. He hadn't wanted the boy to be part of the rescue action but had to admit young Carlos was one of the best and most determined riders on his team. When he tried to speak, the wind blew away his words, or so he excused his inability to speak.

"Senor Adams, Senor Purdy is hurt!"

He caught Carlos's shout. It was enough; they both turned, urging their horses in the direction from which Carlos had come. A dark spot in the sea of white turned out to be a circle of men surrounding a figure on the ground.

Ross dismounted to kneel beside the neighboring rancher. He and Jacob maintained a wary relationship, but he wished the other man no ill. Ripping off the scarf wrapped around his own face, he pressed an ear to Jacob's chest. Over the howling wind, he thought he detected a faint beat. Baring the fingers of one hand, he pressed them against the carotid artery. Even though Jacob was partially covered with snow, there was no mistaking the large amount of blood the man had lost. Several deep slashes marred the fallen man's face, but the deep, bubbling wound across his throat told the story. Jacob had been caught by a flying wire when he'd cut into the fence line stretched taut by the pressure of the dead and dying cattle heaped against it. The fast-moving wire, acting as a thin blade, had severed vital vessels.

Ross pressed a handful of snow against the gaping neck wound, hoping the cold and the pressure would staunch the flow of blood, but it soon became clear it was too late. The thread of breath that escaped the rancher's lips ceased. Pulling back the blanket that protected his face, Ross pressed his ear against the man's chest again in a vain attempt to hear a heartbeat. With the wind and snow swirling and screaming around them, it was hard to be certain, but there seemed to be no sign of life. Ross felt no grief for the arrogant man who'd been the source of the major problems he'd faced since taking over management of the rancho, though there was a stab of guilt for his part in persuading Jacob Purdy to join him in an attempt to save the cattle of both ranches.

Their relationship had been tainted from the start by both men's lust for the Sebastian Rancho and had been further eroded by quarrels over water. Only their common need to save as many cattle as possible had brought them together in a desperate attempt to reach and open the fence. He shook his head and slowly rose to his feet, looking around for Jacob's son.

"Ben?" he shouted against the blowing wind. Even knowing his guilt was misplaced, he felt a need to express his regrets and assure the young man of his support as the younger man assumed management of his father's ranch.

"He and some of the others turned back a long time ago, before we left the willows bordering the creek," one of the Purdy hands announced, his voice muffled by the heavy wool scarf covering the lower half of his face. "He's all right; he only needed to follow the creek back to within a half mile of the ranch house."

Ross's glance went involuntarily to Dominic and young Carlos, then to the other caballeros who formed a circle around the fallen man. He knew without a word being spoken among them that they would never have left him to pursue the cattle without them. They were good men, men he could depend on. He turned his gaze once more to Jacob, but already the dead rancher's cowhands were lifting the rancher's body to lay it across his horse's saddle. He watched them tie down the body before turning into the wind and beginning the treacherous journey back.

Ross stood, letting the snow blow against his bare face and slide down his collar, as he stared helplessly at the white mound before him. He knew it concealed dead cattle and he wondered if Jacob had died in vain and their efforts had been for nothing. He shouldn't have encouraged men to battle a killer storm to protect cattle even if the neighboring ranch faced financial ruin as surely as he did with the loss of so much stock.

"Boss, it's going to be a hard ride back." Dominic stood beside him, holding the reins of Ross's horse. Behind him the Sebastian hands formed a silent line, their heads bowed against the wind and freezing snow. Ross reached out to pull a scarf around Carlos's ears. Ross looked to pull his leather gloves back over his numb fingers but didn't find them. Knowing they were buried in the trampled snow or carried miles away by the wind, he took the proffered reins and swung onto the animal's back. When he was settled, he pulled his coat sleeves as far over his hands as they would go. Fighting their horses' natural instinct to follow any surviving cattle farther south, Ross and his men turned their horses into the wind and made their way to the front of the caballeros to cut a trail back to the ranch.

* * *

She had never seen such a storm. Since she'd been a small child, Iliana had been familiar with the occasional sudden harsh storms that visited the valley each winter, but there had never been one such as this. Taking comfort in the feel of her child in her arms, she rocked Gabe until he fell asleep. After placing him on his bed, she felt too restless to settle and paced from room to room. Once she caught sight of the maid who had been hired to assist Amaya, peering from a window, her face pinched and narrow as she stared into the whirling storm.

"You need not wait," she told the girl. "I will attend to my husband when they arrive."

"Si, Senora." The girl bowed her head to show her respect for her employer. "It is not good for you to wait alone."

"I shall be all right."

"I do not mind keeping their supper warm."

Iliana suspected the girl had her own reasons for wishing to stay up. She'd noticed how the young woman's eyes followed Dominic whenever the caballero was near. With a shrug of her shoulders, Iliana moved to the room her husband called his office but which she still thought of as Grandfather's library. She sensed the girl had withdrawn into the kitchen but had not retired to her room as Amaya had done some time ago. There was something comforting, knowing she didn't wait alone. Loneliness had been part of her life as long as she could remember. First she'd lost her parents, then Grandfather. Grandfather had discouraged a close association with the families that lived in the small houses beyond the stable; she'd seldom visited the village and had never been sent away to attend school. He had tutored her himself. She stood before the wide desk that had been Grandfather's but which now held papers Ross had left in neat piles at one side of the dark wooden surface. She would not think about the possibility that Ross might not return.

A sound disturbed her reverie and she rushed toward the door that opened from the courtyard. Reaching the entry, she stopped in shock. Two ghostlike figures stood hunched together, the taller one supporting the other. Snow caked their bodies from their hooded capes to their boots. White-glazed brows hovered over kerchiefs frozen to their beards and concealing mouths and noses.

Amaya appeared in the opposite doorway, followed by the maid, who gave a frightened scream, shocking Iliana into action. The fully clothed housekeeper hadn't been asleep as Iliana had supposed. Iliana flew toward the man she knew to be Ross. She felt an unfamiliar urge to throw herself in his arms but sensed he was in more need of comfort than she.

"*Mi pobre marido.*" She brushed at the snow, claimed his arm, and tugged him toward the stairs.

"There is warm water on the stove. Raquel, carry it to the senor's chamber. Dominic, you can bathe in the small room off the pantry; Javier will have his hands full with the men in the bunkhouse." Amaya took charge, assuming the role of general. "Iliana, the senor's clothes must be removed and he is in need of warming."

Feeling the cold of Ross's clothing seeping through her gown, she did her best to ignore the unpleasant sensation. After stumbling into his chamber and leaving the door ajar for the maid to bring warm water, she hesitated, uncertain how to proceed. Tentatively she reached for the cords that held her husband's thick poncho closed. Her fingers became cold and stiff as she struggled with the fastenings. But at last the thick, cape-like garment dropped to the floor behind him. He shuddered and she looked up into his face. He attempted to speak, but she couldn't understand his words through the thick, ice-encrusted scarf covering his face.

Something tender stirred in her heart. Reaching up, she brushed snow from Ross's eyebrows then placed her hands over the scarf on either side of his mouth, fearing that pulling away the frozen cloth might pull away skin with it. Her hands grew wet, and she knew that in spite of how cold her fingers felt, they were thawing the frozen scarf.

Raquel bumped the door open with one hip to deposit a tin tub before the fireplace then turned to stir up coals from a fire laid earlier. Iliana drew back from Ross, feeling a hint of embarrassment for being caught in such an intimate position.

"Dominic say you must check his hands. He lost his gloves." Raquel delivered her rapid-fire message, suggesting she was in a hurry to leave.

"Oh!" Iliana whirled back to Ross and reached for his hands. He seemed unable to straighten them from their curled position and the white shade of his skin frightened her. He mumbled something that sounded like "water." She looked around, feeling confused by his request—if it was a request. Spying a pitcher standing beside a china basin, she picked it up.

Looking back to ascertain that water was what he wanted, she was surprised to find he'd hobbled closer. He nodded his head toward the basin and she understood he wanted her to pour the water into it.

As she poured the water, an idea came to her. After setting the pitcher back on the bureau, she dabbed a corner of the towel that waited beside it into the water. The water was cool, but it would do. She lifted the towel to Ross's face and patted the moisture against the scarf. He jerked when the water first touched his face but didn't draw away. Instead he moved closer to the basin and attempted to place his hands in it. Seeing his efforts, she lifted them, one after the other, to set them in the water. He made a whistling sound as though sucking in a painful gulp of air.

Returning her wet hands to his face, she saw one corner of the cloth drop away revealing Ross's mouth drawn into a grimace. She was pleased to see he'd lost no skin and turned her attention to the other side of his face. Soon she drew the rest of the scarf away and tossed the sodden lump aside.

"Thank you," he mumbled. "Best you send for Javier to get my boots off," he continued in a raspy whisper.

"Amaya says Javier has his hands full treating caballeros for frostbite."

Iliana hadn't heard Raquel enter the room again. This time the maid carried two heavy buckets. She poured their contents into the tub and lost no time leaving the room again.

"Sit on the bed." Iliana tried to speak in the same authoritative voice Amaya used when she gave orders no one dared disobey. Ross smiled weakly but allowed her to help him to the bedside, where he sank down in apparent exhaustion. She seated herself on the floor in front of him and reached for a boot. After tugging without success for several minutes, she leaned back to take a deep breath.

"It's too much for you, girl," Ross whispered.

"No. I will do it."

"Perhaps if I set one foot against the footboard . . ."

"Yes, that will help." She understood his suggestion. She stood, then reached for his other leg, swung it onto the bed, and positioned herself so that she could pull on the boot as her husband pushed with his other foot against the heavy footboard.

The first tug was as futile as her earlier attempts, but grasping the boot firmly, she ordered, "Push!" Straining to free the stubborn boot, she felt a moment's elation as the boot began to move. Suddenly she sprawled backward, narrowly missing the tub.

She lay stunned for a moment. From the direction of the bed, she could hear Ross calling her name in that weak voice. Raising herself to a sitting position, she became aware of the large boot cradled by one hand against her chest. "I did it!" It was almost a shout. She scrambled to her feet and hurried to her husband's side to show him the boot.

"Are you hurt?" he asked.

"No, I am fine," she assured him with a triumphant smile, ignoring her bruised behind and skinned elbows. She remembered the second boot, and her spirits drooped. It had to come off too. Just as she reached for it, there was a soft tap on the door followed by a voice. "I have brought more water."

Iliana hurried to the door. Raquel looked at her, keeping her eyes lowered. "If the senor is bathing . . ."

"No, no. I had trouble with his boots. Set the buckets on the floor, then you must help me."

Raquel raised her eyes by slow degrees until she could see Ross was indeed still fully clothed minus his cloak and one boot. She followed Iliana to the bed, where the young women's combined efforts soon freed him from the second boot.

Iliana reached for the buttons of his shirt and Raquel began to back away.

"Carlos, the men? Are they all right?" Ross croaked.

"Si, senor. Amaya say Carlos be strong *hombre*." She turned her head toward Iliana. "Amaya said to tell you to add hot water only little, then little more." She fled from the room in a great hurry.

Ross returned to a sitting position and attempted to fumble with his buttons. Iliana brushed aside his clumsy efforts to finish the task. She felt herself blushing when it came time to unbuckle Ross's belt. When the task was completed, she averted her eyes to slide his stiff denim trousers to the floor.

Once free of his clothes, Ross shuffled toward the tub. She hovered nearby, uncertain how to help. She heard a splash followed by a sharp yelp.

"Is the water too hot?" Guilt assailed her; she'd failed to check the temperature of the water. Dropping to her knees, she knelt to thrust one hand into the water. "It is cold! I shall add this bucket of hot water." She reached for one of the buckets Raquel had left on the floor.

"No!" Ross lifted an arm as if to ward off the hot water. His face appeared drawn with pain. "Let me sit here a moment."

Puzzled, she watched his face slowly relax. He leaned back and his eyes closed.

After a few minutes, he appeared to fall asleep. Concerned that the cold water might further chill him, she picked up the pitcher to use as a scoop. Taking care not to splash hot water on him, she poured a small amount of the heated water into the tub. Remembering Amaya's instructions, delivered by Raquel, she waited a short time before adding another pitcher of the hot water until both buckets were emptied. The water still felt cooler than she would have liked.

Another tap sounded on the door, bringing Iliana to her feet. This time it was Amaya she found waiting. She put a finger to her lips.

"He will soon shake with chills," the older woman whispered. "Give him this and keep him warm." She thrust a thick crockery mug into Iliana's hands. Iliana could feel the heat from Amaya's rich, spicy chocolate through the glazed clay.

When she returned to Ross's side, she found him sitting hunched forward. "Amaya said you should drink this." She handed him the mug and was pleased to see him grasp it in his hands. Slowly he brought it to his lips. She watched a moment. Feeling assured his hands were again functional, she gathered up a nightshirt and turned down Ross's bed.

When he had finished the chocolate, she held out a towel and, seeing the way he shook with cold, urged him from the tub and wrapped it around him. Keeping one arm around his waist, she offered her support as he made his way to the bed.

"Don't fuss," he admonished through chattering teeth when she attempted to pull his nightshirt over his head. She let him pull the shirt on himself but watched with a critical eye until he finished the task and lay back against thick pillows. She reached for an extra quilt at the foot of the bed and pulled it up over his shoulders.

She looked down at him, wondering if there was more she could do. Her world seemed to right itself when she observed that color had returned to Ross's face, though his lips still held a tinge of blue. He was looking back at her with a faint smile turning up the corners of his mouth.

"I've never been so cold in my whole life," he whispered. "Thank you."

"You might have died," she whispered back as tears formed in her eyes. The strength that had kept her seeing to his needs seemed to desert her, and she collapsed against the blankets piled upon his chest. Though she tried to hold it in, a sob escaped her throat.

"I'm fine, darlin'." One arm freed itself from the quilts to wrap around her shoulders. She felt the slight tremor of his hand and knew he still shook with cold.

"You're not fine. You're still cold. I'll fetch another blanket." She removed his arm to slide it back under the quilts. He caught at her fingers and gently tugged her toward him.

"Don't go," he said. She wavered only a moment then stepped out of her slippers to slide beneath the quilts and snuggle against him.

Chapter Nine

Not even the wiry horse wrangler, Willard, with his incessant whistling, could mar Travis's pleasure in a perfect morning. The sun was shining, the long winter was over, he had a good horse under him, and most of the men who'd hired on the previous year had returned for one more foray into Mexico to secure horses. On an impulse he motioned for the men to take the route leading to the Sebastian Ranch.

"Don't we usually stop at Ross Adams's place last?" Willard stopped whistling to question the route Travis had chosen.

"Yes, but I think seeing what he has to offer before we head into the colonies will give us better bargaining power." He didn't go on to speak of the nagging feeling that had been growing stronger the past few days that had been directing him toward reaching the Sebastian Ranch as soon as possible. Several of his Mormon friends had spoken of "feelings" that directed them toward a particular course of action at various times, but he wasn't sure the urgency he was feeling to reach the ranch fell into the same category. He didn't consider himself a religious man.

The afternoon was well spent when the riders approached the outbuildings. An old man and a boy of fourteen or fifteen rode out to meet them.

"Hola!"

"Hola, Javier!" Travis returned the greeting.

"You have come early this year, Senor Travis." Javier cast a questioning look at the dozen riders who gathered behind their leader.

"We thought it advisable to see what we could expect to purchase here before continuing into Mexico. We wouldn't want to find ourselves with too many horses and not enough funds when we stop here on our way back to California."

"You are welcome to camp in your usual place. Senor Ross will be pleased to see you. I shall tell him to expect you in an hour's time." The old man gave a respectful nod of his head before turning back toward the hacienda.

As Travis and his men set up camp near the willows bordering the smaller creek that crossed the ranch, he was surprised to see that, though the tiny stream was nearly overflowing its banks with spring runoff, the distant hills looked dry and the large pond that should have glinted silver in the distance was difficult to even see, signifying it held little if any water.

He took the time to wash up and don a clean shirt before approaching the hacienda. A maid answered his knock and directed him toward the library. Shock washed over him on seeing the thin, wasted figure behind the desk. Ross Adams looked to be in dire health.

Ross didn't rise to greet him as was his usual custom. Instead he motioned for Travis to be seated.

Settling into the leather chair indicated, Travis fumbled for words to express his concern.

"It's no matter," Ross waved aside his fumbling attempt. "We had an unusually severe winter, and I got caught in a blizzard, suffered some frostbite, followed by pneumonia, but with warmer weather I expect I shall soon be fine. Javier tells me you're doing a little advance scouting to determine how many horses I'll be able to sell to you when you return from Mexico."

"I received word from the colonies in Mexico that their numbers are down. Their stock suffered through a difficult winter too."

"We didn't lose many horses because of the severe winter, but a few colts didn't survive. Our greatest loss was our cattle. We were hurt badly by a dry summer, followed by a blizzard that drove the cattle to pile up and die against fences as they tried to move south ahead of the storm. With fewer cattle, we can spare some horses, though not as many as in previous years."

"I shall be happy to contract for as many as you wish to sell. I'm sorry for your loss of cattle and hope you'll be able to make up the loss this year. With the heavy snowfall in the mountains, it seems you should have sufficient water this summer, yet I noticed your stock pond is dry."

A bitter grimace crossed Ross's face. "This ranch is dying for want of water. Before the large stream that comes from the mountains reaches the

Sebastian, it must cross the Purdy Ranch. Relations have not gone well between us. Complicating matters, Jacob Purdy died during the blizzard, leaving everything to his willful son. Ben is determined to force me out and acquire my ranch for himself. He's dammed off the water again. Until I'm well, I can't fight him or follow up on my wife's old grandfather's insistence that there's another source of water in the mountains. He spoke with unmistakable longing of the river that once flowed directly onto the Sebastian Rancho."

Long after Travis returned to camp, he found himself thinking about Ross Adams's plight. He thought too of the land between the Sebastian Ranch and the distant mountains. If the stream of water flowing across that barren land could be found and returned to its ancient channel, that land would be ideal for the ranch he wanted to build. His mind filled with a vision of blooded horses grazing in lush grass beside a swollen river while the sun beat down on neat stables and warmed his back. Toward morning he made up his mind.

"Brother Lewis," he awakened the camp cook, a dependable man the wranglers looked up to and often went to for advice. "I need to ask for a favor."

"What is it?" The man seemed to be instantly awake.

"You know I've been thinking of buying land to start my own place. I've found the piece of land I want, but I need to do some checking on whether there's enough water and who owns the land now. I'm pretty sure it's government land and falls under the homesteading act, but I need some time to check into things. Would you take charge for a couple of weeks, go on down to the villages we've visited before to get as many horses as you can? As soon as I have the information I need, I'll head south to meet up with you."

"Didn't you tell me you own a piece of land in Utah? Why would you want land here, too?" Brother Lewis asked.

"I didn't set out to buy that land in Utah; I was persuaded none too gently at gunpoint to buy an old trapper's claim. The trouble with that piece of land is the location; it's mostly the perpendicular side of a mountain, and it's too small for what I want. Besides I've had a taste of Utah winters and I prefer a more southerly clime."

Brother Lewis expressed some reluctance to go on without Travis but finally agreed to take charge until Travis rejoined them. Travis rode with the men as far as the village, then bid them farewell. He remembered meeting

Ted Williams earlier and learning he ran a small bank in the village, but he also acted as an attorney and informal mayor for the ranchers in the valley and the small community. He'd know what was required to claim the piece of land that ran from the Sebastian Ranch to the distant mountains. Travis turned his steps toward the bank.

It was later than he'd expected when he left the bank and paused to settle his hat on his head and catch his breath. He had been surprised to learn that the old Spanish land grant extended much farther than he'd supposed. Most of the land he'd hoped to acquire, though it lay dry and unused, was part of the large land holding known as the Sebastian Rancho. A much narrower strip that bordered one side of an ancient streambed that disappeared into a mountain canyon was all that was available. Something urged him to make arrangements to acquire the land anyway, and the old banker had insisted that Travis share the canyon with Adams to eliminate any future disputes over water found in the canyon. Travis was agreeable to that. Now it was time to ride back to see Ross Adams and deliver the papers Williams had prepared.

When he arrived at the ranch, Travis was disappointed to learn that Ross Adams had taken a turn for the worse and would be unable to see him. He spent the better part of the day discussing his plans with old Javier, who gave his enthusiastic support and coerced the cook into providing a bag of vittles to supplement the supplies Travis had taken from the cook wagon before sending his wranglers on their way.

He chose to follow the old streambed that wound its way through the barren land. When night came, he made camp but arose and continued the journey before sunrise.

* * *

Feeling himself begin to slide, Travis reached for a scrawny shrub and felt it give beneath his grasp. He clawed with hands and feet for a crack or crevice to break his fall, and to his surprise the small obtrusion his boot struck held his weight. His hands continued to grope for a hold and he sighed in gratitude when his fingers encountered a narrow fissure in the slick rock. He held his position for several minutes, gasping to regain his breath.

When he felt secure, he looked around, searching for a means of regaining the narrow path above him. He turned his head, flattening his cheek against the red rock down which he'd tumbled. That's when he saw it. Twenty feet below him and at least thirty feet above the bottom of the canyon there was a path, long unused, but still unmistakable. As surely as if someone had spoken to him, he knew he should go down, not up, and that the path would lead him to the mystery he sought.

With slow, deliberate movements, he eased his way downward until his hand gripped the rock where his boot had rested. After a few moments, his foot found a new projection and his fingers searched for another hold. At last he dropped the last few feet and found himself standing on the path he'd glimpsed from above. Bending over to rest his hands on his knees, he took in deep gulps of air. Until that moment he hadn't been certain he'd survive his unexpected plunge from where the path he'd been following near the rim of the canyon had suddenly given way.

He'd known it would be dangerous to explore the canyon alone, but he had no other choice and acquiring the land he wanted was dependent on finding water. Before making a claim on the land, he had to know if the rumors concerning a source of water in the canyon were true.

He'd left the Sebastian hacienda before daylight four days ago on General Jack, carrying only those items essential for the trip. He'd followed the old streambed, where no water had flowed for half a century. Riding almost due east to where the rancho ended and the land he hoped to purchase lay, he found no usable grazing land, only rocks, a few half-dead Joshua trees, and a couple of rattlers. The dry stream he followed entered the canyon but disappeared beneath a pile of boulders and old uprooted trees that blocked the entrance to the canyon. He'd thought it best to wait until morning to explore the canyon and had opted to make camp on a small plateau overlooking it. After tethering his horse and setting up camp, he'd gone in search of firewood and had discovered the trail that had enticed him to explore for a short distance on foot. His exploration had ended in disaster as the trail gave way, sending him sliding down the mountainside to what appeared to be another trail, overgrown and long unused.

The old trail he stood on now was partially covered by rocks and debris fallen from above, but it was passable. He wanted to know where the trail led, but it would be dark soon and he didn't wish to leave his horse unattended for long. Small bands of Indians were rumored to still roam these mountains occasionally and his horse wouldn't be safe from a raid. There were likely cougars in the canyon, too, and General Jack could be in danger without the protection of a campfire and Travis's rifle. Thinking of his rifle, he regretted that it had been left back at the camp he'd set up. He'd only meant to explore for a short distance along the narrow trail in hopes of finding a better view of the canyon.

He'd followed the dim trail through thick brush to a ledge that hung over a deeper portion of the winding canyon. From that lofty perspective he spied what appeared to be a continuation of the dry and overgrown streambed he had followed from the ranch until he lost it at the mouth of the steep gorge. Careful inspection indicated a large spring had once gushed from the rocks at that point. As he'd craned his neck for a better view and to perhaps discover why the spring had ceased to flow, he took one careless step that nearly cost his life.

Bringing his thoughts back to his present predicament, he scanned the sheer sides of the lower canyon from the old trail where he stood, searching for a route back up to the trail he'd fallen from and the campsite he'd set up, but saw nothing promising. Looking across the narrow canyon he could see that, indeed, there had once been a good-sized stream of water flowing through the canyon. Only a dry riverbed, overgrown with grass and brush, remained.

It would be dark soon and he was torn between further exploration along the old trail and finding a route back to his campsite. Perhaps if he followed the overgrown path for a little longer, he'd find a place where he could climb the steep cliff. Looking up, he spotted remnants of the higher trail far above his head. It appeared to have collapsed in several places, sending rock slides to cover portions of the lower trail, which caused him to worry that even if he should find a way back up to it, there would be no way to follow the path back to camp. His only hope of regaining the top of the canyon appeared to be following the path he was on to see where it led.

Rounding a bend, he came upon a massive rockslide that had occurred a long time ago. Boulders and debris brought the path he followed to an abrupt halt. If he climbed the slide he'd be a little closer to the top of the canyon, he reasoned. From there he might be able to find a route on up to the ledge from which he'd slipped. He soon discovered that loose rock made climbing the slide both difficult and dangerous. An occasional bush or clump of grass appeared as he approached the highest point. When his foot slipped, he clutched at the grass, only to find himself sprawling backward with the grass clutched in his fist. The shale rock cut like slivers of glass, slicing open his shirt sleeves and opening a gash in his pants. The cuts went through to his skin, leaving a trail of blood to stain his clothes.

Rising on shaky feet, he examined himself and decided the cuts weren't deep and he hadn't lost a lot of ground. He stepped forward, testing each spot where he set a foot. Shadows were beginning to lengthen, warning him he didn't have much time to find his way out of the canyon.

At last he reached the top of the slide debris and wondered if he was hallucinating. He blinked several times, and if his footing wasn't so precarious he would have dropped to his knees in gratitude. Water gleamed like silver in the fading sunset from a short distance below his feet to as far up the canyon as he could see. A long, narrow lake lay behind the dam created by the slide. The story Don Sebastian told had been right. The canyon was the source of water that had made the valley lush when the first Sebastian had arrived to build his empire. Here was enough water to make the ranch he dreamed of a reality and to free the Sebastian Rancho from Purdy's threats—if Travis could find a way to breach the dam. He swallowed a lump in his throat several times as he stood staring at the sight before him.

Turning slowly, Travis looked back the way he'd come. He could see where the old riverbed he'd followed led right to the dam. Excitement filled him as he contemplated a way to return the flow of water to its former path. He'd brought explosives, but they were back at camp. He'd have to study the situation to make certain he didn't send a flood rushing out of the canyon. He had no desire to waste the water nor to wash out the banks of the streams below.

It was logical to assume the slide served as a dam preventing the flow of water from reaching the streambed it once filled. It was also logical to see that the lake had to still have some outlet, or it would have overflowed the dam. He figured some of the water disappeared underground only to reappear as the spring on the eastern slope of the Purdy Ranch. It, too, might have once been much larger than its present condition. He needed to explore more thoroughly.

While staring at the water and visualizing what it meant to him and to the Sebastian Rancho, he lost track of time. Dimming light and a hint of cooler temperature reminded him night was approaching. The critical thing now was to find a way back to his camp.

Chapter Ten

Travis considered how long it would take to retrace his steps then continue on to the mouth of the canyon. On foot the trek would take most of the night. He scanned the shoreline of the narrow lake. A faint impression along the edge of the water suggested the trail he'd been following continued on. For long moments, he stared straight ahead across the water, but not really seeing it as he contemplated which way he should go.

A picture of old Treadwell flashed in his mind. He could see him with bowed head and closed eyes, his lips barely moving before making an important decision. He suspected he'd been praying. Pa sometimes prayed too, and Travis had a faint recollection of Mama kneeling beside him before tucking him in his bed at night. The Mormon riders who helped him with the horses often prayed. He closed his eyes and thought about praying, but he didn't know how, or if even God could help him.

"Which way?" he muttered aloud, opening his eyes and looking toward the sky. Glancing back the way he'd come, then forward to the faint "rabbit trail" ahead, he felt a slight pull to continue on even though the faint path angled away from the spot where he'd entered the canyon. He didn't know if he'd gotten an answer to his question or not, but he began working his way toward what he hoped was a path.

As he scrambled along, he couldn't help wondering what kind of animal had wandered alongside the water often enough to form a path. He felt certain no horse had ever traversed the narrow space. The water rippled close to his boots and he wondered at its depth. It looked dark and black. In several places it lapped across the trail and he took extra care not to slip. He found himself searching for handholds in the rock that rose beside him to ease his way along the more narrow stretches.

What madness had made him think he could follow the treacherous trail with night coming on? One misstep would send him plunging into icy depths. An injury would leave him prey for a wild animal.

Glancing up from the careful placement of his feet, Travis saw a slab of stone that seemed to arise out of the water to block the trail. In the near-darkness he could see no evidence of the path continuing past the sheer cliff that towered over him and projected out into the water. He stared in dismay at water slapping at the bottom of a sheer vertical wall. Returning the way he'd come would be a daunting task in the near darkness.

Leaning his head against the rough stone, he felt an urge to cry. He hadn't cried since the day his mother was buried beneath the willow tree back at the plantation. Drawing his head upright, he shook off the childish urge. His hands swept the canyon wall in angry frustration.

He felt something rough beneath his hand. His fingers delved into a deep indentation. It didn't feel like an ordinary crack or cleft. He swept his hand in a careful arc. Soon he discovered a second one, then another. Something about those indentations in the rock wall stirred something in his mind and he searched out others. He felt excitement building. His hands swept lower, finding a parallel row of step-like gouges.

On an impulse he fit one foot in one of the cuts and grasped an upper indentation with his hand. Moving his right foot to the next cut, he followed with his left to the spot just vacated. He repeated the action, finding hand- and toeholds at regular intervals. Sweat poured down his back and he wondered if he was a fool for blindly following the cuts in the rock. If he fell into the cold, black water below, there was little possibility he could swim to where he could crawl back onto the path. The jagged cuts in the rocks were evenly spaced and perfect for moving parallel to the water and several feet above the lake. Common sense told him the cuts had been made by human hands, and if so, they had to lead somewhere.

That somewhere might be trouble. Renegade Indians and bandits had hidden in these mountains for years; he could be stumbling into some secret hideout. He leaned his forehead against the smooth rock and questioned his own sanity. Some instinct warned there was no going back and he resolutely grasped the next indentation in the rock. At last he worked his way around the point of the rock face. With his face pressed against the rough stone and his feet and hands gripping their holds, he lifted his eyes.

Night had come to the canyon and all he could see was a shadowy cove. His eyes were able to separate land from water, and he could make out a few trees and shrubs on what appeared to be a crescent of land ringed by canyon walls on three sides and the lake on the other.

His movements quickened as he continued his journey to a spot where the cuts ran out and he could leap to solid ground. With cautious steps he moved forward. When his boots struck a ring of stones, he felt certain he'd stumbled onto a campground. His mind flew to stories of Geronimo hiding out successfully in these mountains until a short time ago. *Was it possible some of the Chiricahua Apaches had escaped and still hid out in this place?* He shivered and glanced over his shoulder toward the dense shadows nearer the cliff. All was quiet and there was no sensation of being watched.

Moving closer to the cliffs that framed the cove, he searched for a way out, but with darkness hampering his search, it was impossible to see a way to reach the plateau above. Anxiously he increased his pace. As the curvature of the cliffs brought him to the far side of the small cove and closer to the water again, he recognized the feel of packed earth beneath his feet. The place where he walked was a path, or it had been at one time.

Following what he felt certain was a trail, he discovered a narrow slit in the rocks, one that had been impossible to detect from only a few feet away in the darkness of the canyon. Observing that the packed ground led into the narrow opening, he stepped into it and discovered the opening was wider than he'd supposed. A man on foot could easily lead a horse through it.

The path angled upward and was not pitch dark as he'd expected. The trail followed a fissure in the rock cliff instead of being a cave as he'd first assumed. Overhead he caught glimpses of stars lending light to the night sky. A few minutes later the packed earth disappeared and he heard the sharper sound of rock beneath his boots. Above the narrow slot in the stone walls on either side of him, he caught a glimpse of an almost-full moon.

With no way to judge time, he had no idea how long he'd spent winding his way upward, but after following the steep trail for what seemed a long time, he emerged from the narrow slot canyon onto a tree-less mountainside littered with massive boulders. He filled his lungs with cool mountain air, feeling as though he'd emerged at long last from an underground cavern.

Travis's heart raced. He'd probably discovered a renegade Indian hideout. If the soldiers and posses who had chased the renegades into the mountains had failed to find the hidden cove, he needed to mark the entry to find his way back in daylight. Removing the bandana from around his throat, he secured it with two rocks near the opening of the fissure. He had every intention of returning to that hidden lake.

The large moon, nearing its peak, and the star-filled night provided direction as he moved across the huge slabs of stone that formed the mountain. Soon the rocky mountainside gave way to one of the foothills that led to the mesas and valley below. As he neared the place where he'd left his horse and set up camp earlier, the shrill cry of a big cat reached his ears and he broke into a lope. The puma sounded some distance away, and whether it was announcing a kill or voicing its frustration at a missed opportunity, he didn't want it to come in search of his horse.

On reaching the campsite, he found General Jack pacing and tugging at his tether. He too had heard the cat or possibly caught a whiff of it on the air. Travis lost no time calming the horse and building a fire.

Though aching with fatigue from hours of riding followed by a long hike, he found himself unable to sleep. For a long time he sat near the campfire, thinking and planning his next course of action. His thoughts drifted to his brother and the past. Clayton should be with him to share this adventure. Brother Lewis had brought a thick packet of letters with him when he'd arrived from Salt Lake, and Travis had read them so many times he'd almost memorized them. Clayton wrote of his happiness with Lucy on the old plantation and about another baby expected in the fall. A stab of remorse settled over Travis. Clayton continued to send a letter to the Salt Lake address every month, but Travis had only scribbled a couple of brief notes during the years he'd been trading horses. He'd write his brother a long letter when he returned to California. He'd tell Clayton about buying the land to at last start the ranch he'd dreamed of for so long. A wave of melancholy swept over him and he found himself longing to be with his brother again.

When morning came, he packed up his gear and rode General Jack back the way he'd traveled on foot the night before. Reaching the rocky mountainside, he searched for the red handkerchief he left to mark the hidden entrance to the canyon. General Jack was a sure-footed animal, but even so, Travis chose to lead him across the rocky slope rather than risk a fall on the slippery stone. Before entering the narrow passage that led to the canyon cove, he stood at the opening for a long time memorizing details before gathering up his kerchief and leading his horse down the narrow path.

He looked around the crescent-shaped strip of land in daylight and saw that it had been a campground for a small party not too long ago.

The charred remains of fires were still visible inside several fire rings, and though grass and weeds had sprung up, rounded depressions indicated where shelters had stood. Strapping the supplies he needed to his back, he left his horse in the cove and backtracked around the stone monolith, clinging to the cuts in the stone as he had the night before. With sunlight streaming into the canyon, he moved faster. In a short time he stood beside the mound of rocks and rubble that blocked the water in the lake from reaching the lower canyon and the old streambed.

He could see no way to free the water short of blasting a hole in the slide debris. He lacked the necessary tools and skills to create a diversion canal. Blasting carried a risk of sending all of the water rushing out of the lake, but he hoped the boulders at the mouth of the canyon would slow the flow. The miles of dry desert between the canyon and the Sebastian Rancho would also help to diffuse a flood.

Concerned a blast might trigger another slide and leave him stranded in the canyon, he placed his charge with great care. He wouldn't attempt to clear the whole dam, only to create a small fissure in it. Even a little break would widen quickly, and by the time he returned to General Jack and made his way back to the mouth of the canyon, he'd know whether or not his actions had freed the long-blocked river.

Setting the charge with as long a fuse as possible, he lit it with one of the few sulfur matches he carried, then scurried off the slide and began a fast trot toward the old campground. Before he reached the escarpment separating the trail from the campground, he huddled against the cliff and held his breath. He didn't have to wait long.

The blast echoed through the canyon, reverberating back and forth off the canyon walls. Dust and the distant echo of the explosion seemed to hang in the air for long minutes, followed by a deafening roar. He stared in awe at the water rushing toward the gap left by the dynamite. A jubilant shout left his throat only to be lost in the roar of the rushing water.

Once more he clung to the slashes cut in the rock to reach the campground. His hands shook and he had to slow down to ensure his safe passage. He'd done it! He'd found water, breached the dam, and sent his hopes rushing toward the valley with the river! The conditional note he'd signed at the bank would be in effect before the week was out, and the land would be the first step in realizing his dream of raising horses.

Back on top of the canyon, Travis rode a safe distance from the edge. He caught glimpses of the water streaming down the canyon. At intervals he moved closer for a better view and noticed pools forming in low spots, as well as trees and rocks, forced from the ground, rolling in front of the rushing water. In other places, waterfalls and twisting rapids formed.

He descended from the canyon rim and stopped to ground tether his horse a safe distance from the mouth of the canyon. The rocks and trees carried by the rushing water piled up against the boulders and debris already in place, forming a smaller dam that would keep the lake from emptying too fast. He grinned in satisfaction, seeing the first burst of water shoot over the top of the lower dam, and felt like cheering as a wide stream, emerging from beneath the debris at the mouth of the canyon, began to fill the old streambed. Already a glittering trail of water snaked across the desert, finding and filling the ancient waterway.

Remounting, Travis touched his heels to General Jack's side. He had a long ride ahead of him. The water would reach the upper mesa and tumble over the ledge to begin filling the creek and stock pond near Adams's ranch buildings long before he rode in. He planned to stop only briefly to inform the rancher of the success of his endeavor then move on to finalize his land purchase with old Williams. If he rode hard, he could catch up to his men across the border in a week's time.

On the third day of his return ride, General Jack's comfortable gait almost lulled him to sleep, and he rode in a somnolent haze until he was jolted into awareness by a sharp sting to his shoulder and the unmistakable report of a rifle.

Urging his horse to greater speed, he reached for his own rifle, wincing as the action brought pain to his shoulder. Ignoring the blood streaming down his arm, he scanned the horizon for the shooter.

There, fifty yards to his right, sat a rider with a rifle raised to his shoulder. Bringing his Browning up, Travis fired. Along with the jolt against his sore shoulder, he felt General Jack stumble, and for a moment he felt himself falling. Then all was black.

* * *

Ross watched old Javier thrust his pitchfork into the pile of dry grass then toss it toward a stall. He should have gone with the horse trader. Travis had only planned to be gone a week. Already he was two days late and there was no sign of him. Ross should have left the ranch in Javier's care. He couldn't afford to lose this opportunity to secure a permanent water supply.

No, he clung to a corral post. He would have slowed the trader further. He should be well by now; instead he seemed to grow weaker each day. At first he'd seemed to recuperate well then the pneumonia had set in. Just when he thought he could put being ill behind him, the stomach cramps and dizziness began.

He stared into the distance and worry added to the cramping in his belly. Perhaps Travis wasn't all he seemed to be and meant to steal Ross's last chance to obtain water for the ranch. Ben had been a frequent visitor to the Sebastian Rancho of late and had warned Ross against trusting the Mormon traders. He should have listened. Not that he entirely trusted Ben, but the young man had been grateful for his help in getting his father back for a proper burial and had arrived full of apologies on numerous occasions during Ross's long recuperation. In fact, he'd visited just that morning and they had shared a bottle of fine whiskey the young man had brought.

He hadn't told Ben about Travis's search for the old water source. Even though Ben appeared to have matured in many ways and was behaving in a more responsible manner, Ross hadn't forgotten his earlier behavior nor the evidence that he was tampering with the water supply again. Only a trickle of water was reaching Ross's stock, and Dominic insisted that Ben had replaced his cowboys with gunfighters.

Hearing the thundering drum of hoof beats approaching at a rapid rate, Ross attempted to straighten. Javier leaned his fork against a stable wall and reached for the rifle Ross knew the old man kept nearby.

Dom swung from a lathered horse and hurried toward him.

"We thought you should know—" The cowboy took a deep gulp of air. "It was young Carlos's turn to watch through the army glasses you sent with us. He called for me to come, and we took turns using the glasses to watch a horse that was limping approach the Purdy Ranch from the east." The man swiped the back of his hand across his mouth and took a couple more deep breaths.

"Did the horse have a rider? Was it saddled?" Ross wished the man would get on with his story.

"At first I didn't see the rider. He was all hunched over like he was sleepin' or hurt."

"Was he the trader?"

"Naw. I'd know that big stallion Travis Telford rides anywhere."

"That does it! You better go after Telford. Could have been a gun fight." He doubled over in pain. After a few seconds he straightened. "Send Gonzales and Brown up there to back up the kid and get Javier over here."

"I'm here," the old man stepped forward. Seeing Ross's ashen face, he grasped his arm.

"You must lie down, senor. I will see to what needs done while you rest."

Before Ross could respond, the shouts of a maid leaning out of an upper window of the hacienda interrupted. "See! *Agua*! The water!"

Ross turned in the direction she pointed and spotted a thin silver gleam in the distance. The corners of his mouth turned up. Feeling rejuvenated, he mounted Dominic's horse and spurred it forward in a race toward the creek. As he neared its banks, it became necessary to steer clear of the horns of the cattle that had smelled the water and were also rushing toward it.

The stream spilled over its banks and cattle wallowed in ankle-deep mire as they thrust their noses into the brown water. Turning upstream, he noticed that the farther he rode, the clearer the water became. Travis had succeeded in his quest, but where was he? Ross's elation over the water faded, and with a grim set to his jaw, he urged his horse back to the stable. When he arrived he found that Dominic had saddled another mount and was already on his way toward the distant mountains. Ross dismounted and with Javier's help made his painful way to the hacienda.

Chapter Eleven

THE SUN WAS HIGH IN the sky when Carlos noticed a ring of birds circling something beneath them. His chest grew tight, and he could scarcely breathe as he turned away from the wide stream he had followed and raced toward the object of the birds' attention. Not for the first time, he wondered if he had done the right thing in riding away from the lookout post to backtrack the rider he'd seen earlier.

Coming over a small ridge, he released a yelp of outrage as he caught sight of General Jack lying crumpled on the dry ground. As he drew closer, he saw that the lower half of a man lay pinned beneath the horse. Brown streaks of dried blood were spattered across the ground and over the man's clothing. His eyes were closed.

"Senor Telford!" Carlos leaped from his horse to kneel beside the man. His own pulse was pounding so hard he couldn't be certain whether he detected a beat in the trader's chest or not, but the hand he touched felt warm and limp, not stiff and cold.

He moved quickly to free the injured man of the weight pressing against his legs. Attaching a rope to his own mount's saddle horn and around the dead horse's stiff forelegs, he urged the gelding to slowly back up. Both horse and boy were glistening with sweat by the time the heavy corpse was dragged clear of the fallen rider. Tears glistened in Carlos's eyes as he surveyed the once-magnificent horse. He dashed his forearm across his eyes. There was no time for tears.

Carlos poured water onto his handkerchief, knelt beside Travis, and with slow strokes of the damp cloth, washed Travis's still face. Tipping the canteen, he dribbled a few drops onto the unconscious man's parched lips. While he worked, he continued to whisper Senor Telford's name but without receiving a response.

He'd seen his mother lay her ear against an injured child or cowboy's chest, so he did the same. At first he could hear nothing but continued to listen and thought he felt a faint beat against his ear. After a few minutes he noticed a small bubble forming at the corner of the unconscious man's mouth, a sign that air was passing through his lungs. He continued to bathe Travis's face and, satisfied the comatose man was still alive, began to examine him for injuries. Noticing first that a bullet had passed through the upper portion of Senor Telford's right arm, Carlos cleaned and bandaged the wound, grateful the bullet had passed cleanly through the flesh and that there didn't seem to be any other bullet wounds. The unconscious man's legs were Carlos's greatest concern. They weren't twisted, but they didn't seem quite right, and Carlos didn't know what other signs to look for. He noticed that Travis's face and lips were burned from the hot sun, but there was little he could do about that.

Somehow he had to get him back to the ranch. *Amaya will know what to do.* Seeing no trees from which to build a travois, Carlos pondered how to lift Senor Telford onto the gelding. The injured man was far larger than Carlos.

As he stood contemplating the problem, he heard the pounding of hooves. He felt a moment's panic, fearing that Senor Telford's attacker had returned, but almost at once he recognized one of the horses from the Sebastian stable and to his relief saw Dominic dismount to kneel beside the injured man.

After a brief discussion, they freed the saddle from General Jack and tied it behind Carlos's own. The horse, showing his displeasure with the arrangement, did his best to shake it off. After the young horse settled down, Dom draped Travis's saddlebags and canteen around Carlos's saddle horn and returned to Travis's side.

Kneeling, Dominic lifted the other man to a sitting position. The groan that reached his ears gave Carlos encouragement and he hurried to help heft the unconscious man across Dominic's saddle. It took considerable effort to position Travis in the saddle so that Dom could mount behind him.

The midday sun blazed down, leaving Carlos parched and dry. Sweat stained his shirt and alkali coated his high-heeled boots. Dom stayed close to the stream except where it cut through deep gullies. They stopped frequently to coax a few drops of water down Travis's throat and to allow the horses to suck up whatever moisture they could. Both Carlos and Dominic drank deeply and refilled their canteens often from the rushing water. Once or twice Carlos muttered an audible thank you to the God above for the water and for having allowed him to find Senor Telford.

Carlos rode beside Dom, keeping a watchful eye on the unconscious man. They traveled in silence for several miles before Carlos asked, "Will Senor Telford be crippled?"

"Only God knows." Dom's voice was hoarse as he responded to the question. "I've seen you in the chapel praying beside your mama and the senora. Add Senor Telford to your prayers. Ask that God let him live and walk again."

* * *

Travis opened his eyes and immediately closed them again. Taking his time, he tried to make sense of his position. He had a vague recollection of a rocking motion that had seemed to go on for a long time. He was pretty sure he was now inside some kind of structure and that he lay on a crude mattress. For a moment he wondered if he was back in that half soddie, half cabin in Utah where he'd once sheltered from a blizzard. No, it was too warm for that.

Gradually he became aware of a thick bandage on his arm and memories of the past week came rushing back. He'd been shot! General Jack had fallen and a terrible certainty assailed him that his stallion was dead.

He opened his eyes and stared around. He lay on a rough mattress near a fireplace though there was no fire, not even a glimmer of red coals. A table surrounded by chairs and benches was between him and a small square window, only partially covered by a scrap of curtain. A sound had him twisting to find the source. The movement brought a gasp of pain to his lips.

"Are you all right?" An old man, one who looked faintly familiar, bent over him. Travis wasn't sure where the man came from.

"Where am I?" He didn't recognize the croaking sound that came from his lips.

"Do not worry. You are safe. Two of our caballeros found you and brought you to me. The housekeeper from the hacienda dressed your arm."

"Someone shot me!"

"Did you see who shot you?"

"No. He was some distance away. I fired back, but I don't know if I hit him."

"I think you did. The young man who found you saw a rider who might be wounded heading to the Purdy Ranch."

At last, he recognized Javier, the old man, attired in a nightshirt instead of boots and pants, who worked for Ross Adams. Somehow, Travis didn't know how, he'd reached the Sebastian Rancho. Feeling safe, his mind eased and he drifted back to sleep.

He awoke to the smell of coffee, roasting peppers, and something else that smelled wonderful. He felt his stomach growl and attempted to sit up, only to feel intense pain in his legs. Javier heard his groan and hurried to his side.

"What happened to my legs? I can't move them!"

"Senor, the horse, he fall on you."

"General Jack? Is he all right? Are my legs broken?" He wasn't certain whether he was more concerned for himself or for his beloved horse.

"I am sorry." Javier hung his head. "The horse, he is dead. The legs, I do not find any broken bones, but I do not know if you can walk."

Travis swallowed deeply. The stallion, an offspring of his mother's stallion, Zeus, was possibly his last tie to Mama and Pa. He'd ridden away from Clayton on General Jack that long-ago day when they'd buried Pa. The horse had been his closest companion for eight years.

"Help me up. We'll see if I can walk."

The old man reached for his good arm. Several times Travis thought he might black out as excruciating pain shot through his lower body, but he discovered he could move his legs. At last he stood, though clinging to Javier.

"The pain is good. If there is no pain, the legs, they are no good and you not walk."

Gritting his teeth, Travis moved one foot forward, then the other. Javier was right; the pain was a good sign. His legs still responded to orders from his brain. One more step and he found himself falling. He clutched a chair and sank onto it.

For several minutes, he hung his head, gasping for breath. Slowly awareness came to him that he was clothed in nothing but his smalls. He stared at his legs, not quite believing how swollen they were or their bluish color. It was some kind of miracle that his legs weren't broken. More than that, it was amazing he'd survived both being shot and having a horse fall on him.

After a few minutes, he lifted his head. "I need to tell Ross I found water. There's plenty for the Sebastian Rancho and for the horse ranch I plan to build."

"Senor Ross much sick. He see water fill pond, and the senora, she tell him much water come, but I think he doesn't understand." Javier hung his head, showing his sorrow.

In the coming days, Travis began to mend; walking became easier though the blue color on his legs turned to massive black bruises. He became restless, anxious to continue on to meet his men and acquire the horses he needed to fulfill his contract. Only after his contract was fulfilled could he begin serious work on his own ranch. He also needed a horse for the journey. When he spoke of his concerns, Javier brought Dominic to him.

After thanking the young ranch foreman for his part in saving Travis's life, Travis made arrangements to purchase a four-year-old gelding with an easy gait. Javier would have made a gift of the animal, but Travis insisted he should pay for it. As he bargained with Javier and Dominic, he noticed Ross Adams's beautiful young wife leave the hacienda with a child, a boy about six or seven years old. The two walked toward the stable and disappeared inside. He couldn't help thinking Adams was a lucky man to have a wife as beautiful as the young senora.

"I'd better go," Dominic said. "Senor Adams wishes me to teach his son to ride since he is too ill to continue the boy's lessons."

"Has he been seen by a doctor?"

"The closest doctor is in Albuquerque. He will not travel so far. Father Escudero and Amaya see to the sick and injured in the village and ranches in the valley. You must excuse me now."

Travis stroked the horse he'd just bought and spent a few minutes getting acquainted with the animal before hobbling back to Javier's small house. His arm, though still bandaged, was much better and healing quickly, but his legs were still too tender to attempt riding.

Most of another week passed before Javier deemed Travis ready to undertake the ride south into Mexico to meet the men he'd sent ahead. He regretted that Ross was too ill for him to discuss the water with him, but he could delay no longer. Brother Lewis and the men would be concerned and it was important that he fill the contracts he'd signed. He had two stops to make on his way. He had business to finish with Mr. Williams, and though he didn't expect it would do any good, he planned to report the shooting to the marshal.

Chapter Twelve

Ross lay motionless on his bed. He was dying. He knew it and so did his family who had gathered about him. Iliana dipped a cloth in a basin and laid it across his brow.

"Father, do not go," pleaded his young son. The boy pressed his cheek against the papery-dry flesh of his father's cheek.

Ross stirred as though reluctant to return from a far place. His weathered hand settled on the boy's dark head. "It's time. God willing, I shall meet your great-grandfather before the sun rises."

Iliana stepped forward to stand beside the boy. "I sent Juan for a doctor two days ago. He'll be here soon with the doctor, who will make you well."

"Ben brought a doctor," Ross wheezed. Iliana frowned. She suspected the man Ben had introduced as a doctor from Albuquerque was no doctor. After he and Ben left, Ross had become increasingly ill. That's when she sent Juan for a doctor.

Ross seemed to rally. "There is only time to tell you what I must. I have written it all down and left the paper with Ted Williams at the bank." He closed his eyes and took several shallow breaths before opening them again. His words came with difficulty. "The Sebastian Rancho goes to Gabe. El Rancho de Sebastian was his great-grandfather's ranch, and I gave my word." A deep rattling cough shook his frail body and Iliana ached to offer him comfort. They had grown closer during those first days following the storm, before he'd taken a turn for the worse.

She knew of the bargain her husband had made with her grandfather, and she'd never faulted either of them for securing the rancho through her for her son. Though her marriage hadn't been the fulfillment of a young girl's dreams, Ross had always treated her with respect and kindness. He was a man of honor whom she never doubted would keep his word to her grandfather and the vows he'd made to her. She had come to respect and care for him.

"Husband, you should rest," she whispered as she soaked another cooling cloth, wrung it out, and placed it on his fevered brow.

"No, I must tell you . . ." He caught at her hand. Once more his chest rattled and Iliana feared he would cough out his last breath, but after a moment, he began to speak again in a rasping voice.

"Gabe will have the Sebastian fortune when he is a man, but there is little left of my money. It has gone to restore the herd. Gabe is a child and you are a woman with no money and no protector. I cannot leave you destitute. If there is to be any hope of your survival and keeping the ranch for Gabe to inherit, you must remarry."

"No! I wish only to care for you and young Gabe."

"You are still young and lovely and deserve the respect and honor due a wife. Ben Purdy is in need of a wife and has always cared for you. I have no kin and there is no one else to look after you and protect Gabe's inheritance. Ben regrets the disrespect he has shown you in the past and has agreed to honor the agreement I made with your grandfather. Don Sebastian's grandson will become the owner of the rancho when he comes of age. He and I have agreed. You will go to him two months after I am buried. As Ben's wife you will also become mistress of the hacienda that once belonged to your mother's family as well as save the Sebastian Rancho for our son. God willing, you will give Ben a son to claim the Purdy spread, and two brothers will put an end to the feuding between the two ranches. Marriage will give you honor and respect instead of poverty."

Iliana recoiled in shock. Surely Ross didn't mean what he'd said. Ben was as abhorrent to her as he had ever been. Had Ross's illness sheltered him from learning of Ben's expensive tastes, his gambling, and the deterioration of the ranch his father stole from her maternal grandfather? Did Ross know nothing of the gunslingers who lolled about the Purdy Ranch and took occasional shots at Sebastian cattle? While she, Amaya, and the caballeros were protecting her husband from stressful matters he was too ill to deal with, Ben had been weaseling his way into Ross's good graces.

Ben had never shown respect for her or her people and she didn't suppose he would suddenly change. She'd seen little of him since he'd lain in wait for her on the high mesa that awful day shortly before her marriage to Ross, until the past few months, when he'd become a regular visitor during Ross's illness. She'd avoided him as much as possible during his visits and assumed it was his guilt over deserting his father during the blizzard that brought him to make frequent visits to the storm's other victim of that tragic day. Now she wasn't so sure. *Could it be Ben had capitalized on Ross's guilt over Jacob's death? Surely it was Ben who planted the idea of their marrying in her husband's mind.*

"Ross, you mustn't say such things. You are *mi marido*, my husband. You will get well and all shall be as before your illness." Her desperate plea was almost a prayer.

"No," his bony fingers tightened on her arm. "Ben's land marches alongside that of the Sebastian, and the creek that waters the northern range passes through his land first. It is good that you two should restore cooperation between the ranches as in your grandfathers' day." His words ended in a strangled cough. When he caught his breath, he looked confused but struggled on. "Ben is a hard man. If you do not marry him, he will find a way to remove you from the land, leaving you and our son without a home, and my bargain with your grandfather will turn to dust. If . . . can't . . . won't force . . . the jewels . . . take Gabe." He fell silent with a terrible grimace on his face.

She wanted to storm and protest, to remind him that the trader had found sufficient water and sent it rushing across the dry land, but she feared that upsetting her husband might hasten his death. He'd never recovered from the illness that befell him when a spring blizzard roared out of the north, sweeping cattle and horses before it toward Mexico. Even now when the hot summer sun bore down on grass and adobe, he shivered and clung to his bed. He had grown thin and weak. There was still time to change his mind, she assured herself. Now, he needed to rest.

Sounds drifted through an open window, telling the occupants of the sick chamber that Juan had returned. Amaya went to meet him and Gabe snuggled in a large chair near his father and fell asleep. Iliana rose to her feet in anticipation of seeing that all was in readiness for dinner. As she attempted to free her arm from her husband's grasp, he opened his eyes once more.

"Iliana, my little prairie flower," he whispered. "Our son shall inherit the land, your grandfather's hacienda, and all of the stock. That is the way of life, but I do not mean for you to have nothing. The Sebastian and Medina women's jewelry is yours. It is to be used as you will. If you . . ." He coughed and clenched at his chest for what seemed a long time. At last he lay back, closing his eyes.

Ross's head drooped against his pillow. His breathing became harsh and ragged. Gabe awoke and rushed to his father's side in time to hold his hand as he breathed his last.

* * *

Iliana watched Dominic give the priest a handful of coins. The black-robed man nodded his appreciation and bid Gabe farewell without a glance toward her. There hadn't been a large crowd gathered to say good-bye to her husband in the small chapel her great-grandfather had built at one end of the hacienda. Those in attendance had been mostly the servants and caballeros who worked on the ranch. Ben Purdy had arrived wearing a black suit with large, silver Mexican rowels on his boots. The only other guests had been Mr. Williams, who ran the bank and served as the closest the village came to an attorney or judge, and a handful of neighboring ranchers who had arrived to pay their respects. The priest had been among the last to arrive and had evidenced an urgency to be on his way when the service ended. A few of the gringo ranchers were accompanied by their wives, who paid little heed to Iliana but sat in one corner sipping tea and eating the cakes Amaya had prepared.

Ben had stuck to her side through the service, much to her annoyance. She was grateful for the short, dark veil that hid the revulsion she knew must show on her face each time he laid a proprietary hand on her arm or touched her waist. He lingered after most of the other guests had gone, tempting her to tell him to leave her to mourn in peace. She was slow to realize that he was waiting for the reading of Ross's will.

"I've got to be back to town before closing time," Mr. Williams announced to those assembled in the hacienda's large reception room, "so I'm sure you'll understand that I must speak to the widow, the ranch foreman, Amaya, Javier, and young Gabe privately. If you'll make your way to the library . . ." He gestured for Iliana to precede him. Most of the guests made a hurried exit.

When Ben indicated his intention of accompanying them to the library by linking her arm through his, Mr. Williams frowned. "The heirs only," he pronounced in a solemn voice.

"I shall be Mrs. Adams's husband in a mere two months' time. I think I should be present to look after her interests." Several of the women in the room who hadn't yet reached the door appeared appalled at the announcement, and their husbands coughed or shuffled their feet in a futile effort to conceal their reactions. Iliana struggled to remain impassive as her supposed fiancé puffed out his chest and patted her hand in a patronizing and proprietary attempt to be recognized as part of the bereaved family.

"You're not married to her yet." The gray-haired banker, who seemed to wear a perpetual frown, glared at him. Few men could outface Mr. Williams, and Ben wasn't one of them. With a show of reluctance, he released Iliana's arm.

She took rapid steps toward the room her husband had called an office. If doing so wouldn't shock their guests further and embarrass poor Mr. Williams as well as be inappropriate at such a solemn occasion, she'd have kissed the severe old man's cheek for granting her a respite from Ben's constant attendance. Her thick-skulled neighbor didn't care whether she welcomed his presence or wished to mourn her husband with proper respect.

She took a seat on the wide leather settee between Abuelo's desk and the window. Gabe seated himself beside her, looking grown-up and sad. His cheeks still bore evidence of the tears that had coursed down his cheeks during the brief service. Unobtrusively, she handed him her handkerchief. While he wiped his face, she watched the others settle in the carved chairs that sat before the desk. Mr. Williams claimed Grandfather's chair. He looked out of place seated on the chair she'd considered more of a throne ever since she'd crept into the room as a small child to sit on Abeulo's lap when she was supposed to be taking a siesta in her room. The chair had never quite suited Ross. Only a man as stiff and proud as Don Rodrigo Ignacio Renteria Sebastian could do justice to that majestic piece of furniture.

Mr. Williams wasted no time on pleasantries but came right to the point. "Ross told me he would explain the will to you before he died, so I assume you already know the land, stock, and buildings pass to Gabe as per the agreement reached between Ross Adams and Don Sebastian. That agreement calls for Iliana's son to inherit the ranch. The small amount of operating capital on hand at my bank is to be handled jointly by Javier and Dominic until Iliana remarries. At that time her husband will have charge of it. Iliana is to have the family jewelry to do with as she pleases, and the Sebastian fortune is to be held in trust for Iliana's son until he reaches his twenty-first birthday. Ross also set aside small sums to be awarded to Amaya Martinez and several of the ranch hands who have been on the ranch since old Don Sebastian's time. I took the liberty of filing the necessary papers this morning before the funeral." He looked around as though daring them to challenge his words. When they remained silent, he shuffled a few papers, looked down, then back up, appearing embarrassed.

"There is one other small matter." There was a look almost of apology when his gaze met Iliana's before continuing to speak. "Don Sebastian and Don Ernesto y Medina had an agreement between them to share the water from the creek that runs across the ranch now owned by Ben Purdy. That agreement stood until both gentlemen passed away. Jacob Purdy gave Ross his word he would continue the arrangement, though it seems he did not honor the agreement as well as he should have. Young Ben Purdy and your father reached another agreement a short time ago. Ben won't dam or otherwise divert the water, even in drought years, in exchange for Iliana becoming his wife within two months of Ross's death. The agreement is signed by both Ben and Ross."

Mr. Williams cleared his throat and once again cast an apologetic glance toward Iliana. "I did not draw up this codicil to the original will. It was handled by an attorney in Albuquerque and delivered to my office by a courier."

A look of anger passed between Javier and Dominic while Iliana's own heart seemed to sink to her stomach. Mr. Williams cleared his throat before going on. "The signature appears to be that of Ross Adams. It's possible the document was signed while Ross was suffering one of his fits of confusion during the past month, but it is duly witnessed and has been filed with the appropriate authorities, so I have no choice but to accept it at face value."

Anger threatened to break through the benign, impassive demeanor she had adopted to carry her through the day. She understood the ranch's need for water, but the agreement was unnecessary. There was plenty of water now. Either Ross had been too ill to be aware the horse trader had found water, or he'd signed the agreement before Senor Telford found the old river. Surely Ross wouldn't have agreed to the marriage stipulation if he had known or understood. What the ranch needed was money; it was operating capital they lacked, but if they could hang on for a few years, she felt certain the ranch would provide adequate income again. She loved the ranch, but she wasn't certain she could sacrifice her own future to ensure its continued survival. And she didn't understand why Ross, who had always treated her with kindness, would wish her to marry a cruel man whom she detested. The years ahead promised much bleakness and pain.

Before his departure, Mr. Williams paused beside Iliana. "Ross placed a great deal of trust in you. He was realistic enough to know that you cannot hang onto the ranch alone any more than your grandfather could. One way or another, Ben means to have this land. Perhaps at the end Ross merely made the best bargain he could. In this country a woman can refuse to marry someone she dislikes, but you should consider that as Ben's wife you will not be left homeless as were your Medina grandparents before their disappearance. Your husband said you were more like your grandfather, Don Sebastian, than you know and that he was certain you would do what is best for you and for Gabe. If you need me, my door will always be open to you."

* * *

In the days following Ross's death, life continued pretty much the way it always had. Dominic had assumed the role of foreman on the ranch since before the start of Ross's illness and continued in that capacity. Iliana continued her usual tasks too. She was never quite certain whether she was the mistress of the hacienda or if that title rightfully belonged to the elderly housekeeper. Amaya had been friend, teacher, and confidant for as long as Iliana could remember, assuming a mother's role, as well, since the death of Iliana's mother. It was to Amaya she had turned for comfort and assurance when faced with marriage to a stranger and again at the death of her abeulo.

Amaya had held her, whispering consoling words before reminding her that it was her duty to be obedient to her grandfather. Amaya had also offered to alter Iliana's mother's wedding dress to fit her and to search out the fragile lace mantilla worn by centuries of Sebastian brides. Her fears had been allayed when Ross had agreed to delay the wedding, giving her time to adjust to the arrangement and to discover her betrothed's gentle kindness. It was Amaya who had instructed her in a wife's duties and sat discreetly nearby as Ross courted her. Iliana had come to care for Ross and she missed him now with an ache that would not heal.

Even her body revolted from the future that she faced with Ben, leaving her unable to keep within her the small amounts of nourishment Amaya insisted she eat. No amount of lectures on Amaya's part could convince her she could endure marriage to Ben, but could she deprive her son of his inheritance? If Grandfather could not hold out against the relentless schemes of Americanos to deprive him of his land, how could she hope to do so? Marriage to Ben would be intolerable, but there was no other way to ensure Gabe's future. Besides she had nowhere to go; she'd never ventured further from the ranch than the village. Continuing to feel wan and listless added a new concern as she forced herself to think of the future that awaited her and her small son.

Gabe followed her about the house like an ever-present shadow. He was small for his age and fearful of horses and cattle. That was largely her fault, as she'd sheltered him from dirt and noise, late hours, and anything that might bring on the wheezing and coughing that plagued his young life. She worried about how he would fare under Ben's care. Though Gabe was now the owner of the huge spread his ancestors first received in a land grant, he showed little interest in anything to do with it. His interests ran more to drawing pictures and singing songs than to ranching. The bright New Mexico sun hurt his eyes, and the dust and contact with animals caused him to sneeze and sniffle. She suspected Ben would show no tolerance for her son's quiet nature or frequent illnesses.

In an effort to keep busy and to avoid thinking about marrying Ben, Iliana launched into a flurry of house cleaning. With trepidation she at last approached the suite of rooms that had belonged to her mother. While he lived, Grandfather had ordered the rooms left as her mother, Maria, had left them and had forbidden her as a small child to play there. Ross had not altered those orders when he took charge of the hacienda. She had no doubt Amaya kept the rooms as spotless as when Maria had been alive; still it was Iliana's responsibility to see that all was in order.

When she announced her intention to sort through her mother's belongings and clear the room for whatever use her new husband would choose, Amaya offered to assist her, but Iliana refused the help. This was something she had to do herself.

There were two doors leading to the room that had been her mother's. One door opened from the long hall that had seldom been used since Grandfather's passing. The other entrance connected the room to the one that had been Iliana's father's room. Her father's suite had been used as a sickroom for Ross when he grew too weak to climb the stairs to the rooms he and Iliana had shared since the first day of their marriage.

Gathering her resolution, Iliana opened the heavy door leading from the hall and stepped across the threshold. Forgotten memories swirled around her. A scent that had been unique to her mother still lingered in the air. Common sense told her Amaya likely sprayed a tiny burst of the perfume into the air each time she cleaned the room, but it still brought a familiar ache to Iliana's heart and a longing for the pretty, high-spirited young mother she had adored.

The room was spotless, and there was little for Iliana to do other than place the clothing that still hung in the wardrobe in a trunk to be removed to the storage room. She chose a few things to remove to her own room: a few scarves, her mother's silver-backed brush set, and an ivory statuette of the Madonna and her Child that had been dear to her mother. Last of all, she picked up the carved wooden chest that held her mother's jewelry.

Sinking to the floor with the box, she was oblivious to the jumble of petticoats and the voluminous skirt spread around her. She ran a finger across the delicately carved birds and flowers that formed an elaborate design on the top and around the sides of the antique chest. It was old and had been in her mother's family for generations. Many of the jewels had been part of the dowries of long-forgotten ancestors. It was one of the few items of value belonging to the Medina family that had survived when the Medinas mysteriously disappeared and Jacob Purdy produced a deed for their land and claimed the contents of the hacienda. Thanks to her grandmother's forethought, the jewel casket had been safely placed in the care of their daughter, Maria, the Sebastian bride, before the older couple disappeared. Her mother's eyes had shimmered with tears each time she'd spoken of the tragic events that had ended with the assumed deaths of her parents. In time Grandfather had added the Sebastian family jewels to the box. Iliana closed her eyes and remembered examining the casket and exploring the vivid contents while her mother dressed for dinner or some elaborate entertainment.

At last she lifted the hinged lid and stared in bewilderment. Instead of the dangling earrings, the jewel-encrusted crucifixes, and the many rings her mother had loved, the chest was almost empty. A simple, hand-carved wooden cross, a few once-shiny silver bangles, and a couple of small silver coins were all that remained of a collection of jewels that had been amassed by six generations of women.

Chapter Thirteen

Sickness settled in the bottom of Iliana's abdomen. Tears streamed down her face as she relived that agonizing day all over again when Abeulo had held her on his knee and told her that her *madre* had gone to heaven to live with *Dios*. Her one precious link to her mother that she thought would console her through her coming ordeal was gone. Pressing her hands to her face, she collapsed amidst her skirts, in an agony of tears.

When she'd cried herself out, she straightened to mop at her eyes, and still the hiccoughs that continued to shake her body then she went in search of Amaya. She found the housekeeper in the kitchen chopping vegetables. The spicy scent of Amaya's preparations for dinner filled the air. Instead of being the comfort Amaya's cooking had always been to her, the aromas added to Iliana's sense of loss and grief, sending her to lean over the pail where kitchen scraps were tossed. Amaya rushed to her side to offer her comfort and a damp cloth.

"Amaya, they are gone," she cried when the sickness subsided. She held the almost-empty chest before the woman's eyes.

"Gone?" Amaya dried her hands on her apron before taking the jewel casket from Iliana's hands. "Have you moved Maria's treasures to your own jewel box? This one is old, but it is larger and more valuable. Perhaps you should put everything in this one."

"No, Amaya, you do not understand. Mi madre's pretty jewels are gone. Someone has taken them."

Amaya drew herself up, looking offended. "I have dusted and polished that chest every week since your mama came here as a bride. Never have I opened it other than to take you jewelry to match your gowns for important occasions."

"Oh, dear Amaya, I never meant you. I would never accuse you of such a thing." She threw her arms around the other woman.

Amaya's face brightened. "Senor Adams! He kept important papers and valuables in his safe in his library. He must have placed Maria's jewelry there for safekeeping. Javier will know how to open it and will return to you what is yours."

"Of course! I should have thought of that." She again hugged the housekeeper then brushed furiously at her eyes and attempted a serene smile. "Now tell me what needs to be done. Shall I set the table?"

The older woman's smile disappeared and a thoughtful expression came to her face. "Si. Set the table then you must dress in your prettiest gown. One of the men brought word that Senor Purdy will join you for dinner tonight to discuss arrangements for your wedding."

* * *

Iliana glared at herself in the mirror, seeing her reflection through shimmering tears that almost obscured her dark eyes. The tears added to her anger. She had been taught to control her emotions, yet twice in one day she had wept. It would not do. She straightened her spine. She was not a child and it was long past time for her to be a woman. She must become strong.

She glanced at the dress Amaya had set out for her to wear that evening. She would not wear the prairie green gown. She would wear black. She was in mourning, and after her wedding she would always wear black because she would always be in mourning. The soft, dark curls that framed her pale face refused to submit to her efforts to confine them to a severe bun at her nape, and it was useless to continue trying to force their submission. But she could refuse to add even a hint of blush to her cheeks and lips. If Ben thought her pale and ugly, it would not matter to her. Perhaps he wouldn't wish to marry her if she looked old and worn. She certainly had no wish to marry a man whose touch made her shudder. Ben was nearing his thirtieth birthday, but instead of a lean waist and broad shoulders like Ross had possessed, Ben's shoulders were round and a thick roll of flesh drooped over his silver belt buckle. Worse than the physical revulsion she felt toward him was the feeling she experienced whenever he was near, much like what she had experienced venturing too close to a large snake.

She considered wearing the delicate silver hoops in her ears that Grandfather had given her for her fifteenth birthday celebration, then chose instead to wear only the plain wooden crucifix she'd found in her mother's jewel chest. She unclasped the tiny gold cross she'd worn since

Ross had placed it around her neck the day Gabe was christened and replaced it with the wooden one. There was something dark and foreboding about the black wood with its suffering figure and the hand-carved beads that served as a chain. It suited her mood and she fastened it about her neck.

Gabe refused to hurry when she went to his room to fetch him and she declined to force the issue. Seeing the brightly trimmed shirt Amaya had set out for the boy, she exchanged it for a somber gray one.

Ben stood as she entered the dining room with Gabe at her side. She was surprised to see both Javier and Dominic were present. She should have known Amaya would not permit Ben to see her alone and had included them in the evening meal just as she had allowed her young son to be present. Both wore the usual simple attire they wore when the priest arrived on those rare occasions when he celebrated Mass in their small family chapel, but Ben was dressed as the ultimate Spanish Don. Not even her grandfather had displayed so much silver and ruffles when dressed in his finest. Ben's look of disdain for her when she entered the room was just what she wished. She wanted to discourage his attentions. Dominic hid a not-too-subtle smirk, causing her to suspect he found her plain attire amusing and knew why she'd chosen it.

Deep down Iliana hadn't been fooled by the look of disdain on Ben's face or his fancy clothing and knew his disdain had little to do with her appearance. Though he made no attempt to conceal his lust for her, he didn't respect her or her heritage, and his fancy clothes were merely an attempt to appear anxious to wed her. She suspected his desire to marry her had little to do with her and a great deal to do with his desire to control the Sebastian Rancho.

Pretending not to see Ben's proffered hand, she allowed Gabe to seat her to the right of the chair both Grandfather and Ross had claimed and was pleased when the boy took the seat beside her. Dominic and Ben seated themselves across from her and Gabe, while Javier settled in Ross's chair, looking uncomfortable as he did so. Madre's chair remained vacant, as it had, except on formal occasions, since the tragic day she and Papa had fallen victim to a marauding band of Apache warriors.

They'd scarcely begun the first course when Ben questioned whether she had engaged the priest for their marriage. Without waiting for her response, he elaborated on his expectations for the wedding. Iliana's heart sank. She had no desire to be part of the spectacle Ben described.

"I was thinking of a more simple ceremony here in the family chapel," she said, ducking her head. She couldn't bring herself to look at him. "I am still grieving for Ross."

"No." Ben shook his head. "The joining of the two largest landowners in this part of the territory must make clear to all the wealth and power our names represent. The sodbusters and Mexicans need to be reminded we won't tolerate any incursions on our property or position."

"I'm not sure it is wise to flaunt—" Dominic began.

"You don't understand politics," Ben interrupted with some rudeness. "If we don't take steps to retain control, the scum will overrun our ranches and destroy our way of life. Already there are too many of both. The Mexicans need to be taught their place."

Dominic and Javier both looked affronted but managed to hold their tongues.

"Actually I was thinking of building more individual houses with small garden plots for our permanent hands and encouraging more of the married ones to stay year-round." It took all of the courage Iliana could muster to speak up for the workers.

"You'll do no such thing!" Sauce and spittle flew as Ben banged his fist on the table. "Ross overpaid the rabble he hired, but I thought you had more sense. I shall make certain young Gabe is better trained."

"Oh, and how do you expect to do that?" Iliana sat up straight, not liking the threat toward her son that seemed to linger behind Ben's words.

"When Gabe is in my household—"

"We shall discuss this another time," Javier interrupted.

Ben seemed to realize he'd overstepped himself. He settled back in his chair and once more began gorging himself on Amaya's fajitas, though he sent occasional dark looks toward Javier.

Amaya took advantage of the pause to replenish platters and refill glasses. Her movements were short and abrupt, unlike her usual unobtrusive motions. Something was bothering her.

Javier, breaking his own prohibition, spoke again with clipped finality. "Until the marriage takes place, I have been entrusted with all matters concerning this ranch. It was not Senor Adams's desire to exhaust the ranch's resources on a celebration to encompass half the territory. I agree that the senora should select any gown she wishes, but other than that expense, there will be a minimum of this ranch's resources used to put on a show. Nuptials will be held in the ranch's private chapel with only family and a dozen close friends present. Following the ceremony, only those from the village and surrounding ranches will be welcomed here to sample our finest slow-roasted beef and dance until dawn."

"My friends in Albuquerque and as far away as Austin have already accepted my invitation." Ben's eyes flashed with indignation.

"That is your right, but only six will be permitted to attend the ceremony, and you will be expected to provide beef and servants to accommodate your guests' needs." The set of the old man's jaw told Iliana he would not be swayed and that he knew very well what his defiance would cost him.

"I have told them that el Rancho de Sebastian is the gem of New Mexico." Ben switched tactics, trying to sway Iliana with flattery to support his plans.

"Gem!" Amaya muttered the word in what Iliana knew was a deliberately loud whisper. "Senor," the housekeeper bent near Javier's ear and continued to whisper in a voice louder than was usual for a discreet message. "The senora's inheritance, her mother's valuable jewels, are missing from their chest. Did you put them somewhere for safe keeping?"

"What?" Javier shook his head, confused by the question. Iliana was confused too. It was not the sort of question Amaya should ask of him while he sat with a guest at dinner. It was most unusual for Amaya to be so rude. Iliana cast a rapid glance from beneath her long, thick eyelashes toward the man seated across from her. Ben's eyes were narrowed and sparked with anger. A white line appeared near his clenched lips.

Javier's eyes narrowed too, but his voice remained bland. "When did you discover the jewels were missing?"

"My mistress spent the day cleaning her mother's bedchamber. It was she who discovered her inheritance is missing. Last fall when I gave the room its annual turnout, Senora Maria's jewels filled the box." She bowed her head in a humble gesture as though apologizing for introducing the distasteful topic, but Iliana observed the quick flick of the housekeeper's gaze toward Ben. *Amaya wants Ben to know of her discovery! Surely, she doesn't expect Ben to be of any use in finding the jewels.*

"Who had access to Maria's bedchamber?" Javier asked. His voice continued in that odd, smooth tone, barely above a whisper.

"Only myself and the family." Amaya raised her head and looked him squarely in the eyes.

"It doesn't make sense that Iliana would steal from herself, and Gabe would do nothing to upset his mother. I doubt he even knows the worth of those baubles, so I think we can eliminate them as suspects."

Dominic appeared puzzled by the conversation.

"We can forget Amaya as a suspect," Javier snorted. "She would die before taking one grain of sand from a Sebastian without permission."

"I suppose that leaves you and me, Dominic." Iliana noted there was a cruel smile lurking at the edge of Javier's mustache that didn't bode well for someone. "Seeing as how you haven't been any farther than the village in the past two years and I've heard no reports of you trading beads for any of the wares at the cantina, it's unlikely you are guilty of this breach of honor. That leaves only me—and the guests who visited Senor Ross in the room adjacent to Maria's chamber during his illness."

Iliana's stomach lurched. Javier would no more steal from her than would Amaya. And though she found the village priest cold and indifferent, it would be beneath his dignity to steal a dead woman's jewels. She dismissed Mr. Williams as a suspect; to even entertain the thought that he would stoop to thievery was ludicrous. Shifting her eyes to Ben, she read the guilt there, which quickly changed to arrogant defensiveness.

"I would hardly call it stealing to remove my wife's jewelry to my home, where I can better protect it since she has no male relatives to offer her or her possessions protection." He lifted a stemmed chalice to his lips and drank. With his other hand he made a dismissive gesture.

"I am not your wife." Iliana rose to her feet, heedless of the linen napkin that fell at her feet. Lifting her head in a regal gesture worthy of her Spanish ancestors, she spoke in a scathing tone her son and old Javier had never heard before. "I shall expect the return of my mother's jewels before the sun sets tomorrow or there will be no wedding." She didn't wait for a reply but quickly left the room. Her legs and hands began to tremble, and it took all of her strength to appear in control until she passed out of sight of the men still seated at the table staring after her in various stages of shock.

She leaned against the thick wall beyond the dining room to regain her composure. Fury welled inside her breast, and she fought a desire to scream and throw the first object her hands could reach. She'd never thrown a tantrum in her life, but never before had she been so tempted. *Ben had stolen mother's jewels! Ben!* She had no illusion that he intended to return them to her once she became his wife. Her right to claim her inheritance for herself meant nothing to him. Ben would take all that was dear to her, sully all he touched, and leave her weak and broken. *How could Ross have left me in such a position? I had begun to believe he might actually love me.*

"A silly trifle." Ben's voice reached her ears from beyond the arch that separated the place where she stood from the dining room. "Ross informed me some months ago that he was including the Sebastian women's trinkets in Iliana's dowry. Knowing he failed to provide guards for the hacienda, I saw no harm in providing protection for what is mine."

"Senor Ross never intended those jewels as a dowry. The jewels *belong* to Iliana. They are hers to do with as she pleases!" Javier's voice was harsh, but it comforted Iliana some.

"I think you would do well to return Iliana's inheritance to her at once." Dominic's words carried a threat.

"Don't be ridiculous. New Mexico has no use for those old Spanish customs. Here, a woman's property becomes her husband's. Spanish land grants are of no effect either and can be easily set aside. If Ross hadn't taken steps to secure this ranch in his name after he married Iliana, my father would have claimed it years ago and you two would be as homeless as Ernesto Medina." He spoke disparagingly of Iliana's maternal grandfather, the man from whom his father had stolen the Purdy Ranch.

"This ranch is mine and you had no right to take anything that belongs to my mother." Iliana was surprised to hear her shy young son speak up.

A rude laugh erupted from Ben. "You're a Mexican. Mexicans and Indians can't own property."

"*Embustero*! I'm an American; Father said so. And Mother—"

"Your mother will be my wife in three weeks' time. She'll learn to control her tongue and do as she's told, and so will you. I almost wish you did own this land. It would save me a great deal of time and bother! With full control, I could—"

A loud crash signaled the overturn of one of the heavy dining room chairs. "That's where you're wrong. Ross Adams promised Don Sebastian he would leave this property to the old man's grandson. I heard the reading of the will. The Sebastian Rancho belongs to young Gabriel." Javier was far past any pretense of speaking civilly to their guest. "If you have some foolish scheme in mind to acquire the rancho through Senora Iliana and Gabe, I'll see you dead first. Tomorrow I will send word to the marshal that the senora's jewels have been stolen."

The scraping of a second chair on the floor drove Iliana to seek a place to hide. She hesitated, frozen in place, when she heard Amaya speak. Her voice was mild and smooth, warning Iliana that her words and their meaning were not the same thing. "My apologies, Ben. These two ranches have shared the valley since the days of the early Spanish explorers; it will not do to cause a rift between their owners now. Tomorrow, as a peace offering, send by a messenger that heavy rope of pearls that Iliana wore when she wed Ross Adams, to wear when she weds you, and I shall speak with her concerning her responsibilities."

"Very well, but I will not tolerate any more insolence." A chair made a scraping sound, reminding Iliana she must hide. She lost no time darting behind a heavy tapestry that concealed a deep window enclosure.

Iliana huddled on the window ledge between two layers of heavy woven tapestries, fearful of making any sound or movement that might betray her presence. She wasn't certain what Amaya was up to, but she wasn't foolish enough to take her accommodating words to Ben at face value. She knew the woman well and knew the housekeeper was as enraged as she by Ben's theft of the jewels. She heard the door close, but Amaya didn't return to the dining room. It soon became clear Dominic, Javier, and Gabe had followed to see Ben leave the hacienda.

"It's time for you to go to bed." She knew Amaya was speaking to Gabe.

"Can't you stop him from making Madre cry?" It was the first time she'd ever heard her son ask anything of anyone. Gabe's voice revealed that the boy was struggling to hold back tears. She steeled herself not to add her tears to his. Tears wouldn't help any of them. Somehow she had to be strong for all of them.

"Come, little one. It's time you were in bed." Iliana heard footsteps recede toward the stairs and pictured Amaya taking Gabe's hand to lead him up the stairs. She could no longer hear their footsteps when Javier's voice reminded her that he and Dom were still present.

"I suppose I'll be looking for a new place to live in a few weeks."

"I'm not any more pleased to have that piece of cow dung for a boss than you are," Dominic grumped. "I hate to leave the senora and her little boy, but I don't suppose I'll have a choice in the matter."

"Iliana, too, will do what she must," Javier said. "There's more of her grandfather in her than even she knows."

She wondered what he meant by that statement. She'd heard the same sentiment expressed by Mr. Williams and wondered what these two men knew that eluded her understanding. She was scared half out of her mind and had no inkling of anything she could do about the situation facing her and her son.

Several minutes passed before either man spoke again. It was the more impetuous Dominic who broke the silence.

"Ben won't survive the selling off of stock he has resorted to in order to finance his gambling debts in Albuquerque or his women. He suffered losses as heavy as this ranch from last winter's unprecedented storm. If he hasn't already sold it, I suspect he plans to use Iliana's jewelry to finance his high living next winter. There's a rumor circulating that he has political ambitions, too."

Iliana leaned closer to the curtain, and as she listened to Dominic describe Ben's shortcomings, her heart ached.

"Seems to me he's hatching some plan to steal the Sebastian holdings just the way his father stole the Medina Rancho." Javier's voice was glum. "Senor Ross was ill and sometimes confused those last weeks. I think he was tricked into signing that paper or he knew it wouldn't hold up in court. He was smart and must have had a plan to outmaneuver Purdy, but death caught him sooner than planned. He made an issue of those jewels, and I believe he meant for Iliana to have a way out if she wanted it."

"Perhaps it was the only way he could see to keep her from being left homeless. He knew Ben would go after the ranch, but the marriage would ensure she wouldn't be left with nothing and no place to go." Dominic's voice grew fainter as he moved toward the door. "I assume you'll be riding into Two Creek Junction tomorrow to have a talk with the marshal."

"He's pursuing bandits a long way from here. It could be weeks before he returns to this area."

"What if there's nothing left of the jewels by the time he returns?"

"If the jewels are gone, Ben will be facing more than a wedding in three weeks." Javier's words sent a chill down Iliana's back. "There'll be no more bargains with Ben Purdy."

"With the jewels gone, where will the senora get the money to escape? We've had a couple of bad winters and high expenses. The money Ross left will just meet the ranch's needs if we're careful. Mr. Williams won't let anyone near the small amount Don Sebastian was able to set aside for his grandson until Gabe is grown." Dominic's voice grew loud again, revealing his anger and frustration with the situation.

"We better hope Ben hasn't sold all of Iliana's jewels and that she gets them back. I heard some of those old necklaces and earbobs are worth a great deal. I've no doubt she'll be willing to sell them to avoid marrying Ben Purdy."

"We have to get those jewels back. We can't let Ben win without giving the senora a chance to fire a shot."

Chapter Fourteen

Iliana clapped a hand over her mouth to keep from calling out. Her heart pounded so loudly, she feared the two loyal employees would hear it. Their words filled her with both hope and dismay. It hadn't occurred to her that there might be a way to avoid marrying Ben. She had always been obedient. First she had obeyed Grandfather, then Ross. Was it really for her to decide whether or not she would marry Ben? She'd brushed off Mr. Williams's mention of a choice. She had never considered the possibility that marrying was something she could determine for herself. She knew so little of the world beyond the narrow confines of her birthplace. Javier was right; she'd gladly trade all of her mother's jewelry to escape marrying Ben. But what about Gabe? Could she forfeit his inheritance?

In spite of a glimmer of hope, her heart ached from being placed in the untenable position of having to give up her inheritance in order to save her son's inheritance. She thought briefly of the jewels she'd only ever considered a sentimental link to her mother. She'd never thought of the jewelry as something that belonged to her personally or of the gems' value. Even though the collection was referred to as her mother's jewels, they had been a part of the Medina estate for generations. The gems had never been owned outright by the women who had possessed them. Was it possible that Ross had given them to her in his will to buy her freedom rather than to pass them on to the woman who would someday be Gabe's bride? Had Grandfather had a part in leaving her unrestricted ownership of the family heirlooms? The thought gave her comfort.

Iliana fingered the wooden beads that circled her neck and breathed a quick prayer. She traced the indentations that marked the agony of the figure carved into the wooden cross and decided she would keep this necklace. She suspected it was of little value other than what she placed on it because her mother had often worn it. But if the jewels could be recovered from Ben, she would go to Mr. Williams and ask him to appoint a manager for the ranch until Gabe came of age and ask him if there was a way she could escape marriage to the man she despised.

The voices dimmed and she guessed the two loyal foremen were making their way to the door. She waited until she heard the heavy door close. She had much to think about.

* * *

"Senorita." A small man with a large hat in his hand greeted Iliana after Amaya summoned her from her room the following day. He stood half in shadow under the wide arch that led from the sunny courtyard to the cool dimness of the adobe house. She recognized him as one of the Purdy caballeros. He looked ill at ease as he extended a small bundle toward her. She hesitated to accept it, fearing some cruel trick.

"El Senor Purdy instructed me to place this in your hands and no other."

Schooling her features to hide her trepidation, she accepted the bundle. With care, she unwound the linen to discover her mother's pearls. They appeared dull and tarnished, but she knew they were of great value and would brighten when worn. She'd worn them at Amaya's insistence when she wed Ross, but she had no intention of wearing them for Ben. Her heart lightened with hope. The pearls and their diamond clasp were valuable, but how valuable she didn't know. Could the necklace possibly be her means of escaping marriage to Ben? And if she ran away would her son forfeit his inheritance? The seemingly contradictory concerns circled endlessly in her mind.

She looked up from the pearls to see Ben's messenger backing away. "No, don't go," she called to him on an impulse. "I wish to send a message back with you." He paused then came closer to wait in the entry while she hurried to the library to scribble a hasty message on a piece of heavy parchment. *Thank you for the return of my pearls. I will expect the other pieces you removed from my home by Friday.* She signed her name with a flourish. When she finished, she folded the paper and dropped a small circle of hot wax on it to seal the missive.

With her head held at a regal angle, she handed the sealed note to the caballero. He looked about in a furtive manner. Satisfied they were alone, he whispered, "Do not anger the young senor. There are many hombres with guns who sleep in the bunkhouse now. They are growing restless because promises have not been kept."

Only after he disappeared from sight did she succumb to the trembling that shook her slender frame. Sinking to the floor, she buried her face in her hands, but she did not cry. She couldn't believe she'd found the courage to stand up to Ben Purdy even in a small way, but had she endangered the ranch's loyal workers through seeking the return of what was hers? Twice now she had taken such a bold action! Ben would likely ignore her demand for the return of the remainder of her jewelry—but she had found the courage to make the demand. Only time would tell if her newfound courage would bring trouble.

* * *

"At dawn, you will meet me for a riding lesson," Javier spoke to Gabe that evening shortly following the dinner Iliana and the boy had shared alone in the stately dining room. Gabe's face paled and he looked hesitantly toward his mother.

Javier went on, "It will not do for the master of el Rancho de Sebastian to be unable to ride. I have selected a suitable mount for you."

Iliana saw Gabe's already pale complexion turn pasty and she ached for the fear Javier's words brought her small son. There had been previous attempts to teach the boy to ride and all had ended in failure. She attempted to smile encouragement to him. Once she had dreaded the day Ross would force the child to again undertake riding lessons, but now she felt certain her son must conquer his fear of horses and become comfortable in the world of men. She had turned the task over to Javier, not wishing the possibility of Ben becoming the one to take over Gabe's training.

Gabe turned pleading eyes toward her. He was afraid of the beasts, and she had been content to wait for him to grow stronger before insisting he learn to ride; but the time had arrived when he must overcome his fears, just as she must. Too much was at stake to give in to her son's fears. If she were forced to wed Ben, Gabe must be prepared for the difficulties Ben would inflict on him.

"Your father expected that one day you would become a fine horseman," she told him. "And there are no better horses than those raised on the Sebastian." She turned to Javier. "Which horse have you selected for Gabe?" Knowing he shared her distrust of Ben Purdy, she was finding it easier to speak openly with him.

"Princess Sophia is an excellent mount with commendable patience for those needing assurance," he said.

She smiled at him, showing her gratitude. The mare, steady and dependable, had produced many fine colts and had an easy gait, an excellent choice for her timid son. She turned to Gabe. "Princess Sophia has a fondness for apples. I will accompany you to the stables after dinner so you can take her a treat to let her know you wish to be her friend."

"But Madre—" Gabe protested.

"No. You are no longer a *bebé*. It is time to assume your responsibilities." Speaking with sternness to her son was something she had never done before, but now she suspected she had been wrong to spoil him and protect him from his fears. Ross had been wrong, too, in allowing her to coddle him as Grandfather had coddled her, requiring only obedience of her. She was twenty-four now, a woman, but as she had discovered over the past few days, without Amaya to back her up and tell her what to do, she was woefully unprepared to run her own household or to make the decision that hovered in her mind.

As the week progressed, it took all the restraint Iliana could muster to stay away from the stables when Gabe met with Javier for lessons. Javier hadn't suggested she stay away, but she knew that was his desire, and common sense told her she must not allow Gabe to appeal to her tender heart to escape the old man's charge. The first day, the seven-year-old returned stiff lipped and sullen, refusing to talk about the lesson. The following morning, however, she heard him leave the hacienda for his second lesson, and she breathed a sigh of relief. He returned an hour later covered in dust and exhibiting a slight limp. Again he went straight to his room. She bit her lip and wrung her hands as she paced the floor, reminding herself that she must not sympathize or back down. Toward the end of the week, she began to detect a slight bravado in his step and suspected she need not worry any longer.

Friday arrived and there was no delivery from the Purdy Ranch. Would her mother's pearls and her few jewels, which had been in her own room during her husband's illness, be sufficient to escape to some far place where Ben could not find her and Gabe? She knew nothing of the jewelry's worth or of what funds would be required to establish a new home.

She was deep in thought when someone rapped softly on the door. She looked up to see Javier watching from the doorway.

"Would you care to ride with Gabe and me in the morning?"

The question startled her but pleased her as well. It had been many months since she'd ridden her beloved mare, and she was anxious to judge Gabe's progress. "I would like that."

* * *

The sun was just beginning to make its presence known the next morning when Iliana donned a riding skirt and tied back her hair. She left the house holding Gabe's hand to meet both Javier and Dominic at the stable. Without a cloud to mar the azure smoothness of the sky, the coolness of morning would disappear long before noon. Dominic led Nutmeg toward her, saddled and ready for the ride. In response to her query, he declined to ride with them, citing ranch demands that could not wait.

Gathering up Nutmeg's reins, she allowed Dominic to boost her into the Mexican saddle, with its high pommel and cantle. Grandfather had taught her to use a sidesaddle for special events but had insisted she ride astride when riding cross-country. Javier had encouraged her to ride astride as well, claiming the sidesaddle was foolish and dangerous, though Amaya clucked at this breach of decorum. Iliana was grateful she didn't have to ride in the awkward, dangerous position that limited the freedom of movement occasioned by riding with both legs on the left.

Gabe rounded the stable mounted on Princess Sophia. He was followed closely by Javier on a magnificent gelding that had been one of Ross's favorite mounts. Shiloh was a good choice, Iliana felt, and an excellent match for Princess Sophia since his movements were sedate and his response to commands impeccable. Neither horse was excitable or easily spooked.

Javier led the way and Iliana brought up the rear, keeping the less-experienced rider between them as they left the corrals and headed for a gentle slope leading to a favorite pasture in the foothills. She was pleased with Gabe's posture and the way he held the reins. Princess Sophia was a comfortable horse with a docile temperament, but she wasn't a rocking-horse ride. Though Gabe might never develop a great love such as she held for horses, she was glad he had conquered his fear enough to learn the basics and become comfortable on a gentle mount. In time, he would be able to take his place as a working owner of the ranch.

Iliana enjoyed the climb along the dusty trail with the sharp odor of creosote brush filling her senses and the bright sun bathing the stark mountains in a myriad of colors. She'd spent so many hours at her husband's bedside during the spring and early summer, it had been some time since she and Nutmeg had followed any of the winding trails that led to the upper mesa. She didn't even mind the leisurely pace Javier set and was amused at her son's show of bravado and eagerness to go faster. Perhaps he'd become an avid rider after all.

When they reached the mesa, Javier drew his horse to a halt in the slight shade offered by a patch of trees that grew beside the stream. He motioned for Gabe and Iliana to stop beside him. He stretched out his arm, pointing to a jagged mountain that was barely discernible in the distance. "See, Gabe, the far mountains mark the eastern side, and the western mountains the western side of your land. The new river runs clear to the mountains. The far side of the river you can see to the east now belongs to the horse trader, Senor Telford. The southern edges cannot be seen from here." He pointed again; this time to the north. "See that rocky ridge? That is the northern boundary of your land. The edge of the meadow, where the rocks begin, marks the boundary where your land meets Purdy land."

Iliana's eyes followed where Javier pointed, automatically noting that the grass was still deep and lush beside the narrow trickle of water that made its way from a point near the marker to a shallow bowl where it formed a small pool, then proceeded on its way to meet the larger stream, set free by the horse trader. Here the water tumbled over a precipice, where it provided a wider strip of green leading to a stock pond beyond the stables and kept the creek near the hacienda from running dry.

"It will soon be time to begin moving our breeding stock to this higher grassland for the summer," Javier remarked as he swung down from his horse. He stretched a moment before reaching for Iliana to assist her in dismounting. For a moment she thought her legs might not support her. It had been too long since she had last ridden.

"Look!" Gabe, who was still mounted, pointed to a distant speck. "Someone is coming."

Iliana placed one hand above her eyes to reduce the glare from the bright sunlight. Gabe was right; a rider was approaching from the direction of the Purdy Ranch.

"I'm going to go meet him!" Gabe pressed his heels against his horse's side, and Princess Sophia obediently began trotting toward the distant figure.

"Gabe, wait—" she began.

"Let him go," Javier interrupted. "It will be good for him to ride alone. We can follow at a distance and reach him quickly if he encounters any difficulty."

She knew he was right. To gain confidence in his own abilities, Gabe needed to venture on his own. Javier helped her remount then swung onto Shiloh's back. With their mounts side by side, they moved forward at a sedate walk. Iliana allowed Nutmeg to pick her own way as she kept her attention on the slim figure who was now far ahead of them. The distance between Gabe and the other rider closed rapidly. A sense of unease swept over her.

Javier felt it too. His horse began moving more quickly. The horses they watched approached each other and stopped. Something in the bearing of the other rider and Gabe suggested there was a confrontational element between them.

Javier dug in his heels and his horse lunged forward. Iliana sent Nutmeg racing full speed toward her son. It soon became clear that Ben Purdy was the rider stopped beside Gabe! Her uneasiness grew and she urged her horse to greater speed. Her faster horse soon passed Javier. In spite of her streaming eyes and blurred vision, she saw Ben hand something to Gabe. The angry pitch of his voice reached her but not his words. With a vicious jerk on the reins, he turned his horse away. Before she reached her son, Ben disappeared in a cloud of dust.

Reining in Nutmeg beside Princess Sophia, she held out a shaky hand toward Gabe. "Are you all right?" she asked.

"Of course." The lofty look he gave her showed surprise that she should ask, leaving her feeling foolish. *Why had she been so certain Gabe was in some kind of danger?*

"What did Purdy want?" Javier arrived to take charge of the situation.

"He said he was on his way to the hacienda to give Madre this." With a triumphant grin, Gabe held out a small drawstring bag to Iliana. Javier took it from Gabe's outstretched arm and opened it. After a long look, he silently handed the bag to Iliana.

She wasn't surprised to see familiar earrings, a few ornate finger rings, and a jewel-encrusted cross suspended from a gold chain. The pieces of jewelry she stared at were both beautiful and valuable, but they were only a small portion of the jewelry that was rightfully hers. The brightly colored necklaces and most of the rings were still missing. Though her teeth were gritted and her jaw clenched, she said nothing. Instead she dropped the bag into her skirt pocket.

"He said you will regret threatening to send the marshal for property that will soon be lawfully his." Gabe looked up at Javier, and it seemed to her that some silent understanding passed between them.

She tugged on Nutmeg's rein, indicating her readiness to return to the hacienda. Javier placed his hand on her arm, indicating he wasn't ready to ride yet. Assuming she would obey his silent command to stay a moment longer, he turned again to Gabe.

"Did he say anything else?" There was coldness in Javier's eyes that belied the softly voiced question he directed to her young son. A haughty look came to the boy's face, startling her with his uncanny resemblance to her grandfather.

"He said he ordered a room prepared for me at his ranch so that after the wedding next Friday, Amaya can care for me there." Gabe maintained his arrogant pose for a moment before looking apologetically toward his mother. "I told him I wouldn't be needing the room because my father left the Sebastian Rancho to me. I told him I would be remaining in my own home and he could stay in his."

His words left Iliana speechless. A seven-year-old child could not possibly head his own household. Nor should he speak so disrespectfully to an adult.

"That was all you discussed?" Javier pursued the subject. From the heavy frown on his face, Iliana suspected Javier wasn't pleased with the discussion that had taken place between Gabe and Ben.

Gabe looked offended. "He acted like he didn't hear me. He said I didn't have to worry about anything because he would look after Madre's share of the ranch and mine and that he and mi madre would share the Sebastian Hacienda and Amaya would go on looking after me. He made me angry, and I told him Madre has no share. The rancho is all mine. You are teaching me to manage it and I have no need for his interference."

Iliana felt humiliated and angry. How dare Ben assume he could separate her from her son! Ben was more interested in her inheritance than in her. Even her son assumed her wishes had no part in the matter. And no one seemed to see anything unfair about arranging her life for her.

"He doesn't like me," Gabe went on, sounding like a little boy again.

Her head snapped up. "Did he say something mean to you?"

"When I told him he doesn't have to take care of your share because Father left all of the Sebastian land to me, he got angry. First, he said I didn't know anything and Father promised him that you would get your fair share. Then he said no Mexican brat was going to ruin his plans."

Chapter Fifteen

"Hold still!" Amaya spoke around the pins she held pinched between her lips. Iliana did her best to stop squirming. She also tried to avoid looking at the dress the housekeeper was pinning. She had been smaller, little more than a child, when she'd worn the dress for her marriage to Ross, and it didn't feel right to wear the gown again for Ben, but Amaya had carefully preserved the dress and insisted she must be properly attired for the wedding. The woman had finally had her way, cornering Iliana and insisting she try on the gown so that it could be marked for the necessary alterations. The dress was beautiful, with layer upon layer of hand-embroidered, sheer white silk, but Iliana had no desire to wear it to wed Ben Purdy. She'd rather die than be his bride.

She'd considered ending her life. Amaya would care for Gabe if she were gone, but she quickly repented of such thoughts. Life was precious and she had more than her own to consider.

Besides, her death would solve nothing. It might even push Ben to destroy the lake of water high in the mountains, thus destroying the ranch and all that should one day be Gabe's.

Her eyes caught sight of the lace mantilla that lay across the end of her bed. She wouldn't wear it. Ben would laugh at her for wearing the headpiece dear to the hearts of Latino women, and this one was especially dear to her as both her mother and grandmother had worn it on their wedding days. Resentment burrowed its way deeper into her heart. Ben had ridiculed Gabe, and if her prospective husband looked down on her son because of his mixed heritage, he must think her inferior too. He had always treated her as though she were nothing. Besides, the mantilla was too good for the likes of Ben Purdy.

"Senora?" a soft tap sounded on Iliana's door.

"I'm coming." Amaya rose to her feet and made her way to the door.

"Horses are approaching. They appear to be one of the herds headed for California. They will want water." Iliana recognized Javier's voice. Ross had assigned the old man to do the chores near the hacienda when his own responsibilities took him to the far corners of the ranch, and it seemed Dominic was continuing the assignment. Anyway Javier was old and his hands and knees were twisted and swollen with age and arthritis, making riding and roping difficult. Almost the only riding he'd done in recent years was to accompany her when she left the hacienda and the little necessary for teaching Gabe to ride.

"Why do you come to tell us?" Amaya sounded annoyed. Nevertheless she opened the door to the bandy-legged old cowhand.

"Juan is checking the water in the southern range, and Dominic rode into town early this morning."

"And the young senor? He is the master here now."

Iliana was amused by Amaya's reference to Gabe. Surely no one expected a small boy to take charge of negotiations with a trader. Even Amaya knew that when the trader and his men arrived they would want more than water. They would be looking to acquire horses as well. Dominic would be anxious to sell at least a dozen horses to raise much-needed funds for the ranch.

"The young one rode out also," the old man said.

She should have been informed! Iliana wondered which of the caballeros Gabe had accompanied. Her son was certainly taking his new responsibilities far more seriously than she had expected. She was pleased with his new self-confidence and had noted with satisfaction that he had gained weight and possibly grown a few inches of late as well. Still she should have been consulted.

"Should I permit them to water their animals?" Javier persisted.

"My husband and Grandfather before him always allowed travelers to water their animals and refill their barrels. I have heard no instructions to the contrary."

"Si, Senora. But not all horse traders these days are the harmless traders who have stopped here in the past." He glanced meaningfully toward the north, where everyone on the ranch suspected Ben Purdy was harboring the bandits and gunslingers that were frightening ranchers and townspeople alike.

Glancing at the old man's grave face, she felt a sharp stab of pain. He had reason to hesitate to assume authority. With her wedding to Ben two days away, he had good cause to believe he would be turned away. She wasn't the only one who didn't trust Ben, and she suspected that if she went through with her marriage to him, there would be little she could do for the men and their families who had lived on the Sebastian Rancho all their lives.

"Senora?"

"Give them the water." There was no one else to make the decision, so she would deal with it as she believed Ross would have done. "Saddle Nutmeg and I'll help you watch over them to make certain their stock do not trample the gardens or cause other damage." She understood well the necessity of making certain strange stock didn't mix with the ranch's herds or destroy gardens the workers depended on. In the past few years there had been a steady stream of wagon trains and buggies passing near the ranch headed to new colonies established in Mexico by Americanos. Most of those groups exhibited courtesy and respect, but lately the ranchers had been troubled by groups of well-armed riders behaving like bandits and acting no better than the Apache raiders who had terrorized villages and ranches when she was a child.

Javier looked uncertain. The look he gave her was filled with misgiving. "If anything happens to you, Senora—"

"Dominic shouldn't have left you with so few men. Round up the cook. He can help and he knows how to handle a shotgun." It felt surprisingly good to take charge. It was, in fact, a heady experience.

"It is not proper for you to be seen by strangers—" Amaya protested.

"Hurry! We must be ready," Iliana commanded, and Javier scurried toward the staircase.

"You must not do this." Amaya continued her protests.

Grasping at the excuse Javier's message afforded her, Iliana stepped out of the gown Amaya had been fitting to her and pulled on her more serviceable blouse and long, full skirt. While still tucking her blouse in at the waistline, she moved to the door and opened it.

"I won't allow anyone's horses to go thirsty." She turned her back on the housekeeper to rush to her room and don riding clothes.

She was finding it quite impossible to fasten the divided skirt she'd selected but hadn't worn for many months, when Amaya handed her a bundle of clothing. Iliana looked down at the shirt and trousers the housekeeper had handed her and smiled. Yes, it would be far better to wear the clothing the housekeeper had pulled from the bushes that separated the hacienda and the bunkhouse. It would be good if she appeared as one of the caballeros.

This time the buttons came together with ease. The housekeeper found a strip of leather to fasten her hair high on her head before handing her a hat that concealed the mound of hair she thrust inside it.

"Don't speak—not to anyone," the housekeeper warned. "Let Javier do the talking."

She nodded in silent agreement before racing down the stairs. Before reaching the stable, she spotted the long plume of dust approaching along the road that led to the hacienda. Iliana found her horse saddled when she reached the stable, and from a mounting block she stepped into the saddle. Sandwiched between Javier and the massive black cook, who had arrived at the ranch shortly after the war to make himself at home cooking for the men, she urged Nutmeg forward to meet the approaching riders.

* * *

Dominic entered the sleepy little town shortly before noon. He checked at the marshal's office first and found it still empty. He scribbled a note explaining Ben's theft of Iliana's jewelry and tacked it to the wall behind the lawman's desk. When he finished, he made his way to the cantina.

He took his time wrapping his mount's reins around the hitching post and dusting off his boots before stepping inside the dim coolness of the adobe cantina. It took a few moments for his vision to adjust to the dim light, following the brilliant brightness outside. When he could see clearly, he made his way toward an empty table. Before he reached it, a hand reached out to halt his progress.

"Will you join me?" He recognized the old man who had been a frequent guest at the ranch during Senor Adams's illness.

"Mr. Williams," he spoke the older man's name in the respectful manner he'd long used in addressing those older than himself.

"What brings you to town, my boy?" Williams asked while staring in thoughtful concentration at the glass he held in his hand.

Dominic got right to the point, "I came to report a theft to the marshal." He explained about the missing jewels and Ben's admission of guilt.

Mr. Williams set down his glass and steepled his fingers together just below his chin, peering at Dominic over the top of wire-rimmed spectacles. He spoke with slow deliberation. "Those jewels must be recovered. Adams was certain his young wife would use them to hire a strong man to run the ranch. He left a list of names I should contact if she approached me. If she chose to abandon the ranch to Ben, those gems would have provided a comfortable living for her and the boy until he comes of age."

Dominic smacked his dusty hat against his thigh, his pent-up frustration bursting through his careful control. "Ben Purdy means to own the rancho or destroy it. If the senora marries him, he will destroy her too. It's extortion!" Dominic's voice rose. "It's a clear threat that Gabe will lose the ranch if Iliana doesn't do as Ben demands."

Mr. Williams brought the tips of his fingers to his mouth, tapping them against his lower lip several times. "I fear she will lose it either way."

Dominic suspected the banker knew something he was reluctant to disclose. At last Williams said, "Ross was convinced Iliana would never consent to marrying Ben, but by pretending to agree to the arrangement, he hoped to buy time for her to escape. He was aware of the gunfighters and gamblers who were arriving almost daily at the Purdy Ranch. Young Purdy is deeply in debt and many of his creditors have come to collect or sent someone to do it for them. Those frustrated men are causing havoc from one end of this valley to the other. Some of them have made it clear they're running out of patience, and if Ben doesn't pay up soon, he'll get a bullet for his failure to do so. We made certain Iliana had clear ownership to those gewgaws those old Spanish dames hung onto for centuries. Those fancy things would buy that whole canyon where Travis Telford found water and all of the land between it and the ranch if Telford hadn't already bought it for himself." He smiled a wolfish grin, suggesting he wasn't sharing all his thoughts concerning Ben Purdy and his problems.

"Iliana has no funds. Ben claims he has a right to her jewelry since they're about to be married. He admitted he took them, and though she has demanded their return, he has returned only a few of the less valuable pieces and the pearls he expects her to wear when they wed."

Williams sat up straight, sending his chair slamming against the wall. "What did the marshal say?"

"Marshal Reynolds is out of town and I've no idea when he'll be returning."

"I'll send a few wires, but it could be weeks before he picks one up," Williams mused. "By then it could be too late."

"That's what I fear because we both know Iliana will do anything for Gabe. She'll marry Purdy if she thinks it is the only way she can keep her son's inheritance safe for him."

Williams's fingers drummed against the table, and he appeared deep in thought. Dominic watched him, hoping the old man had a solution for the problem. He truly was concerned for Iliana, but he was concerned for himself also. If Ben took over the rancho, like old Javier, Dominic would lose his job and there would be no way he could marry the shy senorita he had been courting for two years.

The old banker looked troubled and angry, but he appeared as much at a loss to know what to do as Dominic.

* * *

As the riders approached, Iliana counted a dozen men on good mounts with more than eighty riderless horses in the remuda they hazed forward. A buckboard pulled by four strong draft horses held barrels that bounced with each rut the wagon wheels rolled across. She saw the tension ease from Javier's shoulders as he recognized the man who rode at the front. He spurred his horse forward until he could draw his horse alongside the tall, slender man with a reddish beard and blond curls plastered to his damp forehead. He looked slightly familiar to Iliana. The two men greeted each other with obvious familiarity.

"Hola! Javier," the trader shouted, "Have you water?"

"Si! But none to waste. You must be careful." Both men laughed as though they shared a great joke.

"You have my word." The men exchanged satisfied grins.

Iliana dismounted to open the gate for the herd to save Javier the task that was simple for her but would cause the elderly cowboy a great deal of pain. She led her horse aside to be out of the way. Keeping her hat pulled low, she watched with interest as the horses shoved their way toward the stock pond in their eagerness to reach the water.

Watching from beneath the wide brim of her hat, she noticed that the horse wranglers' ages seemed to vary a great deal; a couple had gray hair and thick beards, and some appeared younger than her own age. When she caught the leader staring back at her, she stepped behind Nutmeg. Something in his eyes told her that her attire hadn't concealed her identity as well as she'd hoped.

When the task of watering the stock and filling canteens and barrels was completed, the man in charge gave the signal and the animals began to move again back toward the dusty road. After the last horse passed through the gate, she closed it, making certain it was secure. She turned and was surprised to see the leader had lingered behind. He pulled his horse up close to Javier and the cook, who sat their mounts a short distance away. She heard him ask, "El Senor Adams? He is well? I would like to thank him for his generosity and ask if any of his fine horses are for sale. I contracted in San Bernardino for a hundred horses and have fallen short of that number. I wish, too, to arrange for the purchase of breeding stock for when I start my own ranch next spring."

Javier explained that Ross Adams had died and that Dominic was now in charge of the ranch until Adams's young son was old enough to take over its operation and that the foreman was presently away from the hacienda. Iliana didn't miss the swift glance the man sent her way before turning his attention back to Javier.

Iliana tugged on Javier's shirt and he bent to hear her whisper in his ear. "Tell him they may make camp on Sebastian land near the small stream to the west. Dominic will wish to speak with him." She knew Dominic and her husband had discussed supplementing the ranch's need for cash by selling as many horses as possible to the trader.

Javier looked doubtful but repeated her offer, adding directions to the campsite though the men had camped there before.

"Thank you." The light-haired man touched his hat. "My wranglers and I will be taking this lot to California, but on the chance your foreman wishes to conduct business, we shall accept your offer to camp on Sebastian land for a night."

"I will tell him where to find you," Javier said in a respectful voice.

Chapter Sixteen

ILIANA, BATHED AND WEARING A full-skirted gown over many petticoats, entered the dining room. She looked around and was disappointed to see it was empty. Her son was not waiting for her. She would have to speak with Dominic. He should have informed her before taking her son to the village with him. She assumed Javier had already shared the news about the traders with Dominic, but her first concern was for her young son and how he had fared his first full day away from the hacienda.

She noticed Amaya waiting in the doorway with a concerned frown on her face. Iliana hesitated before taking her chair.

Amaya came forward. "Do you wish to wait dinner until Gabe arrives?"

"I'm not sure." She hated sounding so uncertain.

"Why isn't he here?" Amaya asked. "It isn't like him to take his time dressing for dinner."

"Gabe has never been away so long," Iliana began in a hesitant voice. She didn't wish to imply she questioned Dominic's judgment. Both Ross and Javier trusted him, and her husband had given his young foreman charge of the ranch until she remarried. She only wished she'd been able to prepare the boy for such a long venture. She felt an ache in her heart. Clearly someone needed to prepare *her* for relinquishing some measure of responsibility for her child. "Have they returned?"

"They?" Clearly Amaya knew little more than Iliana did about Gabe's activities that day. A warning sounded in her mind. Amaya always knew the whereabouts of everyone on the ranch.

"Didn't he go with Dominic?" Fear rose like gorge in her throat. She gripped the table to steady herself, fighting the nausea that churned in her stomach. A sense of foreboding made her heart race. "When Javier said he rode out this morning, I thought he meant Gabe had accompanied Dominic into the village." She sank slowly to her chair.

"Go with Dominic? Why would you think he accompanied him? Dominic left before Gabe roused himself from bed this morning. Few of the men were even up when I saw him off." Amaya appeared puzzled.

"And you haven't seen Gabe all day?" She looked at Amaya, almost begging her to tell her Gabe was merely changing for dinner. Amaya's face turned gray and then twisted with anger. She reached out with one hand as if to steady herself before rushing toward the door, screaming for Javier.

She followed Amaya to the door then rushed past her toward Javier's small house. He met Iliana halfway, grasping her by her shoulders to stop her mad rush. "He's gone. Gabe is missing!"

"How long has he been gone?"

"I haven't seen him today." Her voice emerged in a scared whisper. "You said he rode out and I thought you meant he rode out with Dominic for his riding lesson. When they didn't return at the usual time and I learned Dominic had gone to the village, I assumed he was still with him." The sky seemed to swirl around her and she feared she might faint. From somewhere inside herself, she drew on that iron control her grandfather had bequeathed her. She faced Javier, little aware of the bruising grip he held on her arm. His face was white and his eyes revealed a fear almost as great as her own.

"Amaya, I want the house searched," Javier shouted, though the woman was only a few steps away. He seemed to realize he was hurting Iliana's arm and released it abruptly. He spoke to her in a lower voice. "I'll get the men organized. He could be anywhere by now. If his horse has thrown him, he'll need a warm bath and liniment." His eyes didn't hide his fear that the child might be lying somewhere broken and bleeding or worse.

"He rode well when we rode with you last week, but I don't think he's ready to ride alone." Iliana struggled to calm her fears, but one frightening possibility after another rose in her mind. She watched Javier stride toward the door, and the rebellion that had been brewing inside her since Ross's death exploded. "Amaya can prepare for his return. I'm going with you. He may be the owner of this ranch, but he's still a little boy, and I'm his mother."

"Iliana!" Amaya began in a stern voice.

"I'm going." She had never taken such a fierce stand before in her life, but a lifetime of acquiescence dissolved in the face of fear for her child.

Javier started to say something, changed his mind, and turned toward the door instead. "I'll have the horses ready," he threw over his shoulder as he let the door slam shut behind him.

She ran up the stairs to put on her riding skirt, but seeing the clothes she'd discarded after the horse traders left, she again put on the shirt and trousers. Reaching into a high bureau drawer, she pulled out a small caliber pistol. She loaded it with shaking fingers then strapped to her waist the holster made for it. Grandfather had given it to her years ago and taught her how to use it should she happen upon a snake while riding. Since she never rode alone but was always accompanied by Ross or a trusted employee, she seldom carried the small pistol. Today she might need it to send a signal.

Several riders thundered past her as she made her way to the stable. They disappeared in various directions in search of her son, some toward the large stock pond, and she regretted that her son had not been taught to swim.

Javier was just tightening the girth on Nutmeg when she entered the stable. Her mare stood beside his gelding, which was already saddled. She noticed a rifle resting in a scabbard attached to each saddle.

A quick glance told her Princess Sophia was not in her stall. The mare would have returned to the stable if her rider had fallen and was unable to remount.

Without a word, Javier assisted Iliana into her saddle before gathering up his reins and stepping into a stirrup to mount his own horse.

He headed for the trail leading to the high northern mesa, where Iliana had gone with Javier and Gabe a few days earlier. The sun was nearly down and long shadows lay across the trail, but Javier didn't slow his horse and Iliana didn't either. Brush caught at her pants and the scraggly trees that grew near the trail slapped at her face. Even a sure-footed mount such as Nutmeg could trip on the rocky trail, but she refused to slow the mare. She didn't usually ride full out until she reached the mesa, but she didn't hesitate this time. A nagging worry that had followed her all day, which had intensified with the discovery that Gabe was missing, made her oblivious to the breakneck speed. She wanted only to find her son.

When they reached the mesa, Javier pulled his horse to an abrupt stop. Nutmeg slid to a halt beside him. Silently he scanned the high meadow. Iliana, too, searched each rock and shadow as far as she could see. The deepening dusk turned rock formations and the few twisted trees into frightening specters.

"I'll go right; you go left," Javier shouted minimal instructions. "Fire a shot in the air if you find him or become frightened. Call him every two or three hundred yards."

Though Javier's horse took off at a rapid lope, Iliana held Nutmeg to a fast walk. She didn't want to miss anything that might indicate whether Gabe had been on the mesa or was lying injured in the tall grass. More likely, it was Princess Sophia who was injured, she mused as she worked her way north. If Gabe had fallen or been injured, the old mare would have made her way back to the stable, thus alerting Javier that her rider was in trouble. But if the Princess was injured, Gabe may have been reluctant to leave her—or he might have begun walking and become lost.

She rode into each clump of brush and scanned the grass for signs of a horse or a boy's passing. Over and over she called Gabe's name, pausing only to listen for an answering cry. The occasional screech of a night bird was the only response. A chill wind blew down from the mountains, and an eerie silence filled the mesa, made unfamiliar by darkness, and she remembered not many years had passed since renegade Indians had roamed hidden corners of the ranch.

Iliana lost track of time as she rode and called her son's name. The quarter moon that partially lit the mesa had traveled some distance when she heard Javier call out for Gabe, a sign their circuitous search was bringing them near each other again. Despair filled her heart. A short time later, they met near the creek on the north end of the ranch where it met Purdy ranch land. She didn't have to ask to know Javier's search had been no more fruitful than her own.

Seeing the grim set of his face, she knew he wouldn't concede defeat; he would continue searching, as would she. Somewhere in this vast tract of land was a lost and frightened little boy.

Fighting back tears, she asked, "Now where do we search?"

"We'll follow the stream where the grass is tallest. Stay on this side, and I'll cross to the other. We'll have to ride at a slower pace in order to study the grass." His horse responded at once to the pressure of his knees as he turned back to recross the shallow stream, sending a shower of silver spray in his wake.

Iliana allowed Nutmeg a moment to take a few sips of the cold water before urging the animal onward. Across the water she could see Javier moving parallel to her. He was moving more slowly now than when he'd started the search on the outer edges of the mesa. Not only could a small boy be hidden by the long grass near the stream, but it was harder to see rocks or the burrows of small animals that could prove to be stumbling blocks for the horses.

They'd traveled several miles when Javier stood in his stirrups to get a better look at something that caught his attention. Iliana stood too, but she couldn't see whatever it was that the old man saw. Even in the darkness, she sensed a tension in the set of his shoulders.

"What is it?" she shouted.

"I'm not sure, but I think you better wait where you are." He spoke with unusual sharpness. The gelding lunged forward and Javier bent low against the animal's neck. Iliana had no intention of being left behind. She urged Nutmeg forward, forcing her to struggle to keep up with the bigger animal. Once, Nutmeg seemed to stumble but righted herself and hurried on.

She wasn't far behind Javier when he brought his horse to a stop and vaulted from the saddle to run toward the stream. He paused on the bank for a moment before wading into the water, seemingly in a hurry to reach something she couldn't see. Iliana urged her horse closer, but Nutmeg snorted and minced sideways, showing reluctance to continue on.

Iliana swung one leg over the high pommel and leaped to the ground, knowing that with her reins trailing, Nutmeg wouldn't run off. Heedless of any obstacles in her way, she ran toward the place where she could see Javier wading into the water. He paused beside a large boulder where the water was a little deeper than the scant inch or two she'd observed in most of the stream. She had almost reached the water's edge when he looked up.

"Don't come any closer," he shouted. He motioned her back with his hands. She saw him crouch lower and reach for something.

"What is it?" Before she could take another step, she knew. There was no boulder in the stream. The dark object she'd taken for a boulder was Princess Sophia. Sickness rose in her stomach. She'd learned to ride on Princess Sophia. The Princess had been her dearest friend through a lonely childhood.

"Is she dead?" she asked. Dread filled her heart, knowing that if the animal still breathed Javier would have to put her down.

"She's dead." His voice was flat.

Tears filled her eyes, and she moved closer, feeling the water rush over her boots. She couldn't fathom Princess Sophia being gone. The mare was old but she hadn't been feeble or weak. She shook off the memories. She would mourn the faithful mare later; finding Gabe took on greater urgency. He must have been horribly confused and frightened when his mount fell, leaving him wet and alone, perhaps injured. It was becoming increasingly imperative that they find him. "Which way do you think Gabe went?"

There was a long silence then Javier said in a hoarse voice, "He's dead too. It appears the horse fell on him."

"No!" She screamed as she splashed through the water. Javier's blunt words couldn't be true. Gabe was just lost, wandering around disoriented and confused.

She rounded the bulk that was Princess Sophia and saw the kindly old man kneeling in the shallow stream. He was holding Gabe's head above the rushing water. Most of the boy's small body lay beneath the horse. Moonlight painted silver paths down Javier's cheeks.

"I can't believe Princess Sophia stumbled. She's the most sure-footed horse on the ranch." Iliana's mind couldn't grapple with the sight of her child's still face. Her mind searched frantically for some sort of denial.

"The Princess didn't stumble. She was shot."

Stunned by Javier's blunt statement, Iliana almost lost her footing on the slippery rocks, and the world tilted at a crazy angle. She knelt, oblivious to the water soaking her clothes. Her hand went out to caress Gabe's cold, wet face. As her hand stroked the wet flesh, huge gulping sobs wracked her body. Why couldn't she be the one lying dead in the cold stream, not her dear, precious Gabe? Her future held nothing, but Gabe was just beginning his life's journey.

"There's no time for that," Javier's voice was harsh, revealing that he too was having difficulty controlling his emotions. "We've got to get him back to the hacienda and get his horse out of the water before she poisons the stream. You'll have to hold him while I get ropes."

She slid closer and Javier was surprisingly gentle as he transferred his burden to Iliana's arms. She knew letting Gabe's head slip back beneath the water would cause no further harm and, of course, Javier knew that too, but they were in perfect, silent agreement that they must not allow that to happen.

The moon slipped beneath the horizon and the stars seemed to lose much of their luster. A cold wind shrieked its way between junipers and ghostly rock formations. The darkness of the night and the coldness of the water mattered little to Iliana. Her full attention focused on the boy in her arms, her baby. He couldn't be gone. From the day of his birth, Gabe had been her responsibility and her joy. He had eased the unbearable loneliness and given her life purpose. Without him, life was an unending gray vista, not worth living.

Three gunshots ripped the night air in close succession, jolting Iliana out of her absorption with death and grief. She should have expected the shots, but she'd passed over in her mind the need to signal the other searchers to let them know that the search was at an end. From far in the distance, she heard the shots echoed as word spread to the searchers at greater distances.

She was aware of Javier wading across the stream, leading his gelding. Nutmeg whinnied and moved closer to the other horse. Javier attached his lariat to the dead horse and looped the other end of the rope around the pommel of his saddle. He took a second rope that hung from Nutmeg's saddle and fastened it around the dead animal too. Working in tandem, the two saddle horses slowly dragged their longtime stable companion from the water.

As Princess Sophia was dragged away, freeing Gabe, Iliana gathered him closer in her arms. She continued to sit, scarcely aware of the numbness spreading through her lower body from the cold water. With a mother's gentle touch, she attempted to smooth his shirt across his thin chest. A rough spot stilled her hand for a moment then her fingers probed the spot they had encountered. His shirt was torn and beneath the tear her fingers encountered a small hole.

On some level she knew what she would find when she swept a hand across the boy's back. The hole was larger there. Her screams brought Javier running, unmindful of the water he plunged through. He was beside her in seconds to lift Gabe from her arms. Their eyes, grown accustomed to the dim light, met.

"You know?" He spoke softly, but his voice cracked.

She nodded her head. "He was just a little boy. Why would someone shoot my baby?"

Chapter Seventeen

"You probably can't even feel your lower limbs by now." Javier spoke in a determined-to-be-practical voice. "Clasp my belt and hold on until you're feeling steady." She did as he advised and they were soon out of the water and beside their horses. The numbness she felt went far beyond her soaked clothes and chilled flesh; it was as though some vital function in her brain had shut down and some other woman stood in the coarse grass with the night surrounding her.

Nutmeg nudged her back as though offering gentle condolence. Javier gently laid Gabe on the grass while he gathered up the ropes and helped Iliana mount Nutmeg. He lifted the boy to her arms, but once settled in his own saddle, Javier reached to take the body back. She refused to surrender her child, even knowing it was the sensible thing to do, scarce able to bear the ache of her empty arms. Javier gathered up Nutmeg's reins, and trailing the mare behind his gelding, they began the slow descent from the mesa back to the hacienda. Iliana rode as though she'd been turned to stone. Only later would she recall the way Javier had peered into the dark and that he'd kept his rifle cradled close in one arm.

Dominic and several dozen riders met them on the steep trail before they reached the hacienda. In a haze she recognized the horse trader and some of his men, along with almost every cowboy employed by the ranch. When they reached the hacienda, young Carlos helped Javier to dismount while Dominic took Gabe from her arms and passed him to another man. Dominic then reached to pull her from Nutmeg's back and lift her in his arms as though she were an infant, carrying her thus until he could turn her over to Amaya's care. Iliana was only remotely aware of Amaya drawing her wet clothing from her body, urging her into a warm tub, and pressing a warm cup against her lips. Soon wrapped in a thick blanket, she fell into a deep, dreamless slumber.

When she awoke, her bedroom was dark. She held at bay as long as she could the agonizing pain that seemed to rip her very soul apart. Some primal urge begged her to scream, to howl out her pain, but an inbred mandate for self-control held her silent. Gabe, her dear child, was dead—murdered. Murdered! The word hung in her mind. It invoked questions she wasn't ready to ask.

Ignoring the stiffness of her own body, she shut out the questions yammering at her mind. With stoic calm she pulled on the first dress that came to hand before making her silent way to the family chapel.

* * *

"Senora, I wish to speak with you." Dominic stood a few steps behind where she knelt in the small chapel. She turned her head slowly and was surprised to see that the sun, now shining through the colored glass of the chapel windows, cast a rainbow of color across the floor. She raised her eyes to see Dominic dressed in dusty riding clothes with wide leather chaps buckled in place as though he planned to ride through heavy brush in search of stray cattle. Surmising that he had returned to the ranch only a short time before he had met her and Javier on the trail, she did not doubt that he had taken over at once to settle the chaos that had erupted over Gabe's disappearance.

She shook her head, wishing to remain beside the casket that had been hastily built to bear Gabe's body while she slept. It rested on a low dais, and someone, probably Amaya, had found thick candles to set at either end. Their flickering glow lent false warmth to the pale face of her beloved son.

"I shall continue to pray for him while you go with Dominic," the young maid, Raquel, spoke as she and Amaya appeared out of the shadows beyond the flickering candles. Raquel crossed herself before kneeling. It would do no good to argue with both Dominic and Amaya. Iliana started to rise and Dominic stepped forward to offer her a hand to assist her. Amaya's arm circled her waist, lending her support.

She let them lead her to the library, where she found Javier and the horse trader pacing the floor while waiting for her arrival. They too were covered in dust, and both wore guns strapped low on their thighs. She looked at Javier and could feel the barely controlled rage that simmered behind eyes that had received no rest. She was surprised when Dominic indicated she should sit in Grandfather's chair. Not even in play as a young child had she sat in Abuelo's chair. Pain stabbed at her heart as she recognized that the next master of the Sebastian Hacienda to sit in Grandfather's chair was supposed to be Gabe. Slowly she settled onto the seat that was much too large for her.

When she was seated, she wasn't surprised to see Dominic standing at one corner of the desk, with the horse trader at his side. The generally confident young foreman looked at old Javier and hesitated as though waiting for a signal to speak.

"Tell her!" Javier barked. He appeared close to exploding with rage.

Iliana raised startled eyes to him then turned her gaze toward Dominic. The young man seemed to be struggling with the message he had to deliver. She braced as for a blow, frightened by the hesitant behavior of a man who always seemed to be calm and sure of himself in spite of his youth.

"I spoke with Mr. Williams in the village yesterday," he began. "He told me Ben Purdy had been in to see him almost a week ago and that he'd insisted on learning the details of your husband's will. He also said that Purdy had stormed out of the bank in a temper when he learned that Senor Adams had included the terms of his agreement with your grandfather in his will, stipulating that your son or sons alone were to inherit the rancho and that the codicil added shortly before his death didn't change that provision."

Javier's fist slammed down on the desk, causing her to jump. "He murdered Gabe! I know he did or he hired someone to do it for him. And now he plans to make certain a future child of his can claim the ranch."

"Anger won't resolve this. We've plans to make." Dominic attempted to calm the angry former foreman.

"I'll kill him if he sets foot on this ranch," Javier threatened.

Iliana felt the room sway. She'd avoided all thought of sharing Ben's bed or of bearing his children since Ross's death, acknowledging what she knew in some inner recess of her mind to be true. The matter could no longer be kept a secret. She rose on unsteady feet. "No! I won't marry him. I will not give that beast another life to destroy or a son to take all that was to belong to Ross's son."

"You'll have little choice if you stay," Dominic spoke with brutal frankness. "Married or not, he'll get you with child. He won't hesitate to use force, as you well know, and once he has succeeded, you'll have to wed him."

"I am already with child, Ross's child!" Sobbing, she folded her arms in a protective gesture across her abdomen and stood swaying as a frightening blackness crept closer. Stunned silence greeted her words until Amaya stepped forward to gather her into her arms.

Before Amaya could reach her, darkness replaced the bright sun streaming through the window, and Iliana slipped slowly toward the floor. The massive desk halted her fall, leaving her with her cheek pressed against the cool wood. On a barely conscious level she was aware of the old housekeeper's arms encircling her. She'd been fairly certain of her condition for several weeks. At first she wasn't sure. More than once she'd counted the weeks from that short time when Ross had seemed to be getting well. She'd wanted to share her suspicion with him before his death, but the time had never seemed right. Afterward she had felt such stress that all thoughts of her pregnancy were driven from her mind. Even now, facing the reality of her condition seemed of small import compared to Gabe's death.

Neither Abuelo nor Ross would countenance such weakness. The tiny life sheltered beneath her heart required her protection. She straightened, brushing aside Amaya's tender ministrations.

Gradually she became aware of the silence of the men in the room, occasioned by her announcement. Their reaction disappointed her for just a moment; then she saw the reflection of her own fear in their eyes. If Ben killed Gabe, he wouldn't hesitate to kill the helpless child she carried in her womb when he learned of its existence. Neither she nor the men loyal to her husband and grandfather could protect this child if she meekly wed Ben.

A spark of rebellion grew inside her. From the cradle she had been taught gentleness and obedience, but she wouldn't marry Ben, no matter what agreement Ross had made or threats Ben might make. This child mattered more than all of the water or land in New Mexico. She rose to her feet and with all of the dignity of generations of Spanish aristocrats announced, "I will not marry Ben Purdy. I hate him and think Ross must have been out of his normal senses or been tricked to have agreed to the arrangement. Tomorrow when Ben arrives expecting a wedding, I shall be attending to my son's burial. I cannot wed my son's murderer." Her voice broke, "I shall pray for that animal to be hanged."

"Your husband had no business arranging a remarriage for you. A woman in this country has a legal right to refuse any man she finds objectionable. I don't know where he got the idea he could make you marry Ben Purdy." Travis Telford took a protective step closer to her. She had scarcely been aware of his presence until he took her side.

"I think we all took Senor Adams's agreement with Purdy at face value and didn't study it carefully enough," Dominic said with a faraway look on his face. "I had a talk with Mr. Williams yesterday, and he enlightened me to a few aspects of that will I hadn't considered. He hinted that the senor's death was mighty suspicious. Ross Adams was strong, yet each time he seemed to be recovering, he had a sudden relapse. His death occurred just days after he added that marriage codicil to his will. There's nothing anyone can prove, though I intend to bring the matter to Marshal Reynolds's attention when he returns."

"I agree that it would be a mistake for Senora Iliana to wed Purdy, but if we try to stop him he'll kidnap her and force a marriage. The senor knew Purdy wasn't above such an action. I think he agreed to Purdy's demand that Iliana marry him to give us a little time to spirit her and Gabe away. If only he had known that Purdy is a thief and that Telford succeeded in finding water." Javier leaned forward to speak directly to Iliana. "I think it would be best if you aren't here when Purdy arrives tomorrow. Whether or not we can prove what happened yesterday or locate the marshal and get him out here, *we* know what happened. Once Ben gets you away from here, your husband's second child won't draw a breath. The Purdys must have an heir to claim this rancho, and you won't live one day beyond the day you deliver Ben's son."

Cold chills slid down her spine. Javier was right. She must think of the new life she carried within her, which meant she couldn't stay at el Rancho de Sebastian. She must leave, but where could she go? How would she get there? She couldn't leave without seeing Gabe properly buried. And even if the priest arrived to hold a service early tomorrow, there wouldn't be enough time to travel far before Ben arrived, demanding that she become his wife.

"Our men are loyal, and they'll help us hold off Purdy. We can keep him from setting one foot on this land." Dominic's hand rested on the revolver at his side.

"Our cowboys wouldn't stand a chance against the gunfighters and rabble who have replaced caballeros on Purdy's ranch since Ben took over. Open war between our two ranches would spread across the entire territory, stirring up tension between our people, imprisoning us on the land, destroying any chance of rebuilding the herd, and resulting in the loss of lives. There must be another way." Javier arose and walked toward the tall, narrow window at the far end of the room. He stood for several minutes, deep in thought.

"I heard a rumor in town yesterday that those gunfighters are getting impatient to be paid and that Purdy is counting on the sale of stock and furnishings from the Sebastian Rancho and hacienda to pay them off," Dominic offered. "He's furious that even after marrying Iliana he can't use the land as collateral to borrow the money he needs. He'll have to move here and sell his own ranch to have sufficient funds until he has a legal heir. The senora must be gone before he arrives tomorrow. I can escort her to the Gulf, where she can catch a steamer east. If we ride hard, we can reach New Orleans in a few weeks."

"What will I use for money to start a new life? And where will I go?" Iliana felt rising panic. She knew nothing of life beyond the rancho and the nearby village. She'd never traveled by train or public coach.

"You'll have to part with the few bits of jewelry Ben returned to you." Javier softened his voice when he spoke to her. "That's another thing; when the marshal arrives, I'll inform him about Ben stealing your mother's beads and earrings. When we get them back, we can sell them and send the money on to you."

"I already left word of the theft at the marshal's office," Dominic reminded him.

Travis stood and began laying out plans he clearly expected Iliana and her loyal employees to follow. "My apologies, ma'am. Your foreman filled me in on your precarious situation earlier. I can help you if you'll let me." He spoke with barely leashed emotion. "Purdy will assume you rode east into Texas when he finds you gone. His next assumption will be that you've fled to distant family in Mexico. Therefore, you must go west. Last evening Dominic recruited riders from my encampment down by the lower creek to help in the search for your son. My men, with a large number of horses, are headed to California. Your best choice will be to travel with us. We plan to leave at daybreak tomorrow."

"I can't leave so soon," Iliana objected. "The priest won't arrive to conduct the funeral rites before tomorrow at noon."

"You must leave within the next few hours. There's no other way. One of the caballeros' wives can sit with Gabe while Amaya helps you pack whatever you will need for the journey. I'll ride to the camp with you at dusk." Javier seconded the plan and Dominic nodded his approval. Both seemed certain it was the best plan. After only a slight hesitation, Iliana bowed her head in submission.

After Travis made his offer, he strode from the room. Iliana's anguish at the need for a sudden departure brought tears to her eyes. How could she leave without seeing Gabe properly buried? A stronger voice, a voice of reason, told her she must go if she would save the new life she carried.

* * *

Insisting she return to her room to pack, Amaya drew Iliana toward the suite she had shared with Ross before his illness. Iliana watched listlessly as the housekeeper stuffed a skirt and blouse, a shawl, and a single petticoat into one side of the double saddlebags Abuelo had charged a local saddlemaker to hand-tool for her as a gift on a long-ago birthday. In the other side Amaya placed bandanas and Iliana's smallclothes.

Iliana raised no objection when the practical housekeeper added the small pistol, extra ammunition, a strip of beef jerky, sulfur matches, and a rain poncho. Amaya also placed a lace handkerchief and a vial of perfume, which had belonged to Iliana's mother, in the bag. Iliana made no effort to help or to choose for herself what she would take with her. It made no difference to her what Amaya packed.

* * *

Iliana knelt beside Gabe's small casket one last time, with her hands clasped before her. She bowed her head, ignoring the tears that belied her resolve. As she leaned against the rail to brush a last kiss across her son's brow, something dug into her chest in the region of her heart. At first she thought the pain was due to her terrible loss; then she remembered the wooden crucifix that had been her mother's and which she now wore beneath her shirt. It was cutting into her flesh. Lifting her eyes to the heavy beams above her head, she whispered, "Mama, please watch over my son. Hold him when he is frightened and when he misses me." Her hand went to her faintly rounded abdomen. "Only you and his papa can look after him now. I must protect the one that lives beneath my heart." She removed the wooden cross some long-ago ancestor had carved and placed it over her son's small hands. "*Vaya con Dios, hijo mio*," she whispered.

She knelt for a few more minutes before rising to her feet. The heels of her riding boots made a clacking noise as she walked steadily from the chapel, pausing only a moment at the door for one last look behind her. If the new life she carried had any chance of survival, she must leave

Gabe, her home, and all that was familiar behind. “One day, I’ll be back,” she promised herself in order to keep her eyes focused forward.

Chapter Eighteen

Before leaving the rancho, Javier hung Ross's old tin military canteen from the protruding pommel of Iliana's saddle. It dangled beside the intricately tooled leather bag. "You'll need this. It belonged to Senor Adams," he explained.

It had been decided that Dominic, instead of Javier, would ride beside Iliana to the village to seek out Mr. Williams before making their way to the horse traders' camp. In spite of their shared fear of tiring their horses and wasting valuable time, they understood that Iliana could not undertake the long trip and establish a home in California without the money they hoped the banker would advance them on the sale of her few pieces of jewelry.

They rode hard, leaving a trail of dust in their wake. It was nearing dusk when they rode into the sleepy village. Not even a stray dog greeted their arrival. Most of the shops were shuttered and Mr. Williams had closed up the bank for the day as well. Dominic seemed to know where to find the banker's home and turned his mount toward a path leading out of town. After a short ride, Iliana noticed a hacienda encircled by a high adobe wall. Tree tops and vines almost obscured the top of the wall and blocked the view of the house beyond it.

A short, dark-skinned man met them at the gate. He beckoned them inside and offered to care for their horses. "Senor Williams knows of your arrival. He saw your horses climbing the trail. Go to him. You must not keep him waiting."

"Thank you, Fernando." Dominic dismounted. After handing his reins to the man, he assisted Iliana to dismount. Once she felt steady on her feet again, they started toward the house and Mr. Williams called out a greeting to them. He stood in the doorway of a small villa with warm lamplight reaching past him to the cobbled path, inviting them inside.

After the banker welcomed them to the home that far surpassed in luxury any other structure in town and rivaled her own home for comfort, she noted that he didn't seem surprised to see them. With minimal pleasantries, he ushered them into a well-appointed library.

Without preamble Dominic suggested Iliana show Mr. Williams the jewelry. She spread the pieces belonging to her ancestors, as well as the ones that were her own few, on a carved mahogany table that served as a desk. Mr. Williams gave the jewels only a brief inspection before addressing her.

"Your husband said you would bring your jewelry to me when you made your choice, and yesterday Dominic explained the loss of many of your most valuable pieces. I drew up papers and agreed on prices on one of my visits a few weeks before Ross's passing." Williams reached into a drawer and drew out a sheaf of papers.

She heard a strangled sound come from Dominic and followed his pointing finger to the amount that Mr. Williams had agreed to pay for the jewelry. She lifted her eyes to the banker's face. His eyes were filled with regret and he was slowly shaking his head.

"Your husband showed me an antique casket filled with many more jewels than you have brought me. It pains me that I cannot pay such a sum for these few baubles."

"I understand." She bit her bottom lip and bowed her head. What was she to do?

"Mr. Williams, I'm not asking for charity nor do I expect you to pay for these items the amount you would have paid for the entire collection. If you are interested in the box that held them, Dominic can bring that to you. This is all I have to offer that can be exchanged for cash."

Anger darkened Mr. Williams's eyes. "I expect Purdy has disposed of the other pieces by now, but I shall do what I can to locate the buyers who purchased the stolen gems. When the marshal returns, I will be happy to verify the value of the missing pieces."

"The marshal is stretched too thin," Dominic said. "He serves a large area and I have not seen him on any of my recent trips to the village."

"I heard he has been called on to find a number of runaways from farther north who are avoiding federal warrants." The banker shook his head and leaned back in his chair.

"As you have guessed, senor, Iliana has no intention of marrying Ben Purdy." Dominic returned to the need to acquire funds for her escape.

"Little more than twenty-four hours ago, her son was murdered, and we have reason to believe Purdy either killed him or paid someone to do it for him."

"What!" Mr. Williams rose to his feet then slowly sank back down. Real sorrow showed in his eyes. Taking a handkerchief from his pocket, he wiped his eyes and blew his nose. "Little Gabe is dead?"

Iliana nodded her head. She dared not speak, fearing any attempt to voice a response would make it impossible for her to hold back her tears.

"How did this happen?" Williams turned his sharp gaze toward Dominic.

"While I spoke with you yesterday, Gabe rode his pony alone along a trail he and I often rode together. Iliana assumed he was with me and did not miss him until evening." He went on to tell of the events of the previous night. "Javier and I rode to the Purdy Ranch this morning. Ben denies any knowledge of Gabe's death and refuses to delay the wedding which Javier, Iliana, and I agree should never happen at all." His glance rested briefly on Iliana before he went on. "Purdy sees no reason to ask the priest to ride out to the ranch twice and insists he and Iliana will wed tomorrow following the service for her son."

Iliana was beyond being shocked by Ben's insensitivity. Astonishment, followed by disgust, showed on Mr. Williams's face, and he made no attempt to conceal his feelings.

"There is one other factor making it imperative that the senora leave New Mexico at once." Dominic looked apologetically toward Iliana again, then continued speaking. "She is with child, a child conceived during one of her husband's rallies from the illness he suffered following the blizzard. If this child should fall into Purdy's hands, we have no doubt it will suffer the same fate as young Gabe."

Mr. Williams's face paled, and he sat with his fingers tapping at his bottom lip for several minutes before a look of resolve stiffened his features.

"It's a two days' ride to the railhead and almost a week before the next train is expected. How do you plan to evade Purdy until then?"

"I hope Purdy will assume Senora Iliana is on her way to board that train. She won't be. She'll be leaving in a few hours with Travis Telford, the horse trader, and his outfit."

"Telford is a good man. He'll look after her." Williams looked pleased with the plan. "I'd say we have some paperwork to take care of now to get you on your way. Mrs. Adams will need cash and a letter of credit to present to a bank in California, and we must ensure all is in place for you to assume management of the ranch until she selects another manager or her child assumes management."

"Will you provide oversight and assistance to Dominic?" Iliana implored in a soft voice. The elderly man solemnly nodded his agreement.

Half an hour later, Mr. Williams sent Dominic to find two men to witness the signing of the papers they had agreed upon. It was agreed that Iliana could return to the ranch whenever she and her child felt safe doing so.

"Ben will be angry," Mr. Williams confided to Iliana while they waited for Dominic to return. "He's deeply in debt and counting on the Sebastian Rancho to restore his fortune and pay off his creditors. I give you my word I'll do all I can to secure justice for Gabe and force Ben to return your mother's jewelry. If there is any way to preserve the rancho for your child, I will find it."

Iliana bowed her head and remained quiet. She didn't voice her doubt that anyone would ever be charged with the murder of one small Spanish boy. She had little reason to believe her jewelry would be returned either. No one had ever been charged with the deaths of her grandparents or for the theft of their rancho. Mr. Williams was a good man, as were Dominic and Javier, and she didn't doubt they would try to gain justice for her and that they would be in danger when Ben discovered her absence; but they were grown men, capable of protecting themselves, while the child she carried had no one but its mother to protect it. If the ranch was lost and she never saw her home again, she would have to accept it, but the child she carried must have a chance to live.

After a few moments Mr. Williams again spoke of practical matters. "You will be carrying cash; though not enough to meet your needs until your child is grown, it will be enough to tempt a thief." He handed her a thin stack of banknotes and withdrew what appeared to be a silk sash from a drawer. "I suggest you take advantage of these few moments to retire to the chamber across the hall, where you will find clothing suitable for a caballero. You can conceal the banknotes in a pocket you will find in this belt. Secure the belt beneath your clothing." She wondered if the precaution was necessary, but with her customary habit of obedience she followed his instructions.

With the belt firmly in place, and after assuring herself that there were no revealing bulges, she stepped back into Mr. Williams's office just as Dominic returned with two caballeros he'd found eating their supper at the local cantina. Neither could read or write English, but both were willing to sign their names to the papers Mr. Williams set before them. When the papers were completed, Mr. Williams folded one set and gave it to Iliana. The other, he assured her, would go into his safe.

Before Dominic and Iliana left, Mr. Williams took her hands in his. "Your grandfather saved my life many years ago. I was a greenhorn then and would have died if he hadn't found me, lost and half-crazed from thirst. Not only did he give me life-saving water, but he took me to his home, treated my cuts and burned skin, and advanced me the funds to begin my small business. Always he was my friend. Tomorrow I will present myself at the rancho to bid your son farewell and to ascertain that all is as Don Rodrigo Ignacio Renteria Sebastian would have wished for the boy. Be assured the matter will not end there. Now go in peace, child."

Chapter Nineteen

Dominic could see that Iliana was fighting the urge to close her eyes and drift to sleep long before they reached the traders' camp. He'd heard that women in her condition should not ride, especially astride as Iliana did. He'd been surprised by her stubborn insistence that she and her child would be safer astride than perched on a more traditional sidesaddle. Old Javier saw no problem with her riding astride, so Dominic let it go.

Iliana had surprised him of late in other ways too. Until the past few weeks, he'd never known her well or heard her express an opinion. Always Dona Iliana had been nothing other than the epitome of femininity in her dress and deportment. Yet she'd offered no argument when Mr. Williams suggested she attire herself in pants for the long ride ahead of her. She'd politely thanked the older man when he'd sent a servant to fetch several pair of thick, coarse britches for her to add to the small hoard of necessities Amaya had packed in her saddlebags. Dominic couldn't help admiring her courage in undertaking a long, arduous journey in the company of strange men in order to protect the baby she carried. If it were possible he would accompany her all the way to California. Since he could not, he wished he could at least stop to allow her the rest she needed, but he couldn't risk her safety by allowing any further delay. Besides, he must return to the ranch as quickly as possible. The day would bring trouble and old Javier could not be left to deal with Ben Purdy alone.

It caused him some discomfort to think of the responsibility that would now be his. He would rely greatly on old Javier's experience and wisdom, but would it be enough to ward off the gringos who would see a dark-skinned man left in charge of the vast Sebastian holding and seek to take it from him and from the child for whom he held it in trust? Once Iliana left New Mexico, would he ever again see her or the child she would give birth to? Would the *niño* even survive the rigors of the cross-country ride to California? Dom felt a burden of guilt that he'd failed to protect little Gabe. Senor Adams had trusted him. He couldn't bear to fail again.

The camp was already stirring when they rode in, though the sun wasn't yet up. A cooking fire illuminated shadowy figures moving about, and the scent of burning greasewood and warm biscuits filled the air. Travis Telford strode toward them and it was he who reached to assist Iliana to dismount before Dominic could approach. Offering his arm for support, Telford led her to a bedroll spread beneath a misshapen tree, where he urged her to rest until the men had eaten and were ready to ride out. He offered to bring her a plate, but she shook her head before sinking to the blankets.

Dominic accepted the offer of breakfast, and when he'd finished the biscuits and gravy placed before him, he knelt beside Iliana to whisper last-minute advice and to bid her farewell, but he wasn't certain she heard him. She hadn't slept but a few hours since the night her son's body was found. Added to the long ride and the emotional stress she'd faced since then, along with the demands of her condition, too many sleepless hours had passed. Her reserves had been depleted and she could no longer hold sleep at bay. He didn't try to awaken her to say good-bye.

* * *

It seemed she'd just closed her eyes when someone shook her shoulder gently, urging her to arise. She looked into the bearded face of a man who appeared to be a little older than Ross. He smiled and something about him assured her that she needn't fear him. After a few seconds, she recognized him as the man who drove the wagon when the traders had stopped at the ranch, seeking permission to water their herd.

"You're welcome to ride in the cook wagon till you're feeling more rested, ma'am," he offered.

"*Gracias*," she acknowledged the offer, "but I will be more comfortable and of more use to Senor Telford on horseback."

"Sit for a moment," the cook told her. "I'll be right back. My name is Brother Lewis, if you need anything." He handed her a biscuit and a tin cup before hurrying away. She gulped down the water and nibbled at the biscuit as she attempted to clear away the fog from her mind. All that had happened the past few days came crashing back to her, and she found swallowing difficult.

She was glad when Brother Lewis returned leading one of the horses from the rancho already saddled. She rose to her feet, tucked her bedraggled braid into the crown of her hat, and stepped to the wagon to use one of the large wooden wheels as a mounting block.

Her horse shied and fidgeted but didn't attempt to unseat her, for which she was grateful. Looking to the east, she thought of Gabe, soon to be laid to rest beside his father and Abuelo. She turned toward the west, nudged the horse with her heels, and rode toward the herd.

* * *

Dominic appreciated Amaya's thoughtfulness when he discovered a tub of warm water waiting for him when he reached his small house. His bath was followed by only a couple of hours of sleep before Carlos awoke him to inform him that a party of riders had crossed from Purdy land to the Sebastian Rancho and that Ben Purdy rode at their head. Dominic left his bed to cross to the basin, where he removed the thick stubble that had grown since he'd last applied his razor. When he finished, he toweled off the residue of suds on his face and studied his reflection in the mirror for just a moment before rushing to ready himself for the arrival of unwelcome guests.

He dressed in formal attire with the tip of the holster that held his revolver showing just beneath the edge of his coat. Today might very well be the day he proved he was capable of managing the large rancho and that he was worthy of the trust he'd been given by Senor and Senora Adams. He would stand firm for the family he'd pledged his loyalty to since he was a child. Don Sebastian, as well as Senor Adams, would expect him to protect Iliana and the ranch. He'd failed young Gabe, but with the hope of a new Sebastian heir, he would redeem himself or die.

As the riders entered the yard, Dominic leaned over to whisper to Javier. "He's come for a funeral and a wedding." The foreman made no attempt to conceal his contempt for the man he held responsible for young Gabe's murder and for causing Iliana to flee from the home where she should have been able to feel safe and protected.

Javier had made no secret of his approval of Senor Adams's selection of the young man to manage the ranch, and Dom frequently turned to him for guidance and support. A fast friendship had formed between the two men.

"Don't mention Iliana's absence," Javier warned Dominic. "Let her put as much distance as possible between her and the valley before Ben discovers she isn't here. Amaya has a plan." He, too, was impeccably attired and had added a black leather gun belt, which he made no effort to conceal, and his best hat.

A fancy buggy with two benches and a fringed top arrived from the south minutes before Ben and his men rode into the yard. Dominic was pleased to see the priest sitting beside Mr. Williams. Surely the priest's presence would lessen the possibility of violence. Javier lost no time ushering the two men into the chapel, where he was surprised to see the small room filled almost to capacity with the ranch caballeros and their families. He felt a moment's grim satisfaction knowing Amaya had ushered the ranch families into the small space at the front of the chapel, leaving no room there for Ben and his entourage. No doubt a ploy to prevent Ben from realizing any sooner than necessary that Iliana was not among the mourners.

Javier moved as quickly as his creaking bones permitted down the aisle to settle himself beside a slender figure draped in black, a veil covering her face.

No! Iliana . . . Dominic shook his head as if to clear it. The woman couldn't be Iliana. Senor Telford would not have permitted her to leave his encampment. The woman was probably part of Amaya's plan to keep the funeral from erupting into chaos. Javier seemed to be in her confidence, since he showed no hesitation in seating himself beside the veiled woman. The two of them had probably hatched the scheme while he was asleep.

"Take your place beside Javier and Amaya," Mr. Williams encouraged in a kind voice. "I'll take care of late arrivals."

Dominic hesitated only a moment. It was his place to serve as host since there were no male family members present, but he wasn't sure he could greet Ben with any degree of civility. He'd be more apt to shoot him. He moved down the aisle to find the seat reserved for him on the other side of the veiled woman and next to Amaya.

Keeping his eyes focused on the small casket at the front of the room, Javier ignored the brief disruption at the back of the chapel. Father Escudero began the rites, and the old ranch hand stared straight ahead, remembering the small boy who had suffered so many illnesses but found the courage to conquer his fears and became a man too soon.

The last amen faded away, and Javier crossed himself as he and Don Sebastian had done at solemn moments since they were boys. A hand gripped his shoulder, causing him to stiffen before turning to face Ben Purdy.

"Where is she?" the red-faced man spoke through gritted teeth.

Javier looked past Ben to find Dominic. The foreman stood apart from the other mourners with an arm around the young woman Dominic now knew was Juan's oldest daughter, Raquel, who often assisted Amaya in the house, the senorita Dom had been paying particular attention for some time.

"That greaser isn't Iliana!" Ben followed his glance. "And don't give me some kind of rot about her being too overcome with grief to attend her brat's funeral. Get her to the chapel; Father Escudero doesn't have time to waste, and neither do I."

With catlike swiftness Dominic was beside them. His right fist plowed into Ben's midsection, followed by an uppercut to his jaw. Ben went down, but before Dom could throw himself on top of him to continue raining blows, Dom found himself staring into the barrel of Ben's revolver.

"You'll not keep me from marrying Iliana." Ben's voice was laced with venom as he lay sprawled on the ground.

Javier's hand moved toward the holster not quite hidden by his coat.

"Just try to reach for that gun, old man!" Ben shouted. "I'd love an excuse to put a bullet through that smug face of yours!"

"There'll be no weapons fired here today." Mr. Williams's boot came down on Ben's gun arm with an audible crack. Ben screamed and his revolver skittered across the floor.

"There'll be no wedding either." Javier scooped up the fallen weapon. "I'll give you and your men an hour's start, and if I find you on this spread after that, you'll be shot for trespassing."

* * *

During the following days, Dominic kept the men on alert and the stock away from the range land that adjoined the Purdy Ranch. Ben had made wild threats on learning Iliana was gone, and both Javier and Dominic felt it necessary to keep a careful watch for trouble. Dominic smiled in grim satisfaction, remembering the word he'd received a week later of Ben's search between Two Creek Junction and the railhead. Iliana was well away before it occurred to her would-be groom that instead of boarding the train to an unknown destination, she might have gone south into Mexico. In his fury Ben had renewed his threat to shoot both him and Javier. Ben had also dammed off the creek, allowing no water to pass onto the Sebastian Rancho. Fortunately that only affected a small part of the upper mesa since the large stream Travis Telford found was providing ample water for the rest of the ranch. The ranch hands willingly kept watch over the larger stream to ensure no one interfered with its flow.

* * *

Iliana sat her horse with the dignity inherited from a long line of proud Spanish ancestors, though her back ached and she was weary from long hours in the saddle. They'd been riding steadily west for a week across jagged mountains and high mesas. Though she tried to work as hard as the men, she knew she tired sooner and that she was assigned easier tasks than those given the drovers. She felt certain Travis Telford had only agreed to allow her to accompany his party because of the horses Javier had sent to him while she and Dominic were with Mr. Williams. There were sixteen for which he had accepted payment; four more were a gift of gratitude for Telford's acceptance and protection of Iliana. An additional four horses, including Nutmeg, were for Iliana's use. She was well aware of the sacrifice involved in parting with so many horses, but she also knew her grandfather's old friend and foreman was deeply concerned for her and her unborn child's chances of survival.

Grudging acceptance was given to her when her skill with the horses became apparent, and her ability to stay in the saddle as long as any of the caballeros earned their respect, but the men kept their distance from her. She wasn't unaware, however, that all of the men were involved in double shifts as lookouts, and the scouts Telford sent out were checking their back trail as thoroughly as the route ahead of them. Only Travis Telford and Brother Lewis, the cook, made an effort to speak with her, and their conversations were limited to matters concerning the horses and the camps they set up, except on one occasion.

On the second day of their ride, Telford rode beside her for a considerable distance, and she noticed his frequent glances at her face. He seemed about to say something each time he saw her look his way, then hesitated without speaking.

"Senor Telford?" She attempted to give him an opening to say what was on his mind.

"We're going to be traveling together for some time; I would like for you to call me Travis as the men do, and my men prefer the use of their first names as well."

She lowered her head in embarrassment. She'd never addressed an adult male other than her husband, Dominic, and old Javier Rosario by their given names.

"I know you are more accustomed to formality than are we, but I think it would put the men more at ease if you use the names which we use for ourselves. A few of the older men prefer the term 'brother' to precede their names, but the rest of us answer to our given names. Do you think you could do that?"

If ceasing to use respectful titles would set her apart less from the others, she could do this one small thing. "Yes," she agreed to his request. "And if it makes your men more comfortable, I shall be Iliana." The words came out in a near stammer.

Amaya would not approve. But nothing about Iliana's present situation would meet with that lady's approval. She'd be scandalized if she knew Iliana was spending her days and nights with a party that consisted of men only, no matter how much deference and respect they showed her. Iliana missed the woman who had been part mother, part servant, and part confidant Iliana's entire life, but Javier and Dominic had been wise to let the woman think Dominic was taking Iliana to the train and forbidding the elderly maid to accompany her young mistress. Amaya would have been unable to keep up with the half-wild horses and the men who pushed them with unrelenting determination toward California.

Iliana glanced sideways at the handsome cowboy who rode at her side. She knew Travis Telford was aware of her condition. She assumed her pregnancy was the reason he was making it his personal responsibility to see to her welfare. He set up a small tent for her each night, while he and his men rolled out bedrolls near the fire. He personally placed her heavy saddle on whichever horse she was to ride each morning. He'd attempted to persuade her to help with the cooking and to ride in the wagon, but she knew nothing of preparing meals over a campfire and feared the jolting ride the wagon would afford her might cause her to miscarry. Instead she insisted on taking her turn watching over the remuda. Being accustomed to riding, she felt certain her baby would be safer cushioned by the easy gait of one of the fine horses Ross had raised and trained than in the lurching wagon.

The sun's scorching heat was hard to bear. Though she'd lived in sun-drenched New Mexico all of her life, she was accustomed to spending the hours when the sun's rays were at their peak within the thick, cool walls of the hacienda. After three days of the unrelenting heat, she removed from her head the scarf Amaya had said would protect her skin and the thick money belt from beneath her shirt, stuffing them both inside the bags that hung from her saddle.

She soon learned that half of Travis's men circled the herd at night while the other half slept. Iliana noticed that when her night riding shift arrived, it always coincided with Travis's watch and that he didn't maintain the distance between her and himself that he insisted the other wranglers maintain between each other.

He rode beside her now, and though she pretended to ignore him, she was aware of how often he lifted his eyes toward the mountain peaks ahead and that he seemed possessed of unusual nervous energy.

"Can you shoot?" The question startled her, but after a moment's hesitation she nodded her head.

"Si, senor. Grandfather insisted I learn, but I've had little practice of late." Her hand went to the thick lump in the pocket of her pants. Since Ben's long-ago attack before her marriage to Ross, she never rode without the small gun her grandfather had given her.

"I don't mean that little pea shooter," Travis said, and she realized that the weapon she'd taken such care to keep hidden from the men hadn't gotten past the trader's keen eyes.

"I know how to use a rifle also." Both Grandfather and Ross believed a woman living on the frontier should be adept at firing a rifle. Perhaps her son would still be alive, she thought with bitterness and regret, had she carried a gun that day when Ben had attacked her very near the same spot where he had murdered her son.

She closed her eyes for a brief moment. Most of the time she succeeded in shutting out memories of her son and the night she'd found him with a bullet in his small body. It was too painful to think of him lying in the chapel without his mother to grant him a final farewell. She took a small amount of comfort in knowing that Mr. Williams, Amaya, and the faithful ranch hands and their families had been there for him.

"We're soon going to be passing through a narrow pass in the mountains up ahead." Travis gestured toward the stark rock formations rising from the desert floor. "We'll need to keep a watchful eye out for bandits or renegade Apaches. We've heard rumors of attacks on travelers in this area." He slid a rifle into the scabbard attached to her saddle. "It's loaded," he warned, then draped a belt bristling with cartridges over her shoulder. The weight, or perhaps the danger the weapon represented, caused her shoulders to sag.

He studied her face and she struggled not to allow her fear to show. Her mother had died at the hands of Apaches. Since that time she'd dreaded a similar fate, though there had been little sign that the renegades still conducted raids near the ranch or the larger settlements in New Mexico. At some level she'd never ceased mourning her mother, and she felt an odd pang at the realization that if she were to die, there would be no one to mourn her passing save Javier, Dominic, and Amaya.

A slight flutter within her abdomen reminded her of the child she carried. This child was all she had left. Nothing mattered more than keeping it safe. "I'll be ready," she said and turned her eyes to scan the rocky entrance to the passage between steep mountains.

"The canyon opens up into a small valley then narrows again before we reach the other side. There are several smaller dead-end canyons that branch off the larger one," he told her. "We need to push the horses with as much speed as possible and haze them away from the openings to the other canyons. Tom and Bailey," he named two of the wranglers, "have gone ahead to act as scouts." He hesitated a moment. "There are numerous caves in those side canyons. If it looks bad for us, hide in one. If you're followed, be sure there's one bullet left in that pea shooter."

He spurred his horse forward and she felt the pace of the herd increase. To her right a cowboy removed his hat with a swooping gesture and a practiced shout, encouraging the horses forward. By now it was an automatic gesture to pull the kerchief tied about her throat high enough to cover her mouth and nose to ward off the choking dust then with one hand she reached for the rifle. Cradling it in one arm, she urged Nutmeg into a ground-eating run, glad she was mounted on the familiar mare.

Beneath the towering cliffs the air was cooler, but tension kept rivulets of perspiration pouring down the sides of her face and dampening her shirt. The horses picked up the nervous anxiety of the drovers, causing them to prance and break toward each opening they encountered. It took the determined skill of all to keep the animals moving at a fast trot. Iliana found herself breathing a small sigh of relief when the horses burst through the confines of the canyon into a small valley, but she quickly realized it was too soon to relax her guard.

A stream ran through the valley and grass grew tall on either side of it. It had the appearance of an ideal place to rest and water the herd, but even with her inexperience in such matters, she suspected it was also an ideal place for an ambush by anyone wishing to steal the herd. It wouldn't be as easy to pick off the riders here as in the narrower portion of the canyon, but the effort to keep the horses moving could fatally distract the wranglers if raiders lay in wait.

Taking her cue from the other riders, she circled the horses, urging them toward the last segment of the pass. Like wayward children, most of the horses managed to snatch a swallow of the ice-cold water as they splashed through the stream, but soon the riders were pushing them toward the final break in towering rock walls.

Iliana looked at the red cliffs above her as the last of the horses began their trek between the grotesque stone shapes that reminded her of goblins and mystical creatures of legend, and she felt a shiver of apprehension. Looking around to be certain none of the horses were lagging behind, she found she was riding near Travis at the right forward flank of the herd. The rigid set of his shoulders and the frequent glances he sent upward to the jumbles of rock above them proved he still expected trouble. She'd seen nothing to cause alarm, yet she felt an ominous prickle between her shoulders as though she could feel someone watching her.

Trouble struck with a ferocity that left Iliana gasping for breath. A hail of gunfire rained down upon them, and she saw a rider on the left flank slip from his saddle and disappear beneath the stampede of pounding hooves.

"Keep your head down!" She thought she heard a shouted warning. She ducked low against Nutmeg's neck and strained to see through a swirling cloud of dust.

Chapter Twenty

CHAOS REIGNED AS THE HORSES swerved toward a box canyon that branched away from the main canyon. Iliana's efforts to keep the animals moving forward were in vain, and she felt Nutmeg turn with the herd toward the trap the side canyon represented. Soon she'd be imprisoned in the dead-end canyon along with the horses. She suspected that was the intent of their attackers, who seemed to be firing from both the front and back of the herd to prevent either forward or reverse movement of the men and horses and to keep them funneling into the enclosed space. She expected a bullet to tear her from her saddle any moment. She hoped she'd be dead before the frenzied horses trampled her.

Out of the swirling mass of dust and horses a figure appeared beside her. An arm wrapped around her waist and she felt herself leave her saddle to be pulled before her captor. She struggled against his hold for a moment before recognizing the voice shouting in her ear.

"We can make a stand from those rocks!" Travis shouted. She couldn't see the rocks he indicated nor much of anything else because of the dust stirred up by the frightened horses' hooves, but she let herself go with him when he leaped from the saddle to the rocks and pulled her clear of the running herd.

Stumbling to keep pace, she let Travis drag her toward a jumble of rocks she could now see marked one side of the opening to the smaller canyon. Once behind a large boulder, she gasped for breath, but Travis didn't allow her to rest. He pointed upward to where she could just see a booted foot disappearing up a stair step of boulders and indicated she should follow that disappearing figure. She began to climb and was only aware she still grasped the rifle Travis had given her when she found one hand encumbered as she reached for a handhold to speed her climb. Her fingers tightened around the weapon.

Her lungs felt ready to burst from exertion and dust, but she struggled on. At last a hand gripped her arm, half dragging her over the last few feet into a shadowy cave. She sank to the floor, too exhausted to think or consider her situation. For the moment, she felt safe from a flying bullet and that was enough.

After a few moments, her heart slowed its frantic pace and she lifted her head. Three men knelt at the front of the cave. With no one paying any attention to her, she pulled herself to a sitting position where she could lean her back against a rock wall. It took a few more minutes before she became aware that the light only penetrated a short distance into the cavern and there was no way to discover how far the cave extended behind her. It crossed her mind that the cave might be the lair of a mountain lion or some other beast, but the sound of gunfire convinced her she was more afraid of bandits or Indians than of a wild animal.

In front of her she recognized the three men as Travis and two of the horse wranglers. They crouched behind rocks that formed a jagged partial wall at the front of the cave. Each man held a rifle.

Picking up the rifle she'd dropped earlier on the cave floor, she crept forward to kneel beside Travis. Without turning his head, he whispered, "Don't fire. We don't want to give away our position."

"Apache?" her voice quavered.

"Naw," one of the wranglers answered. "If they were Apaches we'd be dead by now. These bandits made a big mistake thinking they could trap us in the canyon with the horses then pick us off before stealing the herd. They didn't want to risk killing any of the horses by shooting at us unless they had clear shots. Gives us a chance to fight back." He scratched at his beard and sighted down his rifle barrel, ready to put up a fight.

Through the gaps between rocks, Iliana could see the herd milling about in the confined space. To one side of the nervous horses was the cook wagon, tipped on its side. It appeared the double-span team pulling it had broken free. There was no sign of Brother Lewis, and she hoped he had somehow escaped. She couldn't see Nutmeg, and the thought of losing the mare to bandits added anger to her fright.

"The rest of the men?" she asked, dreading the answer she might receive.

"Chances are, most of them made it to some kind of shelter," Travis said. He glanced her way for a second or two. "We'll know in a little while."

Silence settled over their hiding place. The horses bunched together at the far end of the small canyon, so even the restless shuffling of their hooves didn't reach Iliana's ears. Her hunched position brought cramps to her legs, and though she strained to see beyond the cave, she could detect no movement. For the moment she was safe, but thirsty, and she wondered how long they could survive without food or water. Her thoughts turned again to Nutmeg. The horse wouldn't understand being saddled but riderless for so long. She wondered if the mare might attempt to return to the stable back at the rancho as she had been trained to do.

Snatches of the ranch flitted through her mind: the cool rooms of the hacienda, deep tubs of water to bathe in, the rush of water falling from the high plateau to the lower grazing land and clear, deep pond. Her skin itched from the layer of dust that covered every inch of her and her throat ached for a drop of moisture.

There didn't seem to be water or grass in the dead-end canyon. In the summer heat, it wouldn't be long before the entire herd would rush the entrance to the canyon in search of water, forcing both Travis and the bandits into acting to prevent the scattering of the herd.

The soft trill of a bird floated in the clear air, and all three men tensed and leaned forward. They seemed to hold their collective breath until the sound came again. Iliana felt a surge of fear. She'd heard of Indians mimicking the calls of birds. Perhaps the traders were mistaken and their attackers were Apache.

"Don't worry none, little lady," the wrangler who had spoken to her before attempted to reassure her. "Ain't no warbler like that'n ever strayed this far south afore. It's just Brother Roberts lettin' us know those ornery cayuses are leavin' their positions to begin roundin' up our hawses."

"Senora Adams, nothing much is going to happen for a little while. This might be a good time to go back in the cave, where it's cooler, to rest for a bit," Travis whispered. Though he'd insisted she call him Travis, he persisted in using her more formal name most of the time.

She knew he was right. She should rest. Even if all had gone smoothly on this trip, she was well aware that the journey was a risk for the child she carried. Knowing that staying at the hacienda would have endangered the new life more was the only reason she'd risked the journey. Giving the darkness behind her a fearful glance, she moved back a few steps to the edge of the darkness and once more sat, leaning against the smooth stone at her back. The coolness was refreshing, but she couldn't relax. What if snakes hid inches from where she sat? Or there might be a puma or some other beast watching for a chance to catch her alone. There were strange markings like a child's hasty sketches on the wall closest to her, and she wondered if long ago someone else might have hidden in the cave. Surely a child hadn't hidden there. Her arms cradled her unborn child in an age-old protective gesture. In spite of her fears, she drifted toward uneasy slumber, rousing frequently with her throat growing raspy and dry as her need for water increased.

A sudden explosion of sound startled her fully awake. Fear riveted her attention on the front of the cave, where all three men were firing their rifles. She crept closer with her rifle, girding herself to do what needed to be done. She wasn't eager to shoot anyone, not even bandits who threatened her life, but if it was the only way to preserve the life of the child she carried, she would do it.

"Give me your rifle!" Travis thrust his rifle and a cartridge bag toward her and reached for hers as she attempted to kneel beside him. She gave up the gun willingly and accepted the one he handed her. It took no explanation to know she would be of greater use to the men if she loaded their rifles instead of joining in the gunfire. Her nimble fingers were kept flying as she loaded one gun, then the next, in a continuous rhythm for what seemed a long time. She was aware in some part of her mind that gunfire was coming from multiple directions and it wasn't all aimed toward the cave where they hid, but it wasn't until the guns fell silent that she dared hope they would survive.

"Are they dead?" she whispered.

"Some of 'em," the talkative wrangler acknowledged. "Most are jist bidin' their time, thinkin' all they gotta do is outlast us."

Without water, how long could they last? To distract her from her thirst and the thoughts troubling her, she knelt beside the array of gun belts and pouches the men had tossed beside her as she loaded their rifles, meaning to organize them. She noticed there were few bullets left. She turned stricken eyes toward Travis. He seemed to read her thoughts. With one hand he lifted the heavy cartridge belt he'd given her earlier from her shoulders. She felt foolish for having forgotten it, but even knowing there was more ammunition than she'd supposed, she knew the cartridges wouldn't last long if there was another gun battle.

The raucous sound of a crow brought her head up, and she studied Travis's face to learn if the cawing sound was another signal. *It must be,* she concluded since she could see his shoulders relax a small amount. He noticed her watching him and gave her a reassuring smile.

"Boss, you think someone oughta mosey down to the wagon to see if Brother Lewis made it?" the quieter wrangler asked. "We're going to need food and water. There's plenty in the cook wagon, and I've been studying on a way to stay out of sight to git to it. I figure I can make it down to that rock the wagon is leaning against without too much trouble," he volunteered. He and Travis discussed the route he proposed to take.

"The sun will be going down soon and the canyon is already in shadow. Give it another half hour and it might be safe to venture out," Travis told him.

Iliana listened to their plans but didn't ask questions. She wanted to know how many outlaws the men thought they were dealing with, how many of Travis's men were alive and armed, and how much risk the man proposing to reach the overturned wagon would be taking, but Amaya had taught her not to question men such as her grandfather and her husband. In some ways Travis Telford was now the authority figure in her life, and she had already forgotten herself in the earlier confusion. She had bothered him with questions when she should have thanked him for saving her life. Still, she would like to know.

So many things had changed in the past few months; she was no longer certain whether the old rules still applied. Never had she thought to be a widow so young, to lose her child, or to run away from the hacienda. If she and her unborn child survived, how would they live? So much had happened so quickly she'd given no thought to finding a place to live at the end of her journey or to what she would need to do and know to care for herself and her infant. Her money, the banknotes Mr. Williams had given her for her few jewels, was in her saddlebag attached to the saddle on Nutmeg's back. Were they lost to her? Surely it wasn't wrong for her mind to be filled with questions or to speak of her concerns.

She stared through the breaks in the rocks in front of her, watching the creeping darkness. Something moved. Or did she just imagine the movement? She peered into the darkening canyon. Again she detected the shifting of a shadow.

"Senor?" Her whisper wavered. She did not wish to interrupt the discussion he was having with the two wranglers, but she must tell him what she had seen. "Travis!"

He turned toward her.

"Something moved below us and just to the left of that dead juniper tree."

Travis squinted, attempting to see what she had seen. The other two men settled back into their previous positions. All three positioned their rifles against their shoulders. None seemed to take offense at her boldness nor question her right to speak.

"I seen it! The gal is right—someone's comin'." Iliana heard the click, signifying one of the men was preparing to shoot.

"Hold your fire," Travis commanded. "It could be one of our own."

"Could be a cat too," the more talkative wrangler muttered. "Might've got trapped in this canyon when we arrived unexpected like, or we could be squattin' in her den." Iliana struggled to restrain a shudder.

"It's not likely to be one of the bandits," Travis theorized in a low voice. "If they decide to rush us, they'll shoot from above or try to ride in from the mouth of the canyon."

Falling silent, they watched for slight movements that might give away the approaching figure's position. All three of the men kept their guns trained on something they seemed able to follow more closely than could she.

"Boss?" A hoarse whisper came from the rocks a short distance below their hiding place, causing her to jump. The voice sounded familiar, but she couldn't be certain.

"It's Lewis!" There was a jubilant note in the voice of the wrangler at her elbow.

"Keep climbing. I'll meet you," Travis whispered back just before he slipped into the darkness that had reached the cave.

It was all she could do to keep the protest that trembled on her lips from being uttered aloud as Travis Telford disappeared into the darkness, leaving her feeling oddly bereft. She found herself straining to see into the darkness, suddenly aware that the blistering heat of the day had given way to nighttime chill. She wrapped her arms around herself in an attempt to ward off the cold and perhaps to provide a bit of comfort. She said nothing. The men beside her were silent as well.

Time seemed to slow to an agonizing pace as she waited. Once she thought she heard a distant shout. She was pretty certain the two men she knelt between heard it too. They both seemed to tense. Then a faint trickle of pebbles sounded just loud enough to signal the arrival of Travis and Brother Lewis.

Beside her the two wranglers lifted their rifles, ready to deal with anyone who might have followed the two men into the cave.

Chapter Twenty-One

"ILIANA." TRAVIS USED HER GIVEN name as he summoned her to the place where Brother Lewis sprawled on the ground. She scrambled backward to reach his side. "He's been shot. The bullet grazed his head just above his right ear, so it's not serious, but he lost quite a bit of blood. He wants to talk to you."

"Me?" If the cook wanted her to bandage his head, she'd try, but she had nothing she could use for a bandage. She knelt beside him. "You wish to tell me something?" she asked.

"It was that horse of yours," he said. "I've never seen anything like her before. I caught a bullet early on, and there was nothing I could do to keep the team from stampeding along with that half-wild bunch of broncos. When the wagon tipped over, I blacked out and when I came to, your mare was standing over me like she was keeping the other horses from stepping on me. I got up slow and careful like and hung onto a stirrup to give me support while I made my way to a pile of rocks, figuring they'd be some protection."

"She's a good horse. My husband trained her to protect a fallen rider." Iliana was pleased to hear Nutmeg was still with the herd.

"I was pretty dizzy and kept fading in and out, but every time I got my senses back, that mare stood twixt me'n the other horses. When my head got to working proper, I could see my team was thrashing around and like to kill themselves, so I used your horse as a shield to get to where I could cut 'em loose. Then I went back to that pile of rocks and removed the mare's saddle to give her a better chance of escaping, if she gets a chance, and to keep her a little cooler. I figured I owed her one." He reached inside his shirt and pulled out a thick leather pouch. "This belongs to you." He handed it to her.

She stared, recognizing the hand-tooled, double saddlebag she'd wondered if she'd ever see again. Her arms closed around it, drawing the soft leather against her chest as she blinked back tears. Brother Lewis could have no idea what the bag and its contents meant to her.

"Th—thank you."

He looked embarrassed. "I wasn't thinkin' about you at all when I took it from your saddle," he admitted. "I saw it and thought the thick leather might protect me from a bullet if I stuck it inside my shirt. I brought along your canteen too." He drew the thong that had secured it to her saddle from around his neck and held it out to her.

Accepting the tin canteen with eagerness, she shook it and was pleased by both its weight and the sloshing sound it made.

"I only took a few swallows," Brother Lewis told her. He hung his head as though embarrassed to have used some of her water.

"I'm glad I filled it this morning," she said, feeling the first urge to smile she'd felt in days. Prying free the cork inserted in the pewter mouth of the canteen, she lifted the water to her lips. Resisting a desire to drink deeply, she took a small sip, holding the water in her mouth for several seconds to extend the sweet pleasure of moisture permeating her parched throat before swallowing.

Rising to her feet, she carried the canteen to Travis. He hesitated then he too took a small sip before passing it on to the other two wranglers. Both men looked at her with gratitude in their eyes before following her and Travis's example by taking only small sips. Without discussion they all understood the water in the canteen must be rationed with care.

Iliana returned to Brother Lewis and her saddlebag. Opening the bag, she drew out the lace handkerchief. In one corner of the white square, she poured a small amount of the perfume Amaya had tucked in her bag. She proceeded to dab it onto the wound on Brother Lewis's head.

"Don't waste any of your precious water on that scratch," he protested.

"It's not water. It's perfume." She thought to appease his protest. Instead he sat straight up with a horrified expression on his face.

"I'll not go about smelling like a brothel!"

"Hush!" She continued to pat the long gash with the damp handkerchief. "The woman who raised me said perfume is as good as whiskey for cleaning a wound and holding back fever."

Hearing a snicker behind her, she turned to glare at the wrangler who was holding his nose.

"I expect she's right," Travis said. "But in any case, don't use it all on Brother Lewis. Who knows who else might need some before we get shut of this place." He looked meaningfully at the snickering wrangler then placed a hand on Brother Lewis's shoulder and continued speaking. "Do you feel strong enough to take my place watching over the canyon for the bandits or any of our crew? Willard and I are going to scout around a bit."

"I'd like to go with you," the cook said, making a move to rise. "I made note of where the rifle fire was coming from."

"Shoot, you can't go," the wrangler she now knew as Willard said. "Them banditos would smell you comin' a mile away."

Brother Lewis glared at him.

"We'll wait a bit for it to get full dark," Travis told him. "Come up to the front if you're rested enough, and tell me what you saw as you made your way here."

While the men talked in low whispers, Iliana crawled a short distance deeper into the cave. Once she felt certain the men couldn't see her, she took the money belt Mr. Williams had given her and tied it once more about her waist under her shirt. No matter how hot and uncomfortable she became, she wouldn't remove it again. That money was all she had to provide food and shelter for her baby. Satisfied her funds were safe, she resumed her place nearer the front of the cave to attempt to rest. Sleep didn't come, and she found herself fretting about Travis and Willard venturing away from the cave. From the men's remarks she understood they stood a better chance of surviving and keeping the herd if they attacked rather than waited for the bandits to initiate a confrontation.

The two men left their hiding place with so little fuss or sound that Iliana wasn't aware of their leaving. One minute there were four shadows crouched behind the rocks that hid the cave from view, and the next, there were only two. She moved forward to kneel beside the two shadowy forms remaining with their eyes focused toward the void in front of them. Not wishing to be separated from her bag, she carried it with her, slung over her shoulder.

Time seemed to crawl, and as hard as she strained to hear any sound, she heard none. Even the horses had ceased their restless movements and frightened nickers. A slim quarter moon cast its dim glow, and one by one stars did their part to lighten the night sky. A few high, wispy clouds drifted in front of the sliver of moon. Except at the bottom of the canyon where the night was the darkest, rocks and trees began to reveal their shapes. Iliana drifted into a trance-like quasi sleep but came fully awake with the yip of a coyote from a nearby mountain peak. Moments later the coyote was answered from farther away.

Whether the coyotes or thirst drove the horses to their feet, Iliana couldn't say, but she could hear the thunder of hooves as the animals milled about in the confined space below. It wouldn't be long until they rushed the entrance to the canyon. Thirst more than coyotes would propel them to break free. Neither the horse traders nor the bandits stood to make a profit if the horses escaped the canyon. She wondered if Nutmeg would be able to find her way back to the ranch and if any of the other horses would follow her. She didn't dare speculate on her own fate or that of her baby if their group was left without mounts.

The remaining wrangler muttered something under his breath. He too seemed concerned about the horses' restless behavior.

With the withdrawal of the hot summer sun, the night turned cold and Iliana shivered. She wished she'd left her rain poncho in her saddlebag instead of rolling it with her blanket behind her saddle. It would have been some protection from the night chill. In spite of the cold and her concern for the horses, Travis, and the men who rode with him, her head began to nod.

She was almost asleep when she remembered the strip of jerky in her saddlebag. She'd had nothing to eat and only a few sips of water since breakfast that morning—or was it yesterday? She might survive for a time without food, but her baby needed nourishment. She searched in her bag for the dried meat, and when she found it, she gnawed out a chunk from the center, keeping the bite she'd taken in her mouth. She gave one of the severed pieces to the two men who waited with her, and the other piece she returned to her bag.

Chewing slowly, she settled back again to wait, and once more she drifted toward sleep in spite of the stone floor beneath her aching body. Her mind drifted back to the hacienda, where Amaya, Abuelo, and then Ross had seen to her needs. She longed for reassuring arms, yet somewhere in the back of her mind she felt a whisper of pride in her ability to manage thus far.

"Look!" the single harsh word from Brother Lewis jerked her back to reality. Leaning forward, she followed the shadowy shape of his arm that pointed toward the mouth of the canyon, where a light flickered.

She rubbed her eyes. Surely the bandits weren't so confident of their victory they had built a campfire! As she watched, a line of small fires flickered across the narrow opening to the box canyon, blocking the only way in or out of it. In what seemed only a matter of seconds, the flames were leaping high in the air, forming a wall of flames across the mouth of the box canyon.

Sudden gunfire erupted from somewhere near the blazing bonfires, filling Iliana with terror. She had no way of knowing whether Travis had met up with more of his men or if he and Willard were battling the bandits alone.

"I should have gone with the boss." The wrangler left behind raised up as though he meant to go to Travis's and Willard's aid. As he did so, he cast a pointed look at Iliana and sank back on his haunches.

She crouched lower, understanding that the man blamed her for his absence from the confrontation below. Feeling mortified that Travis had thought it necessary to leave the man behind to protect her, she urged him to go to the other men's aid. "I can look after myself, and I'm an excellent shot," she assured him.

"The boss'd have my hide if I left ya."

To her surprise, Brother Lewis sided with her. "Go ahead, Frank. We can manage. I've got my second wind now, and between us, we have a rifle and two side arms. You're likely needed more down there to fend off the bandits and keep the horses from breaking through to find water. Mrs. Adams will be safe in my care."

"Well . . ." The wrangler sounded hesitant. But after a moment, he crawled to the edge of the cave opening and disappeared into the darkness. He didn't make a sound, and she wondered how he could find his way in the darkness without kicking stones that might alert the bandits to his position.

"Come up here behind these rocks," Brother Lewis advised her. "They've held onto a little heat, and if we have to shoot, you'll have a better view."

She did as he asked. When she was settled, he spoke again in his slow, unhurried voice, "Are you the praying sort?"

"Yes; first my mother, then our housekeeper taught me to pray." Her hand went to her throat, and she remembered placing her beads, with the cross, in her son's small, cold hands. Her rosary and the gold cross Ross had given her were among the items she'd added to the small hoard of jewels she'd traded for a chance to escape Ben. "My beads . . ." she began.

"No, I don't mean that kind of prayin'. Anyway, I don't suppose any of those prayers you learned fit our present predicament. If you don't mind,

I'll say a few words for both of us." He didn't wait for a response from her but commenced praying. His prayer wasn't like any she'd heard before. It was more like explaining their situation to a good friend and asking Him to look after them and the drovers who were facing a rough patch.

He'd just said "amen" when gunfire opened up from atop the cliff opposite the cave. Brother Lewis seemed to sense her anxiety. "Those shots aren't as bad as they sound," he whispered. "They're a pretty good sign some of our men have made their way to the top and discovered the bandits' lookout."

"Travis?"

"No. He's down there keeping those fires burning."

"Travis started the fires?" She'd been certain they were the work of the bandits, possibly an attempt to burn them out or to force them to show themselves.

"He can't let the bandits scatter the herd. The thieves might make off with enough horses to be worth their effort, but we can't afford to lose even a quarter of the herd. Every man that rides with Travis has put up money of his own and that of their friends and families to buy those animals. He's got to keep them together or a lot of people stand to lose all they own. Horses are skeered of fire, so the boss set them blazes across the mouth of the canyon to keep the horses from charging the opening and leaving us on foot, making us easy pickings for those troublemakers."

The gunshots tapered off, with only a sporadic shot reaching their ears. Iliana waited with her nerves on edge. Had the battle ended or had Travis and his men run out of cartridges? A slight sound reached her ears. She'd heard that sound before. It was the trickle of small stones that had been dislodged by a careless step. Touching Brother Lewis's sleeve, she pointed in the direction from which the sound had come.

Placing his mouth next to her ear, he told her to move back into the cave. Leaving her rifle with him, she retreated into the darkness. Her heart was pounding, and though she hoped the person approaching was Travis or one of his men, the sound hadn't come from the direction they had taken when they left the cave. It had come from the same direction Brother Lewis had made his way from, deeper inside the canyon. She drew her small revolver from her pocket and hoped her hand would be steady if she had to fire it. She thumbed back the hammer.

Focusing her attention on the arc of graying light that outlined the front of the cave, she saw a man step into the space where she'd knelt beside Brother Lewis moments earlier. He carried a rifle in one hand, and the bulge below his hip was sure to be a second weapon. She held her breath, not daring to even breathe.

"Set that gun down easy like," she heard Brother Lewis's voice come from the place where he stood behind one of the boulders that partially blocked the opening to the cave. She saw the man stoop to place his rifle on the ground and heard the clatter of metal against stone.

"Toss your six-shooter over the side and keep your hands where I can see them."

The shadowy form hesitated then did as he was instructed. Brother Lewis eased his way from behind the rock, keeping his rifle pointed toward the man, who now stood with his hands held out from his body at about shoulder height.

"Face down!" Brother Lewis ordered.

As the man began to comply, a second man stepped into Iliana's view. Before she could pull the trigger or scream a warning, the newcomer fired.

Chapter Twenty-Two

"Take cover and stay back from the fires." Travis hissed a warning to his men as the flames caught in the piles of brush he, Willard, and several other wranglers had dragged across the canyon opening. "The outlaws will shoot at any silhouettes they spot around the flames."

Almost in response to his warning, a volley of shots sent the cowboys scurrying for cover, where they commenced returning fire.

The warning was probably unnecessary. All of the wranglers were experienced with stock and wilderness conditions and well aware of fire as both friend and foe. Travis appreciated the badly needed assistance Frank provided when he arrived, but Travis didn't like leaving Iliana and the wounded cook alone. Mentally he counted his men. Four men were serving as scouts and snipers on the high ridges, one man had been killed at the beginning of the ambush, Brother Lewis was with Iliana, and he and four wranglers had made their way to the mouth of the canyon to start the fire. Only one man was unaccounted for. Travis fervently added his thanks to the prayers of his Mormon crew and added a plea for the one missing man.

Settling behind a screen of rocks and brush, he squinted his eyes against the drifting smoke and peered into the darkness beyond the fires. He took care to avoid looking directly at the flames, knowing their brightness would create a kind of blindness. It also prevented the outlaws from pinpointing the positions from which the cowboys fired while causing no such problem for the cowboys who directed their fire toward the tiny flashes that revealed their attackers' positions. For several minutes guns blazed then silence fell over the canyon and the only sound was the crackling, popping sound made by the burning brush.

Waiting for the fight to resume or for an indication it was over, Travis found himself thinking about Iliana while his eyes continued to watch for movement. He'd admired her beauty the first time he saw her. He'd pitied her for the loss of her husband, then her son such a short time later, which led to her desperate need for an escape from her enemy. Now that he knew her better, he admired her also for her willingness to work hard, her courage in facing the situation they now found themselves in, and her generosity in sharing her meager supplies. He wished his contract was fulfilled and Iliana's life wasn't in danger, so they could return to the valley. It would be idyllic to be back there building the ranch he'd longed for almost all of his life, with Iliana his closest neighbor. In time, perhaps she would become more than a neighbor.

From the canyon came the sound of restless hooves. Some of the fires were beginning to burn low, and Travis knew they couldn't risk the frightened animals becoming emboldened enough to attempt an escape. Grasping an armful of heavy brush, he prepared to dash toward the nearest bonfire. Before he could move, he spotted Frank leaping forward to replenish the mound of fire before him. Just as Frank turned to dash back toward cover, a shot rang out from partway up the cliff. Something about that shot bothered Travis. It hadn't been directed toward Frank. He cast a nervous glance toward the cave where he'd left Iliana and Brother Lewis. Three more shots sounded in quick succession. He identified them as the unmistakable reports of a small caliber pistol.

* * *

Brother Lewis crumpled to the ground. There was no time to think as horror gave way to anger and stirred a strong survival instinct within Iliana. Her finger squeezed the trigger, and the stone walls around her magnified the revolver's bark. She felt no emotion as the bandit's gun toppled from his hand and the shadowy figure melted to merge with the ground. Her attention focused on the other man, who had regained his rifle and brought it to his shoulder. She could see outward better than he could see into the black depths of the cave, but she couldn't risk a lucky shot striking her and her baby. She fired again. And again.

The bandit's scream echoed in her ears, telling her he'd been hit, but he didn't fall. Instead he disappeared from her narrow range of vision. She stood in the blackness wondering whether she should pursue him or if he lay in wait for her to show herself. She heard a moan, but there was no way to tell if it came from Brother Lewis or from the first man she shot. Torn between her desire to check on the cook and an instinct toward caution that kept her from calling out his name, she stood, unable to take a step. Time ceased to exist.

At last she took a cautious step forward, then stopped to cast her eyes upward for the briefest of moments. "Oh please let Brother Lewis be alive and help me save my baby," she found herself pleading with Deity much the way the older man had prayed before they were attacked.

"Iliana, are you all right?"

Was she hallucinating, or did she hear Travis calling her name?

With a sob, she rushed toward the man who was emerging onto the narrow lip between the cave and the sharp drop to the canyon floor. She threw herself at him, and he caught her with one arm and held her close while she wrapped both arms around his waist and leaned her head against his chest.

"It's all right. You're safe now." His words penetrated her mind at last. Becoming aware of her arms about a man who was not her husband, she drew back.

To cover her embarrassment, she dropped to her knees to examine Brother Lewis. His eyes opened and to her great relief she heard his breath coming in rasping gasps. With deft fingers she found the puddle of blood on his shoulder and felt a wave of gratitude that the bullet hadn't struck lower.

"How is he?" Travis's voice reached her.

"He's alive, but I think he's bleeding far too much," she whispered.

"Wrap the wound as tight as you can with this." A shirt dropped onto her lap. "Some of the others will be along any minute to help us get him down to the fires so we can see how badly he's hurt." He dropped beside her and spoke to Brother Lewis in a firm voice. "Can you hang on?"

"Yes," the wounded man managed to say before his eyes closed and he drifted into unconsciousness.

"The bandits?" she asked, unable to hide the fear in her voice.

"Some are dead. The others reached their horses and took off. We'll keep a guard or two out until daylight to be certain they don't circle back."

"Is . . . is that man dead?" She pointed to the man who lay unmoving a few feet away.

"Yes," Travis answered in a gentle voice, sensing the realization she'd shot a man was beginning to sink in. "Don't think about him. He's responsible for his death, not you."

"There was another man . . ." she began.

"I know," Travis said. "He tried to descend the cliff too fast and lost his footing. He was already dead when we found him."

"I . . . I shot him."

"It was the fall that killed him."

Was Travis just trying to shield her from knowing she'd killed two men? Fine perspiration filmed her skin and her stomach roiled. Dry heaves shook her body and bile filled her throat. Travis's arm came around her, and when the retching motions stopped, he held an almost-empty canteen to her lips, offering her the last of their water.

* * *

Iliana worked the rest of the night beside Travis to bandage the wounded and assist him in digging a bullet out of the thigh of one cowboy who had been wounded in the initial attack and had hidden in a cave on the opposite side of the canyon from where she and Travis had taken refuge. When she staggered with fatigue, Travis insisted that she rest for a few hours.

The sky lightened by the time they were ready to move out. The cook wagon was beyond repair, but the cowboys salvaged some of the food and rigged packsaddles for the draft horses to carry the rescued supplies. Others built a cart from two wheels and some of the lumber from the wagon. Brother Lewis and two other men who had suffered gunshot wounds were placed on the cart.

Willard brought Nutmeg and handed the reins to Iliana without speaking. She felt a wave of emotion seeing that the cowboy had found her saddle and the precious items that had been attached to the saddle. Some of the cowboys' saddles and gear hadn't fared as well. Once mounted, she leaned forward to pat the mare and whisper encouragement in her ears. The men might think she was being overly emotional, but she felt grateful for being reunited with the mare that was dear to her.

Travis positioned her near him on the forward flank and signaled for the riders to begin moving the horses. She looked back once to see seven fresh graves on a small rise; six held the bodies of bandits and one, a little apart from the others, was the resting place of one of their own. Pain, like something sharp digging into her ribs, cut deeply into her heart, and she knew she'd never be the same woman she'd been just a week ago, before Gabe was murdered and before she became responsible for the deaths of two men who now rested in two of those desolate graves.

* * *

Weeks had passed since the traders' run-in with the bandits, but Iliana still had difficulty sleeping at night. Her inability to sleep was due to more than memories of the terrifying experience or to her advancing pregnancy. It couldn't even be blamed on the ache in her heart for Gabe. She tossed and turned for what seemed like endless hours. Unable to get comfortable, she gave up attempting to sleep and rose to her feet.

Shaking out her boots, then sliding them onto her feet, she left the tent Travis had erected for her. Walking softly to avoid rousing any of the men who lay wrapped in their blankets around the fire, she made her way to the rope remuda that encircled the horses they would ride the next morning. Nutmeg seemed to sense her presence and made her way to the edge of the temporary pen. Iliana dug in her pocket to produce a single lump of sugar she'd placed there when she'd helped wash supper dishes.

"Are you all right?"

She hadn't heard footsteps behind her, but she recognized Travis's voice.

"Yes," she assured him. "I'm just anxious for our journey to end."

"It won't be long now, just a few more days, maybe a week. We're in California now, and we'll soon be passing small towns and a few missions. We'll stop at several ranches in the next couple of weeks where we have contracted to deliver the horses."

"Will you return to Mexico for more horses?"

"Not this season, and perhaps not at all." He was silent for a time, then he added, "I'm thinking of settling down, starting a ranch of my own. After I found the water that rightfully belongs to your ranch, I signed papers to purchase the strip of land on the other side of the new river. With the profit from this trip, I'm thinking I'll have enough to live on and start my own place. I want to acquire good stock with which to build something bigger. If I'm careful, I won't need to trail horses again."

"You wish to stay in New Mexico?" she asked.

"Yes, though for some time I thought I might settle in Utah. An old trapper finagled me into buying his homestead in a pretty valley a couple of days' ride from Salt Lake City. There's an abundance of grass and a small community built around the church. I arranged with the owner to hold it until I return in the spring, but the snow gets powerful deep there in the winter, and I've no fondness for the cold. It's not big enough for raising horses the way I'd like either. Now I think I'll look for a buyer to take it off my hands and invest the money in the New Mexico property. How about you? What are your plans now that we've reached California?"

"I've thought little beyond putting distance between myself and the man who murdered my son and who will kill this child, too, if he finds me." Her hands went in an instinctively protective gesture to the mound that stretched the front of her shirt.

"Javier told me something of the man who wishes to force you into marriage in order to claim your property. He asked me to see you safely to one of the missions along the California coast. Do you have a preference?"

"No." She sighed. "I know nothing of the missions, not even their names. I suppose I must go to one to seek asylum until after my child is born, but after that I don't know what will become of us. I don't think I would be happy raising my child under the regulations of a priestly order." She didn't find it strange to speak so candidly to Travis Telford though she'd never shared her thoughts openly with any man before, not even her husband or her grandfather.

"Some of the mission villages are pleasant, but if you are reluctant to enter one, I can arrange for you to stay at the home of a widow near the boarding house where I and several of my men will winter over. Some of us have contracted to train horses for one of the nearby ranchers through the winter. Fanny Butler is a good woman who would be pleased to have company, and she would be of great use to you when your time comes. Her home is comfortable and clean. She's good company, too."

His words painted an appealing picture in her mind. Father Escudero was the only priest she had ever known, and he had always frightened her a bit, leaving her wary of a community run by a priest.

"I would rather be in a home than at a mission, but my means are limited." The arrangement he described sounded far more inviting than a mission.

"Sister Butler's rates are reasonable. If the two of you don't reach an agreeable arrangement, there's a mission a few miles away you can turn to." His words implied the matter was settled and Iliana felt as though a weight had been taken from her shoulders. It would be good to have another woman near to help with her child's birth. It would be good, too, to have Travis and some of the men she'd gotten to know during the past weeks nearby. Since their ordeal with the bandits, she'd felt a kind of camaraderie with the men, and their deferential treatment of her had become more like what she imagined it would be like to have big brothers.

"You'd better grab some sleep while you can," Travis suggested. "Morning always comes too soon."

She knew he was right, but she felt reluctant to leave his presence. "Thank you for listening to me," she said.

"It was my pleasure," he said with a smile. "I, too, was finding sleep difficult." He placed her hand on his arm, turning her steps toward her tent. Awareness of his proximity and the feel of hard muscle beneath her hand seemed to tie her tongue. She wondered if he felt the same strange sensation since he, too, remained silent as they walked. At the opening to the tent he stopped, and with reluctance she withdrew her hand from his arm.

"Good night, ma'am." She thought he tipped his hat to her, but with her head lowered to hide her confused feelings, she couldn't be certain. She didn't think she was mistaken in hearing a huskier than normal timbre to his voice.

"Good night," she echoed before drawing back the flap to her tent and stepping inside.

* * *

As they moved the herd north, Iliana noticed the abundance of water and the greener landscape. Trees became more plentiful and she caught occasional glimpses of the ocean. It was both strange and beautiful. They reached the first of the ranches where the horses were to be delivered, and she noticed the similarity of the architecture to that of the haciendas to which she was accustomed, with their white adobe walls and clay roofs. Over the following days, the herd of horses dwindled in size, requiring less effort from her and the other riders. She noticed, too, that all of the horses from the Sebastian Ranch were still in the herd.

When lunchtime came she settled herself beneath a large tree and was soon joined by Brother Lewis, who continued his complaints for several minutes concerning the two-wheeled cart that had replaced his cook wagon. Grateful the man had recovered from his injuries and could again take over responsibility for preparing meals, Iliana never expressed weariness with his complaints about his cooking facilities. Her feelings went beyond the haphazard meals prepared by the various cowboys Travis had assigned to the task. She felt a kind of kinship to the cook, as though he were a surrogate father to her.

When his complaints ceased, she asked, "Will you stay in California with Travis and some of the other men to tame horses?"

"No," the man shook his head. "I'm through with this business. I only came for the money to provide my wife and young'ns with a better home. Travis offered me two of the draft horses and enough cash to buy seed for the new ground I added to my farm a year ago if I would cook for his crew. I'm anxious now to get home and be with my family again."

Iliana understood. She missed Amaya. She missed Javier, Dominic, and the ranch hands who had surrounded her all of her life. She was surprised to discover she thought of them as family. It seemed strange that she had grown closer to the men who worked on the ranch since Ross's death than during the years he and Grandfather had been alive. It brought pain to her heart to think she might never see them or the hacienda again. She cut off this line of thinking. It led to thoughts of Gabe. She couldn't bear to think of never seeing her little boy again or of even kneeling at his grave.

When it came time to bid Brother Lewis and the cowboys good-bye she wished them well on their journey just before they boarded one of the cars on the first steam engine she'd ever seen. Unsure whether she could ever ride behind one of the monstrous black engines that belched smoke and steam over the platform, she stood beside Travis, Willard, and a young man called Nephi. Tears filled her eyes when Brother Lewis kissed her cheek and invited her to visit him and his wife if she ever got to Utah.

* * *

Horses from the Sebastian Ranch were among the last consignment of horses delivered to their new owners. Travis and the two other cowboys who had remained behind with him each chose at least one of the horses to keep. Iliana still had her four horses, which Travis offered to board with those of the men on the ranch where they would be working in exchange for use of the animals through the winter or until she decided to sell them. Reluctantly she agreed. She hated being separated from Nutmeg, but she didn't have the means to provide for the animals.

Iliana brushed a few stray curls away from her face and smoothed her hands down the front of the plain black skirt she wore, as though her small effort might erase two months of being bunched at the bottom of her saddlebag. She said a silent thank you to Amaya, who had thought to add one bit of feminine apparel when she'd packed the bags.

"Ready?" Travis smiled in encouragement as he paused outside the door of a neat cottage on the edge of a small town. He'd assured her the town was less than two miles from the ranch where he'd be staying and that he'd ride in every Sunday to check on her.

Taking a deep breath, she nodded her head, and Travis gave the door a brisk rap.

"I'm coming!" a cheery voice called and almost at once the door opened to reveal a small woman with a gray lopsided bun atop her head, laugh wrinkles around her eyes, and a voluminous apron covering her gingham gown.

"Land sakes!" The woman exclaimed and reached for Travis, pulling his head down to give him a kiss on his cheek.

"Hello, Aunt Fanny." Travis patted the woman's shoulder and returned her smile. "I'd like you to meet—" Before he could complete the introduction Fanny Butler held out her arms and enveloped Iliana in them. The exuberant welcome was almost Iliana's undoing. She'd missed Amaya, but she hadn't known how much she hungered for the presence of another female until she felt Fanny Butler's arms go around her. But why hadn't Travis mentioned he wished her to board with his aunt? Or was "aunt" merely a courtesy title?

"It's about time this rascally young man found a wife!"

"I'm not . . . He isn't . . . Oh dear . . ." Iliana stammered and drew back from the welcoming embrace.

"We're not married." Travis's face was as red as Iliana knew her own had become. Fanny turned on him with an angry glare. Her eyes went from Iliana's obviously pregnant figure to Travis. The older woman folded her arms and tapped the toe of one neatly shod foot, clearly expecting an explanation.

"If you don't mind, Aunt Fanny, may we step inside?"

Fanny Butler stepped back and gestured for them to enter her parlor. Once inside the house, Travis lost no time explaining that Iliana was a widow and arrangements had been made for her to travel with him in order to help her avoid a forced marriage to the man responsible for the murder of her young son. Travis went on to say fleeing her home was the only way Iliana could be certain the man wouldn't find a way to destroy her baby too.

"Oh, my dear!" Fanny looked horrified. "You must stay here with me, where that man isn't likely to find you. You can't go trailing after Travis, as others will make the same error of judgment I did. I can drop a quiet word or two to a few people, and even if that horrible man comes to our little town searching for you, no one will tell him a thing."

Iliana trembled. She hadn't considered that Ben might follow her to California. Were his finances so desperate and his obsession with taking over the Sebastian Ranch so strong he'd actually come after her?

Chapter Twenty-Three

Javier rose to his feet, though the movement sent pain coursing through his back and his knees. Since finding Gabe in that cold stream six months earlier, the pains in his joints had grown harder to bear. Schooling his features to hide any sign of discomfort, he held out his hand to the two men who accompanied Dominic to the room where, over Amaya's protests, Javier had resumed management of the ranch's financial affairs. She accused him of being presumptuous to make use of Don Sebastian's library. He'd reminded her that Dominic was in charge and the foreman had made the decision that the library was still the best place for the ranch's books.

Mr. Williams gripped his hand in a firm clasp and Javier struggled not to wince. He turned to the other man, who wore a metal shield on his shirt.

"Marshal, have you any news concerning the blackguard who shot young Gabe? It's likely he's the same coward who put a bullet through that Mormon horse trader." Javier suspected the marshal's attempts to prove the attack was Ben Purdy's doing would be as fruitless as their attempts to bring their neighbor to trial for stealing Iliana's jewelry.

"I have my suspicions, same as you do." The stocky man with a badge on his chest acknowledged Javier's words then went on, "But there were no witnesses and Purdy's men swear he was miles away when the boy was shot."

Dominic snorted none too politely. "And what about the jewelry he admits he stole from her?"

"He claims he returned the jewelry when she requested the items back and that he'd only been safeguarding them for her."

"He's a liar." Javier didn't hedge his denial of Ben's claim.

"I suspect as much," the marshal stated smoothly. "That's why I've requested some discreet checking of inventories at several shops in Albuquerque by officers in that city."

"And I've sent a description of the missing jewels to dealers in more distant cities," Mr. Williams added. "So far, I've heard nothing."

"Is there a reason for your call today?" Dominic got to the point. He was a busy man with the running of the ranch and keeping a guard posted to watch for trouble from the Purdy Ranch. He'd lost at least several cows and calves that had wandered within range of the gunslingers Ben had hired in place of cowboys, and more than one caballero had narrowly dodged flying bullets. The little time he'd had to spare, Dominic had spent worrying about young Senora Adams.

Mr. Williams drew himself up, folding his arms across his chest as though daring anyone to dispute his words. "I asked the marshal to ride out with me today to foreclose on the Purdy Ranch. Ben Purdy is two years in arrears on both his payments and taxes."

Javier and Dominic stared at each other in shock.

"You're booting him off the place?" Dominic directed his question to the marshal with a pleased grin.

"That was my intention, but he isn't there. He left half a dozen drifters with tied-down guns lounging about, but they claim he's been gone for a week, trailing some horse trader he'd learned had been at your ranch about the time Iliana disappeared." The marshal continued, oblivious to the sharp look that passed between Javier and Dominic. "They didn't put up an argument over leaving, though they were plum mad as hornets over not getting paid and made some threats to shoot Ben if they run across him anywhere. I reckon they figure they aren't going to get paid by hanging around, so they might as well ride on. I wouldn't want to be Ben if some of those fellas catch up to him."

"He has no more claim to the Medina Ranch?" Old Javier rubbed his hands together in glee.

"I suggested the men there pack their bags and leave before sundown," the marshal added.

Mr. Williams said, "I plan to send a few people out tomorrow to collect Purdy's personal effects and to salvage anything of value that might be sold to pay some of his debts."

"I don't suppose he left anything like Iliana's jewelry lying around." Amaya's sarcastic remark revealed the bitterness she harbored against their neighbor. The men had been so absorbed in their conversation they hadn't noticed when she quietly slipped into the room.

The marshal's earlier comment concerning Ben following the horse traders troubled Javier, and he wished for a way to warn Iliana.

"Was Ben aware he would lose the ranch?" Javier asked.

"I spelled it out to him on several occasions, and as recently as our last discussion, a little more than a week ago, he assured me that he still intended to marry Iliana in spite of what he called your interference. He seems to believe marrying her will be the end of his financial problems," Mr. Williams said with a sigh. "If he should return to this area, I would encourage caution. He holds a great deal of animosity toward you and Dominic."

"He doesn't hold any position of esteem in our view either." Dom's lip curled in what could only be termed a snarl.

Javier suspected Ben's hatred extended beyond Dominic and himself and extended to Iliana. He hoped she was well hidden in one of California's many monasteries.

"The reason I stopped here," Mr. Williams motioned for the others to be seated and settled himself in one of the chairs drawn up before the desk, "was to run an idea past the two of you."

Javier sank back onto the chair. Mr. Williams nodded toward Dominic to assure him he was included in the discussion. The marshal didn't take a chair but leaned against a wall to listen. "The bank now owns the Purdy Ranch, and I wanted to offer you first refusal rights if you're interested," Mr. Williams began.

Javier saw the way Dominic's eyes lit. The younger man was ambitious and wouldn't be content running someone else's ranch forever. He was a good, hardworking young man and deserved the opportunity being offered him. The Purdy Ranch could be Dom's chance to own his own spread. But how would he pay for it? Ross had paid the young foreman well, but not well enough to purchase his own land. Besides, Dom was a Mexican; how long would it take for another gringo to come along and chase him off the land?

Mr. Williams spun his hat between his fingers for several minutes then broached the subject that bothered Javier. Mr. Williams directed his words to the old man, though he clearly meant them for Dominic. "Some folks object to anyone of your race buying a sizeable piece of land. If Dominic is interested, we could work out an arrangement where I'd let out word that I own the property and employ him to run it along with the Sebastian Rancho. Instead of giving him a salary, I'd pay an agreed-upon amount to the bank each month in Dominic's name plus deposit a percentage of whatever profit the ranch makes in an account for him to use as working capital until he owns it outright."

"Gracias, senor. How soon will Ben's ranch be put up for sale?" Dominic asked, barely containing his enthusiasm.

"These things take time. I'll likely have to carry the papers to Albuquerque myself and find a judge to decide which creditor gets what. Unfortunately none of the gunslingers have contracts I can legally pay off, which won't sit well with them. I'd advise you and your men to steer clear of them until they move on. Purdy's cattle, the few he has left, will be fine left to their own devices on the range for the next few months, but you might check on them from time to time and bring them in with the Sebastian cattle in the fall."

"I'll be riding north come morning myself," the marshal said. "You can ride along." He issued the invitation to Mr. Williams.

"I might as well. I'd like to get this business taken care of as soon as possible. It'll be more comfortable if we take my buggy."

"How do you plan to run two spreads?" Javier gave Dominic a stern look.

"Juan and Maria are in need of a larger house, and young Carlos has become my best hand with the horses. I could send them to keep up the ranch house and to supervise the work there until the senora returns."

"How do you expect to let Senora Adams know Purdy has gone and she can return?" Amaya joined the discussion again.

"Let's not make any decisions until I find out what I'm dealing with in Albuquerque," Mr. Williams cautioned. "We can't be sure it's safe for her to return yet. When it is, I know where to send a wire." He stifled a groan as he pulled himself up by bracing his hands against the desk. "Send a rider into town every three or four days to check for telegrams, and send me word if Purdy returns or there's any trouble." He settled his wide-brimmed hat on his head and headed for the door. The marshal followed.

Chapter Twenty-Four

Something awoke Iliana.

She lifted her head to listen, expecting to hear the wail of her hungry son. All was silent. She listened a moment longer. It wasn't unusual for the child to awaken during the night, demanding to be fed. He was a good baby who seldom fussed, but when he was hungry, he didn't hesitate to let her know.

When no impatient cry reached her ears, she turned back to her pillow, anxious to return to sleep. Sleep didn't come as she'd expected. Instead she felt tense and restless. She'd often lain awake listening for Gabe's cries when he was an infant, but he was thin and weak, not at all like Ricardo, who had greeted Fanny Butler, who served as midwife, with a lusty howl the moment he emerged into the world. Perhaps the sound had come from the shed that served as a stable for Nutmeg. Fanny had insisted Iliana should make use of the small building and the pasture behind it for one of her horses, reminding Iliana she might have an unexpected need for the animal sometime.

She was almost asleep again when a faint scratching at her window reached her ears. Someone was out there! No, surely it was a branch of the bush that grew near the window, scraping against the glass. *But what if someone is trying to get in? Could Ben have found me after all these months?*

She remembered that the only occupants of the house were two women and an infant. The town was small and the houses were not clustered close together. No one would hear their cries if they screamed for help.

She thought of the two bandits she'd shot and swallowed to ease the nausea that struck each time she thought of that night. Then her thoughts went to Gabe, and she knew that if someone threatened Ricki, she wouldn't hesitate to shoot. She would not lose another child! Making every effort to make no sound, she slid her bare feet to the floor. Avoiding the floorboards that squeaked when stepped upon, she crossed the room to the chiffonnier, where she'd hidden her gun in a top drawer shortly after taking up residence in Fanny Butler's house. She hadn't wanted to ever see it again. Still she'd kept it.

She took a moment to slip cartridges into the revolving chamber. Once again she paused to listen and, hearing nothing, wondered if she was being foolish.

A floorboard creaked in the hall outside her room. She turned toward the door with the gun wavering in her trembling hand. She heard the soft rattle of the turning doorknob.

"Ana?"

"Who is it?" she whispered though she knew the only person who ever called her Ana was the widow with whom she boarded. Aunt Fanny had shortened her name right after Travis explained her situation to the woman and asked his former partner's sister to rent a room to her.

Fanny slipped inside the room, whispering, "I thought I heard someone moving around outside and decided to check on you."

"I heard something, too."

"Get your baby and come with me," Fanny whispered.

Iliana hurried to the cradle where Ricki slept and swept him into her arms, praying he wouldn't awake and begin to cry. "Take him." She thrust him into Fanny's arms. "I have a gun and will need to keep my hands free in case I need to use it."

Together the two women hurried down the dark hallway to Fanny's bedroom, where Iliana went straight to the window beside the bed. Fanny laid the baby on the bed before opening the heavy curtains and inching the window open. "The root cellar is just a few steps away. We can hide there. It's as solid as a fortress."

Iliana dropped her revolver onto the bed and reached for the baby.

"I'll climb out first," Fanny whispered. "Then you can hand the baby to me before you crawl out."

A crash sounded from the front of the house, spurring Fanny to disappear through the window. Footsteps could be heard coming nearer. Iliana snatched a quilt from Fanny's bed and wrapped it around her baby before turning back to the window, feeling with her hands for the opening. She couldn't see anything but blackness and the opening wasn't large enough for her to squeeze through carrying the baby. Gathering the corners of the quilt to form a sling, she thrust the quilt-wrapped baby through the opening. When she felt fingers grasp the quilt, she released her hold, praying Fanny had a secure hold on it.

"Someone's coming," she whispered a warning into the blackness. Met by silence, she set one foot over the edge of the windowsill, preparing to follow her friend and her baby. She remembered her pistol and drew her foot back to make a dash for the weapon. As she fumbled for the gun, an arm snaked around her waist, pulling her back.

The back of Iliana's head smacked against her captor's chest, and she struggled to free herself. She could only hope that in the darkness, he was unable to see the open window. A quick glance toward the window revealed only blackness. Screaming and kicking, she fought to free herself.

A stinging blow struck the side of her face, but she didn't lessen her struggle. All she could think of was distracting her assailant from discovering the open window.

A string of obscenities, followed by another blow to her head, left Iliana struggling to remain conscious.

A rag was stuffed into her mouth. "You won't get away again until I'm through with you." She felt the abrasive scrape of rope securing her hands.

Her attacker's voice confirmed her fears. Ben had found her.

Iliana's breath left her with a whoosh as Ben slung her over his shoulder and turned toward the door. She squirmed and kicked, trying to break his hold, but it was useless. Even if she forced him to drop her, she couldn't outrun him with her hands tied. She attempted to spit out the cloth that was gagging her and preventing her from screaming, but her attempts were futile. She couldn't save herself; her only hope was to keep Ben too busy to notice the open window behind the drapes, which had fallen back in place.

"Hold still!" A crashing pain accompanied Ben's words and her world went black.

* * *

Iliana awoke to the acrid odor of smoke and a horrendous pain in her head. In desperation she struggled against the rawhide pigging strings that bound her hands and feet. Fear filled her near to bursting. Had Ben set Fannie's house on fire? In slow increments she became aware she was lying on the ground, thick with dried grass, and that a canopy of trees overhead partially hid a bright moon. No such spot was found anywhere near Fanny's house.

Struggling to a sitting position, she studied her surroundings. She could hear water running over rocks, a sound that filled her with immense relief. There was no stream near Fanny's house. The village's water came from a well, so it wasn't the house that was burning. She became aware of huge trees towering over her and thick brush surrounding a small clearing. She was in a forest, but having no experience with forests, she was filled with dread.

A braided rawhide *riata* was knotted about her waist and led to a tree. Her gag had been removed, which indicated Ben no longer worried about sounds she might make. She decided not to test her theory by screaming. Some instinct cautioned her not to wake the man she could see wrapped in a blanket, lying just beyond a small campfire that smoked and displayed red coals. At least the campfire explained the presence of smoke in the air.

The coals gave her an idea. Shifting to her knees, she twisted and scooted toward the fire pit. Following each small gain, she looked toward Ben, praying he hadn't awakened. Each time he made a snorting sound or shifted position, she froze. Rocks and twigs scraped against her bare feet. Her cotton gown was little protection for her sensitive skin. Closing her eyes, she bit her lower lip to hold back whimpers of pain. She had too much at stake to worry about a few scrapes.

Several feet short of her goal, the tether holding her fast to the tree grew taut and she could go no farther. Tears stung her eyes. How could she come so close, only to fail?

After a moment she decided not to accept failure. She wouldn't give up. There had to be a way! She couldn't reach those hot coals, but perhaps she could bring one to her. She remembered a stick she'd knelt on. If she could make her way back to it . . . and if it was long enough . . .

It took more twisting to inch her way back, but at last she touched the stick with her fingertips. After several tries, she accepted there was no way to close her fingers around it. Her hands had been tightly tied behind her for so long she could barely feel them. It took more careful maneuvering and a mouthful of dirt before she grasped one end of the stick between her teeth. Once more she worked her way toward the coals. Fewer now glowed red.

Perspiration dampened her skin and cramps formed in her thighs as she worked her way as close to the fire as the rope allowed. Taking a firm hold on the stick with her teeth, she attempted to probe the burnt chunks of wood for an ember she could drag closer. Her first attempt sent a bit of charred wood flying toward Ben's sleeping form. It disappeared in the darkness. She held her breath, and when his blanket didn't burst into flames, she resumed her efforts.

Her second attempt proved more successful. Bit by bit, she coaxed a small chunk of wood that still glowed at one end toward her. When she deemed it close enough, she dropped the stick, turned her back, and attempted to position the rope securing her wrists over the hottest spot. A searing pain warned her she wouldn't be able to keep her flesh close enough to the heat long enough to burn through the rope. Gasping in pain, she drew back.

Despair filled her. *Please God*, she found herself praying as she'd heard Brother Lewis and Aunt Fannie pray so many times, *help me get back to my baby.*

As she prayed, a light breeze skimmed across the clearing, carrying a burning stench to her nose. She turned in an awkward motion to see the blanket-wrapped figure still lying motionless in his blanket, his head resting on a saddle. The dying fire looked no different. It took all of the willpower she could muster not to scream when she saw small flickering flames creeping along the rope that tethered her to one of the trees that circled the small clearing. The breeze seemed to be blowing the flames toward the tree where she'd awakened. She couldn't retreat and she could go no farther forward.

A sliver of hope filled her breast. Was it possible the tether would burn through before Ben awoke? She began to work her way toward the side of the clearing. Her heart pounded as the flames began to move faster along the rope that trailed her every movement. Clumps of dried grass caught fire and she feared that flames would soon be licking at her nightgown. Throwing herself flat, she attempted to roll on the rope to put out the fire. That seemed to put out the flames closest to her, but a ribbon of fire continued toward the tree where one end of the rope was fastened; flames were spreading across the grass.

Reaching the end of the tether, she stared in horror at the flames beginning to fill the clearing. Once more, flickers of fire ate their way along the rope toward her, and the small fires ignited by the burning rope grew larger. Panic spread through her like the fire spreading through the dry grass. In desperation, she jerked as hard as she could against the rope over and over. Suddenly she felt it snap. She was falling! A startled scream threatened to escape her lips.

Her instinctive cry ended in a gurgle. She hadn't fallen far and her fall was broken by a splash of cold water. Shaking with shock, she found herself sitting up to her waist in moving water. A stream of water flowed around her, reminding her of the gurgle of flowing water heard earlier.

A slight tug to test the tension of the rope still attached to her assured her she was free of the tether. Relief brought a prickle to the backs of her eyes, but there was no time for tears. She struggled to her feet. This was her chance to escape! But how far could she get with bound feet and hands? A glance behind her revealed an orange glow and filled her with horror. In her effort to free herself, she'd set the woods on fire! With no way to flee, she'd burn to death. *Better to die by fire than to be forced to submit to Ben Purdy!*

Shouts came from the clearing, causing her to cringe for a moment. She didn't know if Ben had discovered her absence or if waking up to find the forest on fire was the cause of the obscenities he screamed. She wondered if he'd be able to escape the flames. A picture of Gabe came to her mind, and for a moment she relished Ben's predicament. Then almost at once she regretted those thoughts of revenge; she really didn't want to be the cause of his death.

She didn't want to become his captive again either. After all she'd gone through, she wasn't going to meekly wait for Ben to find her. She needed to find a place to hide. Before she could make her way toward the bank of the stream, it occurred to her that it might be best to stay in the water. If she stayed in the water, the flames might spare her. Forgetting in her panic that her ankles were tied, she attempted to take a step and came close to toppling over. At the same time she remembered the binding around her ankles, she noticed the rope did not feel as tight as it had earlier. *The bindings around my feet and hands are made of rawhide! Rawhide stretches when wet, then shrinks tighter as it dries.* Working at the knot at her wrists with her teeth, she found it loose as well.

Sitting back down in the water, she worked at stretching the rawhide further until she could wiggle her feet and hands free. She stumbled when she attempted to stand, and her hands at first felt like useless stubs then began to tingle and burn as feeling returned. She forced herself to move them back and forth to speed up the return of circulation in spite of the pain her efforts produced.

Hoping the fire would continue to move away from her, she began to wade upstream. So far the fire was proving to be a barrier between her and Ben, but both fire and wind are fickle. She needed to put as much distance as possible between herself and Ben before either shifted direction.

Something crashed in the brush nearby. She crouched in the water, hoping that she was well hidden from whatever was causing the noise, whether it was Ben or a wild animal. After a few minutes the thrashing sounds became more frantic, and she heard a familiar sound.

It's a horse! She almost jumped from her hiding place but remembered that the horse was bound to be Ben's and there was a good chance he was on the animal and searching for her. The horse sounded distressed. Surely Ben would do something to soothe it if he were riding it. No doubt it was the fire that was frightening the animal. Her mind vacillated for several minutes between checking on the horse and staying in her hiding place. The horse's frightened squeal won her over, and she crept from the water, following the sound.

As she neared the horse, she moved with caution, examining trees and rocks for any indication of Ben's presence. At last she peered through the thick foliage and caught sight of a black and gray horse. A rope that may have served as a hobble trailed from one shank and was wound around several trees and shrubs until it disappeared into a crack in a fallen log. The horse reared and plunged, trying to free itself. Instead the animal's frantic efforts were causing it to become more tangled. Iliana paused for only a moment. Taking time to free the horse was time she couldn't spare—she needed to think of herself and of her baby. But something compelled her forward.

As she worked her way toward the log, she looked around for Ben and saw the fire was moving closer. If the wind shifted just a little, she would be trapped.

"Shh," she crooned. "I'll help you. Please, you must let me come closer."

It didn't take long to discover a heavy knot in one end of the rope that had caught in the fallen tree trunk. Iliana surmised that, panicked by the fire, the horse had broken free of its night stake and, trailing the rope, had fled into the forest only to be caught as the knot lodged in the crack.

With considerable effort she worked the knot free and began untangling the rope. As she neared the wild-eyed horse, she continued to murmur softly to him. The horse stood still on trembling legs, eyeing her with suspicion. When she got close enough to touch him, she expected the horse to shy away, jerking the rope from her hands. Instead, though he visibly shook, he didn't shy away as she slid her hand down his sleek, damp hide. Carefully, she freed the animal from the trailing rope.

Neither she nor the horse took a step for several seconds after she removed the rope, until a loud popping sound startled them both into action. Iliana dropped the rope, grasped the horse's mane, and leaped onto his back. As the horse lunged into motion, she struggled to pull herself farther onto the terrified animal's back.

Grasping the thick mane, she leaned low, feeling the horse's straining muscles against her cheek and tucking her toes against his ribs; she felt as though they were flying. Tree branches tore at her hair and her bare legs burned at the rain of blows from low branches and brush. She was aware at some level of crossing the stream several times and thundering across meadows before plunging back into wooded terrain with no way to control the maddened animal's flight. At any moment she could be scraped from the horse's back or he could trip, leaving her dead or injured. She closed her eyes and prayed the horse would find their way to safety.

Time became a blur, and she had no concept of its passing or of the distance traveled before she became aware the sun had risen and the horse she clung to had slowed to a faltering walk. Hands reached for her, prying her stiff fingers from the thick mane in which they were entwined. Arms cradled her against a stiff leather vest, and her numb brain couldn't find the strength to resist. There was something reassuring about the arms that held her and the deep rumble of words whispered in her ear.

* * *

Iliana's first conscious awareness came along with the hungry screams of an infant. She looked about her, feeling dazed and disoriented, though the room seemed somewhat familiar. The cry of a baby reached her ears again.

"Ricki! *Mi niño!*" Iliana sat up in one quick motion. Fanny sat at the foot of the bed holding Ricki in her arms. Iliana reached for her son.

Fanny settled the screaming baby in Iliana's arms and his cries ceased as he began to suckle. The older woman retired to a chair a few feet away, and Iliana smoothed the dark hair on her child's head as he nestled next to her. Her fingers roamed across his back and touched his plump legs as she assured herself her son was real and that she wasn't dreaming.

After a few minutes, she lifted her eyes to study the room before turning questioning eyes toward Fanny. Fanny seemed to understand her unspoken question.

"Travis brought you here to my daughter's house. He found you clinging to the back of a horse belonging to a ranch almost fifty miles to the south of here. As soon as that man left my house with you, I crawled out of the cellar and ran here for help. My son-in-law notified the neighbors then rode out to the ranch to let Travis know. His boss woke all of the wranglers, and they rode out in search of you. The men searched most of the night and until after dawn in every direction, but Travis rode south, fearing your captor was intent on returning you to New Mexico."

"Yes, I am certain that was his intention."

"You recognized him?"

Iliana fastened her gown, noticing it was not the same soiled and torn one she'd worn earlier. For a moment she fussed with straightening the blanket wrapped around her now-sleeping child.

"Yes, it was Ben Purdy, and he is still determined to force me to marry him in order to obtain my grandfather's ranch." Her eyes were heavy, and she made no further explanation before drifting back to sleep.

Travis was sitting in the chair when she awoke again. He looked tired, but his hair was combed and he wore a clean shirt. Warmth filled her as their eyes met. His concern for her had continued beyond their trek from New Mexico to California. Each Sunday he'd appeared on Fanny's doorstep to accompany Aunt Fanny and Iliana to the simple meetings held in various homes in the village, and he'd stayed after the meetings for dinner with the two women. He'd been the first, after Fanny, to hold Ricardo and had declared him to be a fine boy any man would be proud to claim as his son.

Iliana tried to express her gratitude to him for finding her and reuniting her with her baby, but the words wouldn't come. He reached out to lightly stroke her arm, and with the aid of his comforting touch, she once more drifted back to sleep.

Over the next few days Travis became a frequent visitor, and Iliana learned the fire she'd accidently started had burned several acres before being extinguished by meeting a river it had been unable to jump. Ben's body hadn't been found, and Travis suspected he hadn't perished in the fire and was still a threat to Iliana.

"How did he find me?" she asked.

"I'm not sure," Travis admitted. "I suspect he learned I purchased horses from the Sebastian Ranch about when you disappeared. He could have inquired at the ranches where I sold the horses and learned enough of my proposed route to follow me here. He may have even been told one of my drovers was a woman. He probably snooped around once he reached the valley, found Nutmeg in the shed behind Aunt Fanny's house, and concluded you were staying there."

"Why does he continue to think I will marry him?" She no longer believed Ross had meant for her to go through with marriage to Ben, and she understood better her right to refuse him. Ross was a good man and must have been preparing an escape for her. Perhaps he thought he was only humoring Ben when he added that clause to his will and was convinced he would get well. Whether he thought Ben had changed and would take care of her and Gabe or he'd been somehow tricked into agreeing to the arrangement, she felt confident Ross only wanted for her not to be forced from her home and to keep his bargain with Abuelo.

"Sometimes thwarted hope turns to malice and madness." Travis shook his head, sharing her frustration and reminding her of the question she'd voiced.

"I've thought about that time and it seems strange to me that Ross was getting stronger then suddenly began to grow progressively weaker. I've tried to remember, and it seems Ross always grew weaker after one of Ben's visits."

"Some of the people on the Sebastian shared their suspicion with me that Ben was doing something to harm your husband, perhaps administering small doses of some kind of poison each time he visited."

Iliana began to cry. "I was so fearful of Ben that I stayed as far away from him as possible each time he came to the ranch. I should have stayed beside Ross. All this time I've had a niggling fear that Ross didn't care enough about me and that he let me down; now I think I let him down."

Travis placed a hand over hers, lending her warmth and comfort. "You couldn't know."

* * *

The attack left her uncomfortable with returning to Fanny's house, and she devised and discarded several plans to move on. Travis, Fanny's son-in-law, and the two cowboys who had stayed behind with Travis took turns each night guarding the house where she had been taken following her escape from Ben, but the house was crowded and Iliana knew she must seek another arrangement.

One day Travis walked with her a short distance through a new orchard that grew beside Fanny's daughter's house. He paused and stared off into the distance for several minutes. She studied his profile, seeing beyond his high cheekbones, blue-gray eyes, and the light brown hair that brushed his collar. Something was troubling him. She feared what he was about to tell her. It was almost summer and he'd planned to return to Utah in the spring. She felt certain he was about to tell her his trip could not be further delayed. She dreaded their parting.

"Iliana," Travis began. "I'm no longer needed at the Palmer Ranch and I've made arrangements to depart the first of the week."

Hearing him say the words pinched at her heart. She adored Fanny, but Travis's friendship had touched something deeper inside her. What would she do without him? She'd come to trust in his protection and companionship. She'd never before had a real friend. With him she felt safe, not only physically. With him she could share thoughts she'd never dared voice to anyone else. She felt something more as well, something she'd been hesitant to define.

"I'd like you and little Ricki to go with me."

She stared at him openmouthed, uncertain she'd heard him correctly.

"I can't provide you with the kind of grand house you grew up in or servants, but I'll work hard and be a dependable husband to you and a good father to little Ricardo. I'll do everything possible to keep you both safe. We won't be able to return to New Mexico, but we can live on the property I told you about in Utah."

Iliana's head spun. She'd never considered remarrying. All of her efforts had been focused toward avoiding marriage to Ben and protecting her child, but she could see immediate advantages to marrying Travis. Ben had followed her to California, and she feared returning to Fanny's house, where he could easily find her again. If she changed her name, that would be some protection, and having Travis near her was appealing. He had made no mention of his feelings for her, but she knew him to be a kind man. Was his proposal motivated by pity? Ross had been a kind man. They cared about each other, but their marriage had been primarily a business arrangement. Could she again marry a man who didn't offer his heart?

"You can't stay here," he reminded her. "You have a determined enemy and I can offer you and your son protection. Even Fanny is unwilling to return to her home until Ben is no longer a threat. You and I have spent the better part of a year in each other's company, and we have become friends. I think we should get on well together."

"Then I accept." Even as she said the words she feared she was agreeing out of desperation and that becoming Travis's wife would be terribly unfair to him. Yet she couldn't stay in California, with Ben still searching for her. And not only her own safety concerned her. What of Fanny? And if Ben had been aware of Ricardo's existence the night he broke into Fanny's house, he would have certainly killed the baby. She was as sure of that as she was that Ben was responsible for Gabe's death. No matter the cost, she would protect her child.

Chapter Twenty-Five

THE WEDDING WAS SIMPLE. THEIR only guests were Fanny, her daughter and her son-in-law, and the two cowboys who were eager to return to Utah. Fanny's daughter stood at the back of the room holding Ricardo. Iliana and Travis stood for a few moments in front of a man Fanny called bishop, who Fanny said was authorized to perform marriages, though he wore no robe. Iliana had met him at the church meetings she'd attended with Fanny and Travis, but she didn't remember his name. She repeated her vows in a barely audible voice and signed her name as directed.

At the completion of the short ceremony, Travis brushed her lips with a short kiss, which oddly made her want to linger, just before he slid a plain gold band on her left hand. Fanny helped Iliana pack her few belongings and the items she would need for Ricardo. Fanny's son-in-law brought a buggy around. After loading their few belongings into the wagon, Travis helped her into the rear seat and Fanny kissed Ricardo good-bye before handing him up to his mother. Travis seated himself beside Fanny's son-in-law, and several cowboys from the Palmer Ranch rode their horses beside the buggy. She noticed they carried rifles, and gun belts hung on their hips. Their presence was comforting, though she still found herself scanning the countryside with short, nervous glances.

Four horses trailed behind the wagon: two were hers and two were mares Travis had bought from the Sebastian Rancho and claimed as part of his profit from the drive. She had insisted that Travis sell two of her horses, though he was reluctant to do so. He had plans to acquire a young stallion from a ranch in Texas and wanted to keep as many of the Sebastian Rancho mares as possible. Iliana was glad she could keep Nutmeg and that the mare would be accompanying her to her new life.

They reached a large city near dusk. Iliana stared in awe. She had no experience seeing street after street of houses pushed close together. Ricardo had slept through most of the journey, but now he stared with wide eyes for several minutes before demanding to be fed. Pulling her shawl tightly about them, she shrank low into the upholstery, glad Travis hadn't joined her on the narrow seat. She wondered where they would sleep that night, but they didn't stop until they reached a train station.

It required all of the courage she could muster to board the train. The shrieks and clatter of the black monster, with its trailing stream of soot and steam, jarred her sensibilities, and she felt certain she'd get no sleep while riding the terrible monster. Ricardo cried when the engine's whistle shattered his sleep, and only her long-ingrained sense of decorum kept her from adding her tears to his. Travis took the infant from her trembling arms and held him firmly against his shoulder as they made their way down an aisle to a pair of facing benches. One of the cowboys tucked their bags beneath their seats, touched his hat in a brief salute, then scrambled to find his own seat a little farther down the aisle beside the other Utah cowboy. When the whistle sounded a warning that the train was about to depart, Ricki shrieked and Travis transferred him back to her waiting arms.

Iliana sat with her back stiff as a sharp jerk of the car was followed by a rocking motion that increased at a steady pace. With her arms folded around her baby, she attempted to appear calm and at ease. A half dozen men were seated near them, most of whom slouched in their seats with their hats pulled low over their eyes, clearly prepared to sleep through their journey. Long after the steady motion lulled little Ricki to sleep, Iliana eased the ache that had grown between her shoulder blades, leaned her head against the window, and drifted to sleep as well.

Twisting to relieve a stiff neck, Iliana awoke feeling disoriented. On opening her eyes, she discovered her head no longer rested against the window but against Travis's shoulder. His arm circled her, holding her secure against the lurching movements of the rail car. He was sprawled out with his feet resting on the opposite bench, with her sleeping baby lying across his chest. She didn't move, fearful of awakening these two males who now comprised her family.

The train whistle sounded a long, mournful wail and Travis opened his eyes. He smiled but didn't speak. Neither did he remove his arm from around her. She appreciated his consideration in allowing Ricardo to continue sleeping until the train began to slow.

"We've reached Sacramento," he whispered. "We have time for breakfast and to walk about for a short time before we board the train for Utah."

She found a secluded corner at the rail station to nurse the baby while Travis attended to purchasing tickets and arranging for the transfer of the horses to the eastbound train. Sitting in a quiet corner was more nerve-wracking than riding the train, and Iliana found herself searching each face that she glimpsed, fearing Ben might have followed them. It was a relief to finally board the eastbound train. This time, though he flinched, Ricardo didn't cry at the sound of the train's whistle.

Two days later she stood on a small wooden platform in Ogden, Utah, with the baby in her arms and their small mound of luggage at her feet. Travis, with the aid of Brother Lewis, who met their train, led the horses from their car. She experienced a glow of satisfaction when several men who were hanging around the depot whistled and expressed their admiration for the animals. She felt a sudden longing for the rancho and an ache filled her heart for all she'd left behind. She swallowed to hold back tears. Thinking of her home and all she'd lost was futile. She turned her thoughts forward and wondered what she'd find in this new land. She lifted her eyes to see Travis watching her. He smiled and she felt a measure of comfort knowing he would be beside her whatever this new life brought.

Sitting astride Nutmeg with Ricardo in a sling, Iliana enjoyed the ride to Brother Lewis's small farm tucked against majestic mountains. Sometimes she rode between the two men, who trailed the other horses on lead ropes behind them, and sometimes she dropped back, creating a small amount of privacy for nursing her son. She no longer felt shy around Travis, but Brother Lewis was another matter, even though she'd come to view him as a kindly father figure.

Ricki began to fuss, and Iliana tuned out the men's voices to croon to her baby, who showed signs of becoming weary with traveling.

They were met with hugs and chaos when they reached Brother Lewis's home. He introduced his wife, Lydia, and at least a half dozen children of varying ages. Iliana felt a little overwhelmed by the family's exuberant greeting but soon felt comfortable with the friendly woman. After Ricardo was settled for the night and Lydia's children were also settled in their beds, Lydia invited Iliana for a stroll along a path that led through a small garden.

"I feel I've known you forever," Lydia said. "My husband has told me so much about your skill with horses and your bravery when you were attacked by outlaws. He credits your horse with saving his life."

"Nutmeg is well trained and dependable, but your husband is a man of great courage and resourcefulness. I learned to rely on him through that ordeal."

"We were thrilled when we received a wire from Travis a few days ago informing us of his imminent arrival. In it he mentioned that he would be bringing his wife and son to Utah along with four horses." Lydia gave Iliana a warm smile. "Lorenzo and I will be moving shortly to the colonies established by a group of people of our faith in Mexico. He mentioned that the colonies are only a week's ride from your ranch. I hope we can stay in touch."

Iliana bit her lip, feeling uncertain how much to explain to Lydia. "I think we'll be staying here in Utah. If you pass through New Mexico, it would be best not to mention my name to anyone. I faced great danger there and was followed to California by a man who wishes to harm me and my son. That is why Travis married me and brought me here."

Lydia looked startled then spoke softly, "I saw the way he watches you. It is not just to protect you from an evil man that he married you. I think Travis has finally found a woman who touches his heart."

Iliana felt a blush rise to her cheeks. Travis was a man who took responsibility seriously. But did he see her as more than a duty he'd assumed when he agreed to escort her to California?

On the third day of their visit, Travis received a telegram from Fanny. He read it then sought out Iliana. He handed it to her silently. She read it twice before turning panic-stricken eyes toward him.

"It's Ben," she whispered, referring to Fanny's wire. A stranger in town had enquired about Iliana's whereabouts. When he was told she'd left town with her baby, he shot out the general store window and riddled a horse trough with bullets. "He knows about Ricardo and he'll keep asking questions until he finds us."

"He'll not find us," Travis attempted to reassure her. He reached for her, pulling her into a tight embrace. His arms were comforting and she felt a measure of reassurance. Travis was resourceful; he'd proved that when they'd been attacked by horse thieves, but could he keep her and Ricki safe from a man with no scruples, who was determined to have his way?

"Everyone calls you the Mormon horse trader. He'll guess we've come to Utah."

"Utah is a big territory and it won't be as easy to find us as he might think." He lowered his head and lightly brushed her lips with his own.

It was barely a kiss, but it was the first time he'd kissed her since their wedding, and it ignited a strange flutter beneath her breastbone. "You need to get to bed early. We'll be leaving in the morning." He released her and walked away. She stood for several moments, feeling dazed; whether it was because of the confirmation that Ben was still pursuing her or because of Travis's kiss, she didn't wish to analyze.

* * *

Something was different. Opening her eyes cautiously, Iliana took in her surroundings. She was in the big bed where she'd slept for three nights. Only this time she wasn't alone. Turning her head a tiny amount, she discovered she was lying wrapped in Travis's arms. She'd gone to bed each night in the room the Lewises had assigned her and Travis, but each night he'd come to bed long after she'd fallen asleep and had departed while she was still asleep. But for the times Ricki needed to be fed during the night, which gave her occasion to watch her husband sleep, she couldn't have been certain he'd even shared her bed those nights.

"Good morning!"

She felt a moment's panic on hearing his voice and knowing he'd awakened while she lay beside him.

"Better get a move on." He rolled away from her and stood beside the bed as though there was nothing unusual in awakening with her in his arms. She blushed and pulled the blanket higher. She heard the rustle of clothes as he dressed and moments later he stood beside her. "Don't go back to sleep. Ricki will be awake any minute," he whispered. "Get packed and we'll leave as soon as we've had breakfast." He leaned down to leave a kiss on her lips, a kiss that ended much too soon. She stared after his disappearing back and touched her lips with her fingers, wondering at the swarm of feelings that filled her with a longing she couldn't quite explain even to herself. She'd been a married woman for eight years, but she'd never felt quite the way she felt at that moment. Remembering Travis's admonition to hurry, she scrambled from bed and hurried to dress and attend to Ricki's needs.

After breakfast Travis and Iliana, with little Ricki riding in a sling before Iliana, left the Lewis household to resume their journey. They passed through Salt Lake City and stopped only long enough to mail a letter to Clayton, Travis's brother, informing him of their marriage and their intention to settle on a piece of property two days' ride from

Salt Lake City. Travis collected at least a dozen envelopes, which he tucked in his saddlebag before leading the way along a broad road that led toward a formidable mountain range.

Leaving the city, they entered a mountain canyon. Travis seemed in no hurry to reach their destination once they left the city, and when he found a likely spot, he set up camp beside a cool stream. He erected a small tent well away from the trail. That evening he fried trout he'd caught in the stream and mixed biscuits as though he'd had plenty of experience cooking over campfires. After they finished their meal, he announced plans to stay in their secluded camp for several days, possibly a whole week.

It was the first she and Travis had been truly alone since their hasty wedding. Iliana wondered at her lack of nervousness at being alone with a man other than Ross but shrugged away the question. Travis was her husband now, and when he met her eyes across the smoldering campfire she felt a quiver of excitement. When he took her hand and led her inside the small tent, she snuggled close to his side.

Iliana relished the quiet time and was amused by Travis's efforts to teach Ricardo to crawl. She found something satisfying in the chubby baby's enthusiastic smiles and giggles when Travis played with him and felt assured her baby would grow up with a good father. Sometimes she drifted to sleep on a blanket spread on the grass under tall pine trees that reached toward endless blue sky and awoke to find both Travis and Ricardo sleeping beside her. With plenty of grass and water, the horses, too, seemed content, which added to Iliana's sense of security. Nutmeg would issue a warning if an intruder approached their camp.

She was pleased to discover Travis's outdoor cooking skills far surpassed her own. Nights spent inside the canvas tent in his arms filled her with joy. She was surprised to discover she was happy. She'd given no thought before his proposal to the possibility that she might remarry, yet her heart filled with a peaceful assurance that she was falling in love with her husband—or perhaps she'd been in love with Travis for a long time without knowing it. Of one thing she was sure: though Ross had been a good man, Travis filled an ache in her heart Ross had never touched.

"It's time to move on," Travis announced one morning. "We need to be settled before winter."

Iliana looked back several times as they made their way back to the road cut by pioneer wagons and improved by more than forty years of immigration and commerce entering and leaving the Salt Lake Valley.

Travis stopped beside her and looked back too, then at her. His head dipped, and he brushed his lips against hers then settled into a deeper kiss that left her longing to return to their idyllic camp site. Her heart sang. Though the words hadn't been spoken aloud yet, she sensed he cared as deeply for her as she'd come to care for him.

Another day's journey brought them to a picturesque valley, hemmed in on three sides by mountains. Its beauty thrilled her, but she wondered if it would ever feel like home to her or if she would always miss the vistas that seemed to stretch on forever in her native New Mexico. No, she mustn't dwell on the past. With Travis and Ricki beside her, the mountain valley would soon feel like home, she assured herself.

A sagging cabin with a dirt roof and a thin wisp of smoke rising from the crumbling chimney came into view as they topped a rise, and her heart fell. Sensing her disappointment, Travis reached across the space to touch her arm. He seemed to know her thoughts. Perhaps he even shared them. "It'll be all right," he promised. "I'll make it tight for the winter and in the spring I'll build us a new house."

When they reached the cabin, a small man wearing buckskins and sporting long hair and whiskers emerged from the cabin. He danced around in glee when Travis introduced Iliana as his wife. The man began gathering up odds and ends, which he thrust into a large bundle. He lost no time strapping the enormous bundle on the back of a burro he led from a lean-to beside the cabin. Travis handed him a small leather pouch, and the man scrawled his signature on a piece of paper Travis produced from his pocket. With a jaunty wave, the man mounted a second burro and departed.

"It's all ours." Travis held up the paper, eying it with satisfaction. Iliana looked at the dirt floor and greasy walls and stifled an urge to cry.

Chapter Twenty-Six

The hills glowed with color, and there was a sharp tang in the early morning air. Iliana walked swiftly through the long yellow grass with Ricki on her hip. She'd done all she could to make the cabin habitable in the weeks since their arrival, but she could hardly bear to be inside its one dreary room. On nights with Travis lying beside her, she could forget the bare log walls, the splintered plank floor she'd at first thought was a dirt floor, and the thatched roof that still smelled musty after Travis had replaced the grass thatching, but with Travis away, she found she could not bear another minute inside the shadowy interior.

Travis had hesitated leaving her alone, but if they were to survive the winter in a crude cabin built by trappers, they had to have supplies. It was already late October and there was a chill bite in the air even on bright sunny mornings. They'd agreed that it was best that she and the baby weren't seen in the small town of Heber, the closest settlement, so Travis had ridden out alone the previous morning on one horse and taken a second one to use as a pack animal.

Iliana climbed the hill behind the cabin as she'd done numerous times since their arrival in the secluded valley. When she reached the slight promontory she'd come to think of as her own, she paused to catch her breath and stare out over the grass and trees that spread before her. The valley was beautiful, and she understood why Travis loved it though it wasn't his first choice for a home. She could grow attached to this beautiful place as well but for the cabin, and she knew Travis was dreading the onslaught of winter. She shuddered, thinking of the terrible winter that had brought about Ross's illness. That had been one storm; could she endure months of similar storms?

Ricki began to fuss to be put down. Her arms ached and it would be good to rest them a moment. With one hand she loosened the cloak Lydia had given her and spread it on the ground. She'd been reluctant to accept the gift, but Lydia had assured Iliana she had another one and that she needed to do something kind in turn for the person who had nursed her husband through his gunshot wounds. As the fall days grew increasingly chilly in the high mountain valley, she'd become increasingly grateful for the cloak. Seating herself on it, she allowed the baby to explore to its edges before gathering him up to nurse him.

She sat dreaming with her back against a tree while the baby nursed. Their funds wouldn't stretch far beyond the food items they needed, but she hoped Travis would be able to buy a cow and a few chickens. Next summer she would plant a garden like the one old Javier grew each year behind the hacienda. In time there would be fine horses running through the alpine meadow and the bottom land would be plowed and planted with crops they could sell. In the spring they would enlarge the cabin. She smiled, remembering how handsome her husband had looked riding away in the crisp tan shirt she'd ironed with the heavy iron that had been another parting gift from Lydia.

Ever on the alert, Iliana saw a flicker of movement in the distance. Ever since Ben had found her at Fanny's place, she'd expected to see him around every corner. Though Travis took precautions to cover their trail, the fear remained in her mind that Ben would not give up. He was obsessed with owning the Sebastian Rancho—and her as well. She watched as a single rider appeared only to disappear then appear once more along the narrow track leading from the valley to the cabin.

For just a moment, her hopes arose that Travis was returning earlier than expected. Seeing no pack animal following the rider, her hopes were dashed and her fear escalated. The rider could be anyone, a neighbor, a hunter, someone looking for a place to establish a homestead, and she was probably worrying for nothing. A prickling at the back of her neck warned that the approaching man had no such innocent purpose. She touched the weight that sagged her apron pocket. She was never without the small pistol.

She considered making a dash for the cabin. She could bar the door. Common sense told her that the approaching rider would see her cross the open meadow to reach the house, and if it was Ben, a bar across the door wouldn't keep him out. Looking back at the baby lying peacefully on her cloak in the small grove of quaking aspen, she knew what she had to do. Gathering up the sleeping child and forming a sling to hang around her neck from the cloak on which he lay, she began to climb toward the steep bluffs that towered over the valley. Some premonition warned she had to find a secure hiding place.

* * *

"Afternoon, sir!" The blacksmith passed a massive arm across his sweaty brow. "I'll be with you as soon as I finish shoeing this horse." He bent again to pound the metal shoe in place on a large sorrel horse.

"I can wait," Travis said in a conversational tone. He stood watching the big man give the horseshoe a couple more taps then lead the sorrel to a nearby hitching rail. When the smith returned, he gave an appreciative whistle.

"That's a mighty fine lookin' mare!" His eyes widened when he saw a second horse trailing on a lead rope. "There be two of 'em!"

Travis chuckled. "Any chance you'd have time to tighten a shoe on this one?" He indicated the second animal, which carried a large pack.

"I reckon I could." He took the lead rope and drew the horse closer. Together they removed the pack on the animal's back. "You new around here?" the blacksmith asked.

"Been here a while." Travis didn't want to give too much information in case anyone came looking for Iliana. The less the locals knew about him and his family, the safer they'd be, he reasoned.

"Fella came by here earlier askin' about new folks in the area. Said some old geezer at the train station in Salt Lake was braggin' 'bout sellin his claim to some young whippersnapper with a good-lookin' wife and a young'n. Figgered he might be meanin' you." The blacksmith thrust several nails in his mouth before reaching for his hammer and lifting the mare's hoof.

"Who was he?" Travis struggled to keep alarm out of his voice.

"Don't rightly know. Never seen him afore, but he ain't a church-goin' man or I'd know 'im fer sure." He spit the nails out to answer the question then thrust all but one back in. He tapped the nail into place.

"Do you know where I might find him?" Travis asked.

"Naw!" The blacksmith hammered a few strokes. "I suggested he look over at the old trapper's cabin up that canyon a bit." He waved his hammer toward a deep cleft in a nearby mountain and seemed unaware that his words caused Travis to stiffen. "I heard the old guy livin' there was anxious to head to a warmer place before winter sets in and he'd already made some prearranged deal with the fella who bought it."

Travis quickly remounted his horse. "I'll be back for the mare," he shouted, digging his heels into his mount. His horse responded as though set for a race. Several miles out of town, Travis slowed to veer up a trail that led into the mountains.

"It doesn't look like we're the first to head up this trail today," Travis spoke aloud to his horse, spotting tracks left in the dust. Two sets of tracks pointed the same direction he was traveling and set Travis's heart to pounding. He prayed he wouldn't be too late.

He pushed his horse hard for what seemed like a long time before pulling back on the reins to stare aghast at a plume of black smoke rising in a dense cloud above the trees. He closed his eyes in a brief moment of fear and agony before urging his horse to a faster pace. The mare responded as though sensing his desperation. Rounding the last curve, he approached the cabin at an all-out run. He could see flames licking at the cabin's log sides and foul, black smoke escaping from the sod roof.

Vaulting from his saddle, Travis rushed toward the burning building. The heat struck him like a blow to the face. Still he flung open the door, screaming, "Iliana! Iliana!" When there was no answer, he groped about the small space until his lungs threatened to burst. Stumbling upon a saddlebag, he dragged it with him to the door.

Bending forward with his hands on his knees, he struggled to catch his breath. Coughing and wheezing, he attempted to assure himself that Iliana and Ricardo were not in the burning cabin.

Then where are they? Travis cast his eyes upward and struggled to think. There had been no tracks leading away from the cabin, only toward it. He began a worried survey of the meadow. *She's here somewhere and so is Purdy. I have to find them!* Iliana was a smart woman and protective of Ricki. If she even suspected Purdy had found her, she'd hide. Travis seemed to be grasping for any slender bit of hope.

Her horse! Travis took off at a run toward a thick stand of aspens and pines where he'd built a corral among the trees. Nutmeg and another mare whinnied and trotted toward him, nervously tossing their heads. Wherever Iliana was, she hadn't taken her horse. She was afoot somewhere among a sea of trees and boulders.

A sudden picture of a small glen on a knoll overlooking the cabin came to his mind, and he remembered Iliana's preference for the view from there. Travis took a moment to switch his saddle from his spent horse to Nutmeg, a horse he suspected was more sure-footed than the remaining mare, then hurried up a faint trail. He'd almost reached the crown of the small hill when something caught his eye. He dismounted to inspect a clearing that appeared empty at first glance.

He strode to where the grass had been flattened by a blanket or perhaps a cloak spread beneath a nearby tree. Examining the area more closely, he discovered a thread of dark green wool clinging to a prickly shrub, and broken twigs suggested someone had left the clearing by squeezing between the shrubs instead of following the trail back down.

"Someone else was here!" he muttered aloud. He knelt beside telltale marks in the hard ground where someone wearing spurs had hunched down to examine something.

Purdy may not be alone, Travis worried. He remembered there had been more than one set of tracks on the road leading to the cabin. What chance would Iliana have against Purdy and one of his gunslingers?

Chapter Twenty-Seven

SOMEONE WAS FOLLOWING HER. SHE could hear him coming. The sound of movement behind her had been drawing closer for some time. Her eyes searched frantically for a place to hide. Carrying Ricki was slowing her down; he was a plump baby and almost ready to take his first steps. With each step she took, he seemed to grow heavier. He could awaken at any moment and his cries would give away their position. If only she could find a place where they could hide! The towering cliffs filled with deep clefts seemed her only option.

The trees were not so close together now and the ground was growing rockier. There was too much open space between the trees and boulder-strewn peaks. Perhaps she should have found a thicket to hide in, but the bushes that grew on the mountainside were almost bare of leaves, leaving little cover. She feared Ben would spot her as soon as she left the shelter of the trees. Her mind grasped for another means of escaping. If she climbed to the top of one of the large pine trees she'd be hidden from view and he might pass by without discovering her. No, the idea was ridiculous. She could barely carry her son; she couldn't possibly pull herself up a tree with just one arm while carrying the heavy baby, and besides, her tracks in the damp soil would lead right to the tree she chose. She must reach the rocky ground higher up, where no tracks would show.

Somehow in her flight and desperation she'd found a trail and followed it. Now some instinct told her that though the path made movement easier, it would also lead her pursuer straight to her. She veered off the path, striving to leave nothing disturbed that would be a clue to the direction she'd taken. She searched out rocky spots to hide her footsteps. Instead of continuing upward, she moved sideways. If she found another route down, perhaps she could circle behind her pursuer and reach the corral where Nutmeg grazed.

Her arms ached and her lungs were near to bursting. A whiff of smoke puzzled her for a moment but she dismissed it. She collided with a boulder and heard Ricki whimper. *Please don't cry.* It was almost a prayer. If she could just rest for a few minutes. Her head felt fuzzy and it was hard to think. Fatigue and altitude were sapping her last reserves of strength.

She looked down and to her horror discovered she'd stumbled onto a narrow, rocky ledge. Inches from her feet was a sheer drop-off down the mountain that would mean certain death if she fell. Looking back the way she'd come, she could see she'd followed the ledge for about twenty feet. How could she have become so numb with fatigue and fear that she'd been unaware of where her feet were leading her? The heavy thud of footsteps and snapping brush warned her she couldn't rest nor return the way she'd come. Her pursuer was much too close. Cautiously she took another step forward, then another toward a tree that grew out of the side of the cliff. If she could reach it, she could crouch behind it to hide from Ben's view.

The bundle she carried shook as Ricki struggled to free himself from her cloak. He was a strong baby who had more than once demonstrated a stubborn determination to get his way. At that moment he wanted free of the restraining cloak. Iliana grasped at the rock wall beside her to steady herself. Any moment he would begin to scream. If only he had continued to sleep! Freeing him from the cloak, she let it drop over the precipice and tried to keep her voice steady as she whispered soothing words in his ear.

"Send the brat after the rag you been carrying him in!" Ben's wheezing voice carried to her, startling a scream from her throat, and Ricki began to howl. How had Ben caught up to her so quickly?

She flattened herself against the cliff wall behind her, holding Ricki so tightly his cries turned to screams. Too frightened to attempt to quiet him, she could only think to plead with God to spare them.

"Get rid of him now or I'll shoot him and come after you. I have plans for you, and they don't include that squalling brat. I'd shoot you now if I didn't need you to get the land you and that crooked banker cheated me out of. You and the Sebastian should have been mine years ago!"

He was insane! He had to know she was already married and that she could not be forced to marry him. In a protective gesture, she twisted her body to shield Ricardo from him.

"You've already ruined my life and left me to die in a fire you set, so don't think I won't shoot you and your stinkin' brat if you don't do as I say!"

Ben's voice sounded nearer. She risked a quick look and saw he'd stepped out onto the ledge and was taking slow steps toward her.

* * *

Nutmeg shied, and Travis ducked as an object flew toward them, catching in the prickly needles of a nearby spruce tree. Riding closer to the dangling object, Travis swore when he identified it as Iliana's cloak. A shrill cry echoed through the air. Searching for the source of the cry, he let his eyes drift upward, examining each ledge and outcropping until he spotted two figures on a narrow ledge far above him. His heart began to hammer. A blowing skirt and long, dark hair assured him he had found Iliana. Focusing on the other figure, he saw a man edging toward her. His movements were slow, indicating he had a fear of heights. Iliana stepped away from him. Travis sensed her fear, and rage coursed through him. A ray of sunlight lit a silver glint in the man's hand, alerting Travis that the man was armed. Swinging his foot over his saddle horn, Travis leaped to the ground, dragging his rifle from its sheath. He scrambled toward a pile of rocks. He needed an unobstructed angle.

His heart pounded, and desperation warned that if he didn't stop Ben, Iliana would die. *Please God,* he begged, *don't let me lose her. Horses, land, nothing matters more to me than she does.* He caught a glimpse of a blue chambray shirt farther up the valley, reminding him Ben wasn't alone.

He worked his way around a pile of boulders that lay jumbled together from where, at some time, they'd tumbled in a slide from the cliffs above. He paused at the highest point to scan the valley and the steep mountainsides around him. A movement caught his eye again on the opposite side of the narrow valley. He was surprised the man he'd spotted minutes ago had traveled such a great distance since he had last seen the stranger, though Travis was aware a person could travel faster through forested terrain than through the jumble of rocks he'd encountered. The man on the ledge, moving slowly but steadily toward Iliana, was his first concern. Travis would worry about the other man after he dealt with the immediate threat to Iliana.

From below him came the rustle of a heavy creature moving toward him through the brush. Not even the possible threat of a bear or a moose could sway Travis from taking careful aim at Ben, who was closing in on Iliana. She clung to a ledge not more than forty feet from where Travis stood. Even if she somehow made it to the tree growing out of the side of the cliff, there was nowhere to go from there but straight down more than a hundred feet. Travis knelt, bringing his Browning to his shoulder.

* * *

It took all the strength she could muster to hold her sobbing, struggling child with one arm while groping with her opposite hand for the pistol in her pocket. At last her hand closed around the hard grip. Fearing she might drop the small gun, she held it with an iron grip as she withdrew the small pistol and leveled it. She had hoped never to draw the gun again in her life, but she had to protect Ricki! With a shaking hand, she pointed the gun toward the advancing threat. Ben's gun hand raised, and there was no mistaking his deadly intention. Her finger pressed against the trigger, and she instinctively turned away to protect her child.

The cliff and the surrounding mountains distorted the soft *snik* of a bullet hitting its target. Reports of gunfire bounced eerily in the mountain air, echoing like a small militia attack. Iliana waited for the pain. When it didn't come, she twisted for a better view of her son, still clutched in one arm. With his cheeks wet with tears, he struggled to be set down. She saw no blood, and fearing a second shot, she lifted the pistol again, preparing to fire the small caliber repeater once more. With a slight turn of her head, she looked over her shoulder. Seeing an empty ledge where Ben had stood moments before, she stared at the empty space, uncomprehending.

Expecting a trick, she eyed the trees at the edge of the precipice then turned her attention back to the ledge. Her shot had gone astray; she knew it had! She'd been shaking too hard from fear and fatigue to even hold the gun steady. It had to be some kind of trick.

She had to get off the ledge, but if she returned the way she'd come would Ben leap out of the trees to ambush her? She looked toward the stunted tree blocking the other end of the ledge. It might be safer to continue on. She took a tentative step.

"Don't move!" A faint shout reached her ears. She knew that voice, and it wasn't Ben's! Turning toward the voice, she gasped in amazement. A man stood on a rocky projection a little lower than the ledge where she clung. He held a rifle with one hand, but he didn't appear to be threatening her. She stood frozen, unsure what to do, as the rifleman scrambled down the rocks and disappeared from view.

"Wait there!" This time the shout came from behind her. She turned and nearly lost her balance at the unexpected sight of Travis bursting from the trees and stripping off his slick, high-heeled boots before beginning the perilous walk along the ledge toward her. His voice carried across the diminishing distance between them in the same lilting tones she'd heard him use countless times to soothe a frightened horse. Ricardo hushed his cries and turned his head, searching for the source of the familiar voice.

Her mind couldn't assimilate what had happened. How had Travis known she needed him? He reached her side and it took all the restraint she could muster to keep from throwing herself into his arms. Only an awareness that a sudden movement could send all three of them plunging to their deaths held her in place on the narrow ledge.

"Travis!" His name was the only sound she could form as she struggled to keep tears from obscuring her vision.

"You're safe now," he whispered, still in that soothing voice.

Fearing a miscalculated move could send all three of them plunging to the rocks below, she held herself steady as Travis pried Ricki from her cramped arm. For agonizing minutes, she attempted to restore circulation by moving her arm back and forth. The pain added to her confusion.

"Ready?" he asked and she saw the concern in his eyes. "I can take the baby across then come back for you."

"No, I can walk." She wasn't sure she could navigate the ledge again, but she didn't see any way Travis could leave Ricardo alone once he carried him off the ledge, short of tying the baby to a tree. The baby would crawl over the edge of the cliff or be found by Ben while Travis returned for her. A new fear added to the trembling in her legs: a fear that Ben would spring from the trees at the other end of the ledge to kill Travis as well as Ricki and herself.

It took all of her concentration to begin the careful steps that led back to safety. Never daring to look down, Iliana forced each step until Travis, with the baby tucked under one arm, reached back to pull her the last step. Collapsing against him, she clung to him while he patted her back and hugged her to him.

After a few moments, he drew her farther from the edge of the precipice and urged her to sit on a patch of grass in the shade of a large pine tree. There he sat beside her to kiss her thoroughly while keeping one hand attached to the back of Ricki's long linen shirt.

"We must go before Ben . . ."

"Shhh." Travis kissed her again. "Ben will never bother you again. You don't need to fear him anymore."

"He's dead?" She couldn't take it in.

Travis went on speaking, "I didn't think I could be any more frightened than when I saw smoke rising from the cabin where I left you and our son, until I caught sight of you on that ledge with Purdy holding a gun on you." Travis's voice choked with emotion. "I don't think I could go on if I lost you."

Iliana reached up with a scratched, aching arm to pull his head down again to hers. When the kiss ended, she made a quiet admission. "I love you. You and Ricki are my family, my life. Not even Grandfather's rancho matters more than the two of you. I couldn't bear to be without you."

"You'll never be without me. I love you, and I've waited a long time, since before I had a right to hope, to hear those words from you."

She didn't see the stranger until he stepped from the trees, bearded and scruffy with a rifle tucked with easy familiarity under his arm and a tied-down holster on his hip. Travis scrambled for his gun, but the stranger ignored him. He spit toward a nearby bush then looking straight at Iliana said, "Good shot." Iliana stared at him in astonishment.

"I didn't . . . My shot went wild . . ." She didn't know what to say. She turned to Travis.

Travis looked confused. "I'm certain my shot was off. I fired too soon. I thought you . . ." He blinked several times then looked at Iliana and his voice trailed off. The stranger grunted, then gave a thin smile that revealed a hint of satisfaction before walking away.

They both stared after him until the unmistakable sound of a horse making its way down the mountain reached their ears.

Iliana reached for her son, but the boy wrapped his arms around Travis's neck. "Ben? Are you sure . . . ?" Iliana whispered. She had to know.

"He's dead. If the bullet didn't finish him, the fall did."

Climbing over rocks and picking her way downhill without the additional weight of a sleeping child made the distance seem much shorter to Iliana than it had on her panicked upward race. Still she was pleased when she followed Travis into a thicket to find Nutmeg grazing near a spring that released a tiny freshet of water toward the valley. They drank their fill of the cold water before continuing on, with Iliana seated on the mare's back and Travis walking beside her with the contented infant in his arms.

They spoke little until they were almost in sight of the rubble that was all that was left of the cabin.

"Did that man shoot Ben, or did you?" Illiana ventured.

"I don't know for sure, but I think he did," Travis answered after a long pause. "Looks like while Purdy was trailing you, someone was trailing him. We might not ever know for sure whose bullet killed the sorry cuss."

* * *

Iliana's lip quivered, and Travis wasn't certain whether she was holding in laughter or tears when she saw the rubble that was all that was left of the cabin. He knew how much she despised the cabin even if she'd never said so.

"Where will we sleep?" She slid from Nutmeg's back and stared at the charred remains. Her clothes were bedraggled, her cloak gone, and she shivered in the cool mountain air.

Travis's shoulders slumped. "I'll build a new one," he promised.

"I mean now, tonight. Our blankets, everything we owned was in the cabin."

"Not quite everything." Travis suddenly grinned. "We've still got four horses, one of which is in Heber getting a new shoe. I left the pack holding all of our winter supplies there too. That should get us back to the Sebastian."

"We're going back to New Mexico?"

"Well, I suppose we'll have to find a boarding house for tonight, and the sheriff may want to speak with us before we leave. It may take a day or two to settle everything."

In her exhausted state, it took a few seconds for Travis's words to sink into Iliana's dazed mind. They could go home! There was no longer a threat hanging over her head! Ricki could one day take Abuelo's place as the owner of the Sebastian Rancho. Soon she would see Amaya and all the familiar faces of the people who had loved her enough to protect her from Ben. And Travis could follow his lifelong dream.

"You will raise the finest horses in all of New Mexico," she whispered, flinging her arms around her husband and her small son.

"*We*," he corrected. "*We* will raise the finest horses in all of America, and we will raise the bravest sons and daughters to match our heritage. In time they will know their cousins in Alabama and seek out their Medina family in Mexico." He bent his head to press his lips against hers. Her heart seemed to swell in a soaring song. "If we hurry we might be able to travel with Brother Lewis and Lydia since they're planning a trip to the Mormon colonies before snowfall."

"Mama!" Ricardo erupted in an outraged cry.

Iliana drew back then reached for her son. "He's hungry."

"Sit over there," Travis gestured toward a tree stump. "You can feed him while I collect the other horses." He whistled as he walked toward the corral.

She hunched her shoulders and longed for her warm cloak for only a moment; a sense of peace and happiness crept over her. She and Travis would surely face trouble and inconveniences in the years ahead, but there would be joy, too. She looked forward to the experiences they would face. Never again would she be an outsider in her own life. Together they would face each day, and each night would find them safe in each other's arms.

About the Author

JENNIE HANSEN LIVED A NOMADIC life during her early years and can remember living in twenty-two different houses and attending eight schools. The two colleges where she earned degrees, Ricks and Westminster, make ten. She worked as a model, secretary, newspaper reporter and editor, legislative page, teacher, and librarian. Through it all, she kept writing. To date she has twenty-four published novels, numerous short stories, and many magazine and newspaper articles to her credit. She has written reviews of LDS fiction for *Meridian Magazine* since 2001.

She and her husband have five children, all of whom are married to wonderful people, and thirteen grandchildren. Two days each week Jennie and her husband can be found serving at the Oquirrh Mountain Temple, a fifteen-minute drive from their Utah home.

You can learn more about Jennie Hansen by visiting her blog at http://notesfromjenniesdesk.blogspot.com or by contacting her publisher at Covenant Communications, PO Box 416, American Fork, Utah 84003-0416.